COLOR HER DEAD

A SUSAN CHASE MYSTERY

STEVE BROWN

ibooks
new york
www.ibooks.net

DISTRIBUTED BY SIMON & SCHUSTER, INC.

For Sara Paretsky

A Publication of ibooks, inc.

Copyright © 1999 by Steve Brown

An ibooks, inc. Book

Distributed by Simon & Schuster, Inc.
1230 Avenue of the Americas, New York, NY 10020

ibooks, inc.
24 West 25th Street
New York, NY 10010

The ibooks World Wide Web Site Address is:
http://www.ibooks.net

The Chick Springs Publishing World Wide Web Site Address is:
http://www.chicksprings.com

ISBN 0-7434-7973-4
First ibooks, inc. printing January 2004
10 9 8 7 6 5 4 3 2 1

Printed in the U.S.A.

Acknowledgments

I would like to thank Skye Alexander, Mark J. Brown, Susanne Moore, and many thanks to Cathy Wiggins and Lesta Sue Hardee of the Chapin Memorial Library for their fact checking. Thanks also to my favorite Generation Xer, Stacey, for making me sound slightly hip, and, of course, Mary Ella.

Author's Note

Although cities, locations, and organizations mentioned in this book are real, any references to them, and all characters and events, are for the purpose of entertainment only and are part of a fictional account.

Chapter 1

I was guarding the beach one afternoon, a steady breeze cooling off a hot and humid day, when Pick stopped by and told me Mrs. Rogers wanted to see me. She wanted me to find her daughter.

Now that's pretty weird in itself. Jenny never goes anywhere without parental consent. She's totally under the thumb of her mother, who's a real bitch anyone would be wise to stay away from.

Easy for me to say. I haven't hung with Jenny for quite a while. She used to dig up information to help me find runaways until I got my own computer, so I was kind of committed to stopping by. Kinda.

"But I'm not putting on any damn dress," I told Pick from my lifeguard stand.

Pick squinted up at me, the glare off the ocean making it hard for me to see him. The boy's face was blank, as it usually is. Pick's a retarded kid who hangs around the marina and picks up odd jobs, hence the name. He seems to know where to find me, or perhaps looks longer than most. A good-looking kid, Pick's mind stopped growing somewhere along the line, but his heart never did.

"She didn't say anything about a dress, Susan."

Being a lifeguard, I couldn't make extended eye contact. Some idiot was bringing a speedboat ashore. Not that it wasn't a hot-looking gunboat, but this is a bathing beach.

Dropping from the stand and taking my buoy with me, I walked to the water's edge with Pick tagging along. The beach was about as lively as possible: Boomers lying in the sun and complaining about how much more crowded Myrtle Beach is now than when they'd come here as children. What'd they expect? Back then, dinosaurs still roamed the earth.

A slender but muscular guy was at the wheel and as he stepped out of the boat I strode over to where they rent jet skis, sailboats, and other shit. Along with him came a girl, bent over, suffering the dry heaves. She wore a yellow bikini.

"What's your problem, fella?" He was a real hottie: with a nice-looking bod, a strong line in a tanned jaw, but he needed to brush back his unruly brown hair.

"She's seasick. I had to bring her in." And before I could chew his ass properly, he apologized for coming ashore among the bathers.

"You gonna need EMS?" I asked.

The girl was dark-haired, skinny, and would've been helped by any kind of a boob job. She shook her head as she bent over, clearing her throat as she waved off the suggestion. When she straightened up her face was white and she held onto the cute guy's arm.

"Can you watch the boat?" he asked. "I'll send someone for it."

"Sorry, fella," I said, scanning the beach in the opposite direction, "but I'm on the job."

"Look, I'll pay you." When I turned back to him, he

was taking a checkbook from a fanny pack. "Will you take a check? It's good at any bank along the Grand Strand."

"Any?"

"Sure." He gestured at the speedboat. "And you've got the boat."

The guy was simply too cute to be taking his money. "Keep your check. I'll watch the boat, but I leave at four." When his girlfriend shot me a look I didn't care for, I added, "If you want to be righteous about this, you could be here and help me stack the chairs and take down the umbrellas."

He nodded with that strong chin of his. "I'll be here."

"Chad, just because I'm a little sick doesn't mean I can't go out again." The girl glanced at me. "Later."

"Let's get you out of the sun and find something to settle your stomach." To me he said "thanks" before helping the girl off the beach. "There's the cab," he said encouragingly.

When I looked at the public access area, I saw a yellow cab.

"What do I tell Mrs. Rogers?"

"What?" I turned back to Pick. I'd forgotten about him.

"Mrs. Rogers wants to see you."

"Tell her I'll drop by after my shift's over."

Then again maybe not. The cute guy was waving at me over the top of the cab. Flushing, I returned my attention to the beach.

By 4:30 I had the umbrellas and chairs stored away. The good-looking guy hadn't returned, but he did send two guys in a sport-utility vehicle. They hustled out to where the boat was beached and examined the craft as if no one had been responsible for it.

What you talking about? I'd skipped lunch to watch that frigging thing. Oh, well, if the guy wanted to find me, he knew where to find my stand. Or I could call him. The name on the sport-ute: Rivers Water Crafts and they could be found in Conway, South Carolina.

Along the coast of Carolina there's a strip of beach called the Grand Strand. Myrtle Beach believes IT is the Grand Strand, but everyone along that strip has his hand out. You know the drill.

Yes, sir, that'll be ten dollars. Five dollars here, twelve-fifty there; fifty for the two of you.

Even I have my hand out, if you want me to find your runaway—if I don't turn your kid over to Child Protective Services. With CPS looking over their shoulders most parents are eager to talk. Even listen. Sometimes for the first time.

The Rogers lived in the Second Row—that's anything off the beach. The house was concrete block and stucco, built when Myrtle Beach exploded. In other words, when the Snowbirds got tired of driving all the way to Florida and began stopping here. Near the street was a set of date palms, then a walkway up to an empty porch and shrubbery cut back to a skeleton of its former self. The windows were protected by bars, even the one overlooking the street from a peekaboo attic.

In the adjoining yard two Chicanos relined brakes on an old Ford, and behind them, on the porch, a gray-headed woman rocked back and forth, her lap full of brown babies. Across the street a young man strummed a guitar. When I stepped down from my jeep, the guitar player broke into song, something along the lines of the Anglo girl with the blue cutoffs on. As I walked around the vehicle, he sang of how he wanted to love me, to treasure me, as only a man such as he could do. His only complaint: my legs. They were too skinny.

The mechanics stopped their work and gave my legs the eye as I went up their neighbor's walk, but the baby-sitting grandma ignored me as if she knew what became of a woman who let herself be seduced by a man's tender words. I'm taller than most, with gray-blue eyes, wear the shoulders of a lifeguard, and have a larger than average chest. When you're a blonde, that means you have to dress down or you attract guys you won't be able to talk to afterwards.

One of the mechanics took issue with the balladeer's song, using his hands to argue in favor of my legs.

I appreciated that and said so. *"¡Si, Señor. Usted tiene muy gusto!"* Spanish wasn't the only language I'd learned growing up along any number of waterfronts.

The Chicanos returned to their work, clanking metal on metal and muttering things I didn't want to hear. Across the street the balladeer dropped a chord or two. On the Rogers' porch I rang the doorbell.

"Who is it?" demanded a shrill voice.

"Susan Chase."

"Who?"

"Susan Chase. You wanted me to drop by."

"Come to the window where I can see you."

I did.

From a window overlooking the porch, Mrs. Rogers pulled back the curtain—enough for her to see me, not enough for me to see much of her.

"Do you have any identification?" When I hesitated, she raised her voice again. "Miss Chase, a person my age—we have to be certain about these things."

So I took out my license—South Carolina requires

me to be licensed as a private investigator, even if all I do is look for runaways—and held it up to the window. That wasn't good enough and not because the picture sucked big time.

"Can't see that. Pass it through the little door."

"The little . . . door?"

I heard locks and bolts being thrown, then a tiny door opened, cut from the base of the larger one. Something that might be used by cats or dogs—or people who didn't want to have contact with the outside world but still liked to eat.

I stooped down and held out my ID. When I did, a liver-spotted hand snatched the photostat away, then slammed the little door—almost on my hand. I stood up and gritted my teeth.

"Is there anyone with you?" asked Mrs. Rogers.

I glanced around, and as I did, realized whatever the old lady had was catching. "I don't think so."

"'No, ma'am,' don't you mean, young lady?"

Taking a breath, I reminded myself that this was the mother of a girl who'd listened bunches of times to problems with my so-called love life. After letting out the breath, I said, "Yes, ma'am. No, ma'am." The old bitch was worse than Jenny had said. Best to go in there, all business, and get out fast.

More locks were turned, bolts thrown, and chains dropped; finally the door opened.

Mrs. Rogers stood there in a dress that hung on her like a sack. Around her neck were pearls, on her feet a pair of scuffs. Her hair was gray and hung in a long braid down her back. Wrinkles creased her face and flesh sagged under her chin.

"Come in," she said, returning my ID and looking beyond me. "A woman can't be too careful these days.

One of those people could jump up on my porch and force his way in here."

I glanced at the street. The mechanics were busy with their work, the grandmother with her babies, and the balladeer with his song, this one likening insanity to an undertow that sucks you down and pulls you under.

"I see what you mean." I dropped the photostat into my fanny pack and stepped into the living room.

Rogers shut the door behind me. Firmly. Locks, bolts, and chains were refastened; but I gave up after counting as many as seven.

Coming inside from the afternoon sun, the house seemed to be in permanent dusk, drawn curtains blocking out most of the light. Behind the curtains hummed a pair of air conditioners, one in the living room, one in the dining room. The dining room table was dominated by an empty pewter bowl; its floor was bare. In the living room an Oriental rug covered most of the wood and against the street-side windows sat a red velvet sofa. The sofa was flanked by slender tables with marble tops and legs that ended in lion's feet. Lamps gave the room its only light. Across from the sofa sat a Queen Anne chair and an intricately carved rocker. A too-tall table displayed a couple of framed photographs: a middle-aged man and a doe-eyed young woman. Jenny.

"I was expecting someone a bit older, Miss Chase."

"Older than who?" slipped out before I could stop it or wanted to.

She looked me over. "You could be any number of girls on the beach—with that outfit you're wearing." Meaning my one-piece, covered by a tank top and cut-offs, along with running shoes and the fanny pack.

"When I go looking for someone, Mrs. Rogers, it's

best I don't look like her mother." I took a seat on the sofa.

"Would you like some tea?"

"If it's no trouble." Actually, I was dying for something, a beer, a wine cooler, anything; I'd even drink water. It had been damn hot out there today.

"No trouble at all, but you'll have to take decaf. The other stuff keeps me awake at night."

"Decaf will be just fine."

"Very well."

After she disappeared through a swinging door on the far side of the dining room I got up to take a better look at the photographs. The late Mr. Rogers wore slacks and a business shirt open at the neck. He was overweight, going gray, and laughed at the camera. He held a cigar, and on the table in front of him—he, too, sat on the red velvet sofa—sat an ashtray full of ash, a glass filled with drink.

Jenny had been photographed in the same spot, wearing her brown hair straight to her shoulders, a dress with few frills and little color, granny glasses, and no makeup. Around her neck hung a tiny gold cross and her hands held each other across her lap. No cigarettes or drink at hand, but Jenny had something neither parent had: large, round, brown eyes. Those eyes gripped you, like the kids in the paintings sold at Wal-Mart, begging you to take them home.

Question was: What had given this mouse the nerve to break with her mother? Someone told me Jenny had taken a leave of absence from her job at the library to paint. To paint? Last I'd heard, Mrs. Rogers had been ill and Jenny had been spending too much time hanging around the hospital.

I returned to the sofa before Mrs. Rogers pushed

her way through the swinging door with tea in china cups. Oh, jeez!

She placed my cup on the coffee table, then took a seat in the Queen Anne chair and sipped from her own. I stared at the drink. Perhaps it was time to test the theory that hot liquids were good for you when you're hot—not!

"I called you, Miss Chase . . . ."

I looked up to see her staring at the photographs, the ones I'd picked up. "Yes?"

She shifted the position, ever so slightly, of Jenny's photograph, canting it around to face her father. That still didn't make the girl smile.

"I called you, Miss Chase, because the police won't lift a finger to help me find my daughter."

"You may not want my help either. I charge a hundred dollars a day, plus mileage and expenses."

"But I thought you did this in your spare time."

"I do."

"But a hundred dollars a day . . .?" Her cup was put down.

"If I worked full-time, Mrs. Rogers, my fee would be three hundred. A day. Plus expenses."

"That much? Really. But I thought Jenny did things for you . . . sometimes."

"And I paid her. Besides, I agree with SLED. Jenny will come home when she's good and ready."

SLED (State Law Enforcement Division): Grand Strand was a coordinated effort among law enforcement agencies along the Grand Strand. It was staffed by those forced on the locals: a middle-aged guy pensioned off after being shot in the line of duty plus one of the few black men on SLED's staff. Kind of tells you what SLED thinks of their operation at the beach.

"You've already talked with Lieutenant Warden?"

"Before I came over. Consider it a freebie." Warden's exact words had been: "Thank heavens for small blessings" and "Get that woman off my back." Warden was the cop who'd been shot in the line of duty, then pensioned off by NYPD.

"But you don't understand. My baby could be lying in some alley, mugged or worse!"

"Probably not."

"How can you be so sure?"

"This time of the year SLED runs a daily printout. Jenny's name hasn't appeared in any morgue, hospital, or jail along the Grand Strand. And there are no Jane Does her age or description—"

"You don't believe me any more than that man does!"

"Oh, we believe you, Mrs. Rogers. We just interpret your daughter's disappearance differently. Jenny's simply run away from home—"

"And I want you to find her and bring her back."

"You're willing to pay my fee? Plus mileage and expenses?"

The old lady sat there considering my offer, and I sat there wondering what was in it for her. A beginning artist couldn't be selling all that much.

"Yes," Rogers said finally.

"Fine—then consider yourself a client."

"Er—Miss Chase, these expenses you mentioned?"

"Anything necessary to find your daughter. You'll receive an itemized statement of all money spent and you can challenge anything that doesn't meet with your approval." I learned this line of bull from hanging around fishing boat captains. In any service business you firm up the terms by being as specific as possible and using legalese.

"Do you offer a senior citizen's discount?"

I crossed my legs instead of digging out my cigarettes. "Never thought about it."

"Well, you should. We seniors could use a little help. I know I could. All I have is the money from my husband's insurance."

"I'll consider it."

"You do that, Miss Chase." She squinted at me. "You don't smoke, do you?"

I uncrossed my legs. "I won't around you or your daughter."

"Well, I hope that goes for any drinking, too."

"Would a little wine be okay? For medicinal purposes?"

She considered this, then said, "Well, you look like a nice enough young lady, though I would've thought you'd wear a dress to meet a prospective client . . . ." She paused, giving time for the idea to sink in. It didn't.

"So I think I'll take a chance on you."

"Thank you. Did Jenny leave a note?"

"A note?"

"Yes, like in 'Good-bye, Mom. I'm off with Ralph.'"

"Ralph?"

"A boyfriend."

"Certainly not one named 'Ralph.'"

"Did Jenny have a boyfriend?"

"Absolutely not."

"Mrs. Rogers, how old is Jenny?"

"Twenty-six." When I said nothing, she asked, "Does Jenny have to have a boyfriend for you to find her?"

"Not at all. But it does make things easier and might save you some money."

"Oh," then very quickly, "Jenny didn't leave a note, but she has been seeing the wrong crowd. Those hippies at Pawleys Island. Maybe you could start there."

Pawleys Island is to the south of us and allows working artists to live there at discounted rates—another attempt at heightening the mystique. Perhaps you've seen their bumper sticker: "Arrogantly Shabby, Pawleys Island."

"Did Jenny hang with anyone in particular?"

"Hang? Oh, yes, Kristy O'Key."

"The painter?"

"Do you know her?"

"Only by her work." One of my friends had tried to get me to appreciate O'Key's work—in black and white. A painter working at the beach and not using colors? I don't think so.

"Kristy O'Key's the one who put the notion in Jenny's head that she could paint."

"Could she?"

"Of course not. All Jenny's paintings were horrible things; made no sense at all."

"She does abstracts?"

Rogers gave me a blank stare.

"Where forms flow together and aren't always recognizable?"

"Absolutely not. Jenny painted landscapes, people, bowls of fruit—the usual things. It's how they turned out that was so strange."

"Do you have a sample, something I could look at?"

"Not a single one. I threw them out. All of them. They were too disturbing to look at." She sniffed. "We didn't have any trouble in this family until that Kristy O'Key came along."

"You're speaking of Jenny's painting again?"

"Worse than that. Kristy told my daughter to turn her back on her family. Turn her back on her mother—imagine that. That's what Kristy O'Key did to this family."

"You didn't encourage Jenny to paint?"

"Of course not. It was a terrible waste of time, locking herself in her room and working all hours, sometimes not coming out to eat, going days without bathing. Jenny had a good job and she could've had as much overtime as she wanted. There's always someone who wants off, someone who won't put in her hours. Painting was such a waste of time, and that leave of absence . . . ." She shook her head. "You know, Miss Chase, the library doesn't pay you when you take a leave of absence."

"When did Jenny take hers?"

"About six months ago."

"And she continued to paint? Here? At home?"

"Absolutely not. I wasn't going to encourage such foolishness." She shuddered. "Absolutely dreadful, some of the ideas she came up with."

"Such as?"

"Miss Chase, I'd rather not discuss my daughter's painting. I'd rather discuss finding her."

"All right, then while she was working—"

"She wasn't working. She'd taken that leave of absence, like I told you."

"What I mean was: While Jenny continued to paint, while she was on her leave, she lived here? With you?"

"What'd you think I'd do? Throw her out? No, sirree, I stood by my daughter while she was going through this . . . phase." Her chin elevated. "It's a mother's duty."

"When did Jenny disappear?"

"A month ago yesterday."

"And you immediately contacted the police?"

"That very night."

"And they said?"

"That Jenny would turn up when she wanted to. Can you imagine? And from a public servant."

"Does Jenny own a car?"

"Yes—it's locked up in the garage behind the house."

So much for that line of investigation. "Have you tried contacting O'Key?"

"I couldn't locate her, but I did reach her mother, actually her stepmother, and told her I was hiring a private investigator to find my daughter."

That must've been a real treat for the new Mrs. O'Key. "And she said . . . ?"

"She said to do what I thought was best."

"And?"

Rogers looked like she'd bitten into something that didn't taste so good. "And let her know if there was anything she could do to help."

"Was there anyone else Jenny might've contacted? Friends? A priest, a minister perhaps?"

"No—there's no one else. I'm all Jenny has." She glanced toward the street. "We stopped going to church when the neighborhood began to change. I told Lieutenant Warden he was shirking his job, that I was a taxpayer, too. I even wrote the mayor, but what good will that do? This time of year he's only interested in the tourists."

"May I take a look at her room?"

"Jenny's room—what in the world for?"

"For some clue as to where she's gone."

"No," she said, shaking her head, "you won't find anything in her room."

But I did. Not a clue to where she was, but why Jenny felt she had to leave.

Chapter 2

Jenny's room was vacant, vacant of personality, empty of character. No pictures hung on the walls and no personal items lay on the dresser. No curtains at the windows. Venetian blinds only.

Rogers said, "You don't know how hard I had to work to get the paint off the floor."

The air conditioner was silent and the room felt stuffy. The door stuck, and I had to help Mrs. Rogers push it open to get inside. Romance novels filled the bed's bookcase headboard. More of the same drab clothing, similar to that worn by Jenny in the living room photograph, hung in the closet.

Mrs. Rogers fingered one of the pale, frill-less dresses. "Just look at all these nice clothes going to waste. You know, jeans and men's shirts aren't very becoming to a young lady."

I didn't mention I was more comfortable in the same and why should boys have all the fun, but continued to dig around in pockets of Jenny's clothes until I came up with a receipt for $42.36—in a pair of jeans, of course. Paints, brushes, and a bottle of thinner had been purchased from the Artists' House. The store was located off the King's Highway, in the direction of Pawleys Island.

"What's that?" asked the old lady.

"Perhaps a clue."

In the dresser were a few colorless tops, more chains with tiny crosses on them, some spare underwear. Taped to the back of the dresser I found an oversized envelope holding a half-used sketchbook. Mrs. Rogers gasped as I flipped through the pages.

Jenny's father was all mouth and painted in bright colors, the sun peering over his shoulder, but Mama was a devil in black and white, complete with horns and tail. One sketch was nothing more than an elaborate but empty frame entitled "Fiddler." In another, Kristy O'Key was the mountaintop guru from the comic strip "B.C."

Mrs. Rogers snatched the sketchbook out of my hands and ripped it to pieces, even fighting her way through the cardboard cover. "I thought I'd gotten all that trash out of here!"

"Then I take it you wouldn't care to hear about some of the real treasures I find while searching teenage boys' rooms."

"I would not! I'm a lady, Miss Chase."

Could we put that to a vote? Before we had the chance, she added, "I really don't think I like your manner."

"It comes from people telling me how to do my job."

"I don't see where I tried—"

"The sketches might've helped me find your daughter."

"I sincerely doubt that."

"Me, too, but I'm not fool enough to tear up anything that might be a clue."

"Are you calling me a fool?"

I bit my tongue. This old woman was certainly that, but she was also scared—scared of what might've happened to her daughter and how it might affect her life. She'd have to live alone in this neighborhood, with all its real and imagined monsters.

"Perhaps you'd prefer to have someone else locate your daughter?"

The old lady stood there weighing the hassle of finding someone else versus continuing to deal with me. I came out the loser. She didn't fire me.

"I won't interfere again, but I want to see whatever you find in here."

"And I'll be happy to show it to you, but I work best when left alone. Now if you don't mind . . . ."

Leaving the room, she said, "I should've expected something like this by the way you're dressed."

The painting was under Jenny's bed, its frame easily mistaken for part of the foundation. I took the artwork with me so her mother wouldn't shred it.

"I may need to show it around Pawleys."

"Well, just make sure you return it."

No way. *Lady.*

The painting was of the Grand Strand, not done in the traditional greens, blues, and whites, but in reds, yellows, and fiery orange. Hotel Row pulsed, as if ready to explode. Along the beach, the ocean had reached the boiling point, heaving up and stirring around. The picture seemed to come alive in my hands, drawing me into its world.

I didn't know what to say, and for me that is quite remarkable. Just like her mother, I'd used Jenny for my own purposes. All those times I'd spoken with her across the counter in the reference department of the library . . . I suddenly realized how one-sided all those conversations had been.

In the garage I went through Jenny's car, with Mrs. Rogers keeping an eye on me from the screened-in back porch. The car was an oven, and opening all four doors didn't help. My bathing suit became soaked, as did my tank top, which clung to me as I dug under the seat. A great place to come across all sorts of Lowcountry wildlife.

All I found was a six-month-old gas receipt from a station near the library. The glove compartment was a bit more helpful. Along with a receipt from where Jenny had bought her last set of tires, I also found a letter encouraging her work, not what she did at the library but her painting. The note was wrinkled and worn like it'd been read more than once.

> Dear Jenny,
>
> I know what you're going through. I had similar problems. Once you discover art is actually work and difficult work at that, the temptation arises to drop it. After all, no one's paying you to knock yourself out like this. Not to mention the money's always going to be somewhere between slim and none, and Slim just left town. (A joke.)
>
> Seriously, hang in there and you'll find your own style and not be considered just another of Kristy's Klones.
>
> My best,
> Emma

Even a high school dropout like myself could tell the
difference between Kristy O'Key's work in black and
white and the picture under the bed, the one that'd
made me dizzy. I'd probably find this Emma what's-
her-name on Pawleys Island—if she was worth talking
to. But before going down there I dropped by the landing and left the painting in the care of Dads.

Dads isn't his real name, but Harry Poinsett. He is a
descendant of the fellow who christened the scarlet-
leafed plant you decorate your house with at Christmas, but I prefer "Dads." Harry says "Dads" implies
intimacy without being close. Harry says stuff like that.
He's a retired diplomat whose wife didn't appreciate
his taking early retirement. Now the old bat lives in the
capital and runs with the university crowd while Harry
lives aboard his schooner, sailing up and down the
Waterway, rarely venturing out to sea. A balding fellow
in his early sixties, with a polite but graying beard,
Harry knows the school system gave short shrift to my
generation. We were expected to learn new math in
open classrooms, fill in the blanks when it came to sex
and drugs, and never think about how lucky we'd been
to have survived The Pill.

Harry thinks he can remedy my predicament, but in
the process makes me feel like I'm being home-schooled.
I don't know why I put up with this. But people like me
belong to the Cleanup Generation, following along behind the Boomers, picking up the pieces and holding
society together. And you can't blame us if we're only
picking up the pieces that make sense to us.

Where I live is called Wacca Wache Landing. I know,
I know, it sounds like some tourist trap in Florida, but

these "Friendly Waters" are located at mile marker 383.4 along the I.W. The Intracoastal Waterway is a series of rivers, bays, sounds, and inlets, all linked by the Army Corps of Engineers. Over the years the Waterway has become home to those who don't want to ride out the weather along the coast or pay the price of beachfront property. People live aboard boats and in shacks or homes that could grace the cover of *Southern Living*. The water is calm, about twelve feet deep, and if you're of a mind, you can travel all the way up to Boston or as far south as Miami. My father's shrimp boat is permanently moored there and *Daddy's Girl* is about the only home I've ever known.

When I arrived Dads was supervising Pick, who was replacing grommets in the mainsail of Harry's schooner. It was a case of the ignorant instructing the limited. I took the hand-held machine and got Pick started, which freed up Harry to check out what I'd drug home.

"Princess, do you know what you have here?"

I told him and stood even taller.

"Susan, I don't think you understand. This could be worth thousands of dollars." He glanced at where the painting had been lashed across the roll bar of my jeep. "How did you say you came by it?"

"It was part of a bed frame."

Harry studied the painting again. "Maybe I should have Paul Zidane examine it."

"Better you than me."

"Snobs have their uses, Princess. What are you doing with it?"

"Looking for Jenny Rogers."

"She's missing?"

"Run away from home."

"Run away . . . how old is she?"

"Twenty-six."

"Oh." He glanced at the painting again. "Amazing this could come from someone so young."

"Yes—she's not much older than me."

"Point taken." Glancing at the jeep again, he asked, "And where did you come across it?"

"I got it from her mother."

"Well, I'm sure she'll want it back."

"She won't get it. She hates Jenny's work."

"Yes, yes, I think I heard something like that, but I thought it was a marketing ploy."

"Dads, why didn't you tell me Jenny had become famous?"

"I don't think 'famous' is quite the word. I'd say she's notorious. There's quite a controversy as to whether Jenny did her own work or if someone did it for her. Besides, Princess, when did you become interested in art?"

"I guess it starts now."

Pawleys Island is a blend of rich and poor, Bohemian and sophisticated, each rubbing shoulders with the other and feeling quite superior about it. I saw women who could pass for fashion models and hippies who could be artists, or wanted you to think so. But the biggest segment of the population is made up of vacationing Boomers who spend up to five grand a week for the opportunity to rent one of the houses on the island. Because of those prices, their womenfolk put the best face on all the cooking that has to be done. "You wouldn't believe how much closer the vacation brought our family," they say.

O'Key lived in the old Maritime Hotel, a wooden structure on the backside of the island. O'Key's place

was on the top floor, the fourth, and there was no elevator. The stairs were swept clean but worn black from
use. Edges of wallpaper peeled up from the constant
heat and humidity and lights burned without cano-
pies—except over the stairwell. Most of those lights were
permanently out. Too difficult to replace, I imagine.

The wall separating the stairs from the hallway ran
from landing to ceiling, making it a handy place for
rapes and muggings, so I kept a firm hand on my fanny
pack and trudged onward and upward. Whenever I go
looking for runaways, I always take my *pistole* along.
All in all it makes for a more pleasant day.

Hard to believe this woman was related to some of
the bluest blood in the Carolinas: O'Keys of the Keys,
as they were called, having a beach house on one of
three tiny islands lying in line off the coast to the south
of us. Two hip-looking dudes gave me the eye as we
passed in the hall, then they turned one of those blind
corners and disappeared downstairs.

I finished those four flights, and those four flights
about finished me. Mrs. Rogers was right. I shouldn't
be smoking—on or off the job. Then again, without a
vice or two how would a gal know if she was being good
or not?

O'Key's name was on the apartment at the far end
of the hall, on a slip of paper like the one over her
mailbox in the lobby. I rapped on the door.

No one answered.

I tried again, this time with more vigor, and the door
creaked open. Just a crack. Enough to cause me to
glance toward the stairs. Seeing no one there, I put a
knee against the surface and gave the door a little shove.

"Hello?" I said.

Still no answer.

"Anyone there? Ms. O'Key?"

I pushed back the door, using my knee again.

The apartment had been tossed. Dresser drawers lay upside-down; books had been pulled down from their shelves, clothing thrown out of closets; a Murphy bed was out of the wall with its bedding torn apart. Through an open door I could see into the bathroom where the shower curtain lay half in and half out of the tub. The microwave had been shoved into the sink and the door of the refrigerator hung open. That explained the odor. Finally, O'Key's easel, paints, brushes, and spare easels were scattered across what had been an empty corner of the apartment that caught the morning light. The windows were closed; one held an AC, the other led to the fire escape.

Seeing no one in the bathroom or behind the kitchen counter, I stepped over to a window, opened it, and looked down. A skinny guy wearing shorts and flip-flops was taking out the garbage. Behind him ran the shell road, and behind that, the marsh separating us from the mainland. The fresh air made the room bearable. Turning on the AC helped even more. The phone lay on the floor, and underneath it, a letter from Paul Zidane, who owned the Golden Fleece Art Gallery. Zidane was looking forward to seeing O'Key's latest work, panting for it in the most urbane and sophisticated terms.

I picked up the phone, and as I did, noticed a brochure stuck behind the refrigerator. I slid my hand between counter and fridge and retrieved it. The brochure touted the delights of Rio and said to contact Lois Wyman for First Class Travel. Clever. I dropped the brochure on the counter, and for the first time realized the inside of the fridge had been splattered with paints; all dry now. The paints and the heat caused the odor, not spoiled food.

I called the cops and reported the break-in. The dispatcher told me to stay where I was and not to touch anything, that a squad car was on its way. I said I'd give them about ten minutes.

I doubled-checked the bathroom and found nothing on the counter or under the basin, just a few over-the-counter medicines and out-of-date prescriptions. On the bathtub rim and under a corner of the torn-down curtain were bottles of shampoo and conditioner—and enough scum to prove O'Key wasn't any better housekeeper than I was. The closet was empty except for a paint-smeared smock and old pairs of running shoes. In front of the closet lay several boxes used to store sketches, some odd pieces of clothing, and O'Key's income tax returns for the last five years. O'Key wasn't making any more money than I was. So much for living the artist's life—or guarding the beach.

Crossing the room again, I stepped over several out-of-date bathing suits, scarves, a few pieces of mismatched underwear, a couple of sweaters, and some photographs of O'Key with her father. I was retrieving a cushion for the recliner when someone spoke behind me.

"What are you doing in here?"

I whirled around, dropping the cushion and reaching for my fanny pack. The guy was about my age and not much larger. Still, it had been dumb of me to turn my back on the door.

"Fixing this chair."

He stepped inside. "Who are you?"

"Susan Chase. And you?"

"George Fiddler. I live across the hall. Really, what are you doing in here?"

"Waiting for the cops."

The guy wore jeans, a Coastal Carolina sweatshirt, and a pair of sandals, and had the underfed look artists cultivate. His clothing was old and worn but his face young and fresh. Hair grew to his shoulders, and across his lip, a weak attempt at a mustache.

Looking around the apartment, he said, "She made a real mess, didn't she?"

"Who?"

He stared at me. "You just let yourself in?"

"More comfortable than sitting in the hall."

"But won't the cops be mad?"

"They usually are and there's little I can do about it."

"You a friend of Kristy's?"

"Jenny Rogers."

"Jenny? Jenny hasn't been here for weeks. Kristy's gone, too. Out of town."

"Know where?"

"No." More staring. "How do you know Jenny . . . Miss Chase?"

"She did some work for me."

"What kind of work?"

"At the library."

He leaned against the sofa. "Jenny's not into that anymore. She's a painter now."

"So I've heard. Have any idea where I might find her?"

"No—I haven't seen Jenny in weeks."

"Who tore up this place?"

"I don't know."

"Yes, you do." I sat down in the recliner and opened my fanny pack and took out my cigarettes. This guy was harmless—to me and any other woman. "You almost blurted it out when you came through the door.

You think some woman did it."

Fiddler glanced at the floor. "I can't be sure."

"Speculate for me, George," I said, lighting up. "It'll be a while before the cops arrive."

"Why would you want to know?"

I let out a smoke-filled breath and stared at him. He caved first. "Emma Coker, I think."

"Who's she?" I asked, remembering the person who'd written the stupid note Jenny Rogers had treasured.

"Another painter."

"Where can I find her?"

"She lives here—on Pawleys."

"Where?"

He gave me the address.

"Why would she ransack this place?"

"She was pissed at Kristy."

I gestured at the mess. "This is more than being pissed off."

"Look—are you really a friend of Jenny's?"

I pointed at the phone. "Call the library. They'll vouch for me."

"No, no, I believe you. I just don't know if you'd understand Emma and Kristy's relationship."

"Try me."

Fiddler looked as if he were organizing his thoughts, then said, "Well, it was like this: At one time Emma and Kristy were friends, but Kristy broke it off. Then they started competing. Competing for people. Jenny was one of those people. When Kristy threw her out Jenny went to live with Emma."

"But if Jenny lived with Coker why would she trash O'Key's apartment?"

He shrugged. "I don't know. All I know is I heard her in here raving and ranting and tearing the place apart.

I came to the door and told her to hold it down, that I was trying to work—I'm a playwright and I need my quiet. Later, when she left, I heard the door slam. She slammed that door awfully loud, Miss Chase. Kristy and I rent these rooms because there's not much noise back here."

"Then you didn't actually see her?"

"No, but it was Emma."

"But it could've been anyone—right, George?"

"Who?" He looked beyond me. "A burglar would've taken the microwave and not made as much noise."

"I was thinking of Jenny."

Fiddler came off the sofa. "No way. She'd never do anything like this."

"Why not?" I asked, switching the cigarette to my left hand. "Kristy threw her out."

"She couldn't . . . she was . . . ." He looked at the floor again.

"In love with Kristy?"

His head jerked up. "Absolutely not! She idolized Kristy, that's all."

Not making much progress with this line of thought, I asked, "How would Coker have gotten in?"

Fiddler considered my offer. "Probably with Jenny's key, left over from when she lived with Kristy."

"Why'd Kristy throw her out—Jenny, that is?"

"They disagreed over Jenny's work."

"That's enough to throw someone out?"

"For Kristy, it was. She thinks she knows everything. About art. About everything."

"You think her work is any good—Jenny's, I mean?"

"Sure it is." He took a seat on the arm of the sofa again. "Different from anything I've ever seen."

"In what way?"

"Well, you know how some artists' work is so weird

you can't make out what they're getting at, then there's the traditional stuff that gets old pretty fast. Jenny's work combined the two, and when you saw hers, you couldn't forget it. I remember a bowl of fruit she painted. The apple had a worm with its head sticking out of it. I asked Jenny who the worm was supposed to be because it looked like the worm had a face."

"A face?" I could see we were pushing the outside of the envelope here.

"I know it sounds funny. Jenny asked me who I thought it was and I said the face looked like my father."

"So?"

"Jenny'd never met my father. She had no idea what he looked like. My father doesn't come down here. He's in the plumbing business up in Charlotte. I know the image was blurred, but that's what it looked like. To me."

Trying to get back on track, I asked, "When did this happen?" and gestured at the mess again.

"A few weeks ago."

"And you didn't report it?"

Fiddler shook his head. "It's none of my business what goes on between those two women, Miss Chase, and if you're smart, you'll stay out of their way, too."

"Seen Emma Coker around lately?"

"Here and there."

"Was Jenny with her?"

Fiddler had to think about that. "No."

That didn't sound so good. "When did Kristy throw her out?"

"A few weeks ago." He looked around the room again. "But Jenny wouldn't do anything like this."

"Uh-huh. Is it normal for O'Key to be gone so long?"

"Sometimes months at a time."

"Think Jenny might be traveling with her?"

"What? No. I mean, I don't think so."

"Had Jenny and Kristy fought before and made up?"

"Uh . . . yes."

"So they could be together now."

"Yeah. I guess it's possible." Fiddler's shoulders sagged.

"You had a crush on her, didn't you, George?"

"No, no . . . ."

In my best schoolmarm voice, I said, "George!"

A guilty smile appeared on his face. "Yeah—I guess I did." He slid into the couch, his legs over the arm. "But Jenny wasn't interested. She wanted to be independent and she had her trust fund to do it."

My ears perked up. "Trust fund?"

"Jenny receives a thousand a month from a fund set up by her father. It's not a lot, but enough for an artist to live on. The money went to her mother until Jenny turned twenty-five. The money's all her mother's interested in." He swung his feet off the arm of the couch. "Is that why you're here? Did Jenny's mother send you?"

I didn't have to answer that because at that very moment a cop walked though the door. After making sure we weren't the bad guys, he told us we'd have to wait in the hall. We did. Fiddler seemed to want to question me further but was too intimidated by the presence of the cop.

Fifteen minutes later the chief of police reached the top floor and came around the corner, huffing and puffing. He leaned against the wall and caught his breath, then saw us, stood up, and straightened his

Sam Browne belt. He was a heavy Boomer and his shirt was as damp as his face. He wiped it with a handker- chief pulled from a back pocket.

"They oughta do something about those dad-blamed lights. Somebody's gonna break their neck. You Chase?"

I nodded.

The chief gave me the once over, taking in every- thing, even my running shoes.

"They were inside when I arrived," said the cop.

"Why'd you do that?" asked the chief, stepping to- ward us.

Fiddler gave ground. I didn't. "To call you."

"You might've used another phone."

"I didn't like those stairs any more than you did, Chief." Or that my cell phone needed to be pumped up. Again.

"You could've disturbed the crime scene."

"I was trained by SLED not to."

He looked me over again. "I'll bet you were." He jerked a thumb toward the door. "Inside, Chase."

"Oh, we're going to disturb the crime scene again?"

He snorted as we went into O'Key's apartment. Both Fiddler and the patrolman craned their necks, watch- ing us through the door. I was cool with that—as long as the door stayed open.

The chief checked the bathroom, then looked out the window, all along wiping his face. The air condi- tioning was making inroads against the heat, still the cloth quickly became soaked.

"Okay, give, Chase."

"I was looking for a friend, but she wasn't here. When I knocked, the door opened. I saw this and called you."

"What else?"

"What else, what? Am I a suspect?"

"No—you have a reputation for disturbing the tourists and we don't like our tourists disturbed on Pawleys Island."

There was little I could say to that.

"I can have your ticket lifted for noncooperation."

"So I'm cooperating—what's your problem? You putting on this tough guy act for your patrolman. If so, I've seen others, and on a scale from one—"

He stepped toward me. "Listen, girl . . . ." He glanced at the door and stopped. "You'd best remember who you're talking to."

"You, too. I'm a woman."

"Come on, Chase, don't be giving me such a hard time. What were you really looking for?"

"Who, Chief, and I don't have to tell you."

"But you will," he said with a sly smile, "won't you?"

"Only because you'll get it out of the guy in the hall."

"You bet I will."

"Jenny Rogers."

"Who's that?"

"Another painter."

He glanced around the room again. It hadn't improved with age. "What's your interest in this?"

"In her, Chief, in her. Rogers is missing, I'm looking for her, and O'Key and she were buddies."

"You got a client?"

"Usually do."

"Just answer the question. You want to play detective, you gotta play by the rules."

"Rogers' mother," I said, suddenly wanting this over.

"You have any proof of employment?"

I unzipped my fanny pack and turned over Rogers' check. I hadn't had time to get by the bank to cash it.

"A hundred dollars," said the chief, taking the check. "Dad-gum, how long you planning on dragging this thing out—a week?"

"Ought to be finished by tonight."

"But the check's dated today."

"I'm a fast worker."

He eyed me. "So how'd you really get in? Pick the lock?" He glanced at my fanny pack. "Maybe I should check that pack. It might have a set of burglar tools in it. Possession of burglar tools in this state—"

"Dammit! I told you the fucking door was open!"

"Watch your language, young lady."

"And you stop the lecturing. I'm a licensed investigator and you have no right—"

He jerked a thumb toward the door. "Get out of here, Chase. We don't need your help or your mouth."

"Yeah—right," I said, snatching the check out of his hand. "That's what others have said before."

Chapter 3

Emma Coker lived in a building that was someone's idea of what a turn-of-the-century house along the coast might look like. It had a broad, sloping roof and a deeply recessed veranda, the latter to channel breezes through. Workable shutters hung at the windows, as if someone remembered what winds could do to anything built along this coast. Coker's condo was on the fourth floor—like O'Key's—but just because there were only four floors didn't mean the damn place couldn't have an elevator. Someone was taking this turn-of-the-century stuff a bit too far. There was no answer the first time I knocked and that gave me a chance to catch my breath.

I knocked again.

No answer again.

The third time I knocked the door opened abruptly and a woman filled its frame, and fill the frame she did: wide shoulders, thick neck, jeans, jogging shoes, and a paint-smeared smock. She was fortyish, with an oval face and black hair that looked like it had been cut with a pair of shears and a cereal bowl. One hand held a paintbrush, the other was positioned to shut the door in my face. This had to be Emma Coker or that new middle linebacker the Carolina Panthers were touting.

"Knock it off! I'm trying to work in here."

"Ms. Coker?"

"Whatever you're selling, I'm not buying."

She tried to close the door, but I stepped forward, putting my shoulder into it.

"What the hell you doing?"

I was digging through my fanny pack. "Getting out my card."

"I don't want to see your fucking card!"

"It's not just for getting laid."

"I don't . . . ." She stopped and the resistance against my shoulder lessened. "Was that supposed to be some kind of joke?"

"Depends on whether you understood it or not."

She took the card and read it, then gave me the once-over, and I felt more attention in that one look than any woman might ordinarily give another. Involuntarily, I stepped back. She thrust the card at me. "Not buying any detectives either."

"I'm looking for Jenny Rogers."

"Don't know her." And taking the card with her, she slammed the door in my face.

I blinked, then knocked again.

No answer.

Again I rapped on the door.

Still no answer.

I took out a cigarette and lit it. After a couple of drags, I knocked again. A couple of puffs later I hammered some more. Across the hall a door cracked open, then shut quickly. Some retiree lived there: Never

enough to do but always indignant whenever interrupted. I finished my cigarette and went at the door
again, enough to bruise my knuckles.

The door opened and Coker lunged out, grasping
the jamb. "Knock on this door again and I'll throw your
ass down those fucking steps."

I held up the letter I had found in Jenny's car.

She glanced at it. "That doesn't mean a thing.
There's plenty of Emmas around here."

"But you're the only one who knew Jenny, her work,
and her relationship to O'Key." I put the letter away.
"Come on, Emma, tell me what you know, then I won't
keep bothering you."

"It'd take more than you to bother me, twerp."

I fished out my ID. "You see this? This is a license
to do just that and you're at the top of my list."

"And you might lose some teeth."

I shrugged as I put away my license. "If that's the
way you want it, okay, but you can forget about being
able to concentrate for the next few days."

After a long sigh she said, "Damn. I'm beginning to
think that little twit isn't worth the trouble." She opened
the door and stepped back. "Come on in."

I did.

Her living room, or studio, ran lengthwise and was
empty but for an easel and paints and a couple of
director's chairs which sat on either side of a Parsons
table. Lying on the table were a few magazines, the top
copy *Architectural Digest*. The far wall was all windows,
with a view of the water, and in front of the windows
stood Coker's easel with its back to me. The smell of
oils filled the room. Sheets of newspaper lay under the
easel—pages from *The Wall Street Journal*—and the floor
was polished to such a shine that the wood could glare

at you just like its owner. Walls and trim were also white. There were doors at opposite ends of the room, but you had to look hard to find them.

I took a seat in one of the director's chairs and Coker assumed a position in front of me, hands on her hips. She was a formidable-looking woman, and ugly. Beady eyes stared at me from under those bangs and she had shoulders that wouldn't quit; hands made for working with stone, not painting, or maybe for strangling bothersome folk who interrupted her work.

"You know," she said, "I've a mind to call the cops."

"Be my guest," I said, pulling out my cigarettes. "I still get paid, even if the cops do all my work. And the cops are more likely to get involved if you complain." Boy, what a line of bull. The last thing I wanted was another do-si-do with the chief of police of Pawleys Island.

"Listen, you, I have no idea where Rogers is."

"Come on, Emma," I said, lighting up again, then sucking the smoke down deep into my chest. "You can do better than that."

"And where the hell do you get off calling me by my first name? I don't even know you."

I crossed my legs, leaned back in the chair, and exhaled. "It allows me to get closer to you, so you'll pour out your heart to me."

She sneered at me. "You're a real smart-ass, aren't you? That come with the badge or from watching old movies on TV?"

"You want to play games, I'll play. You tell me where Jenny is and I'm out of here."

"And I'm telling you I don't know where she is. The night she showed up I was just as surprised as anyone."

I still didn't say anything.

"You don't believe me?"

"I'm listening—seeing if what you tell me fits in with what I already know."

Cigarettes and a lighter came out of the paint-smeared smock and she took a seat in the other director's chair. After a drag off her weed, she said, "I don't know why the old bitch won't let her go."

"She's her daughter."

"Yeah, and it's a fucked-up world, too." She reached into her smock and pulled out my card. "So the old bitch hired you to find her. Pretty sleazy work if you ask me. What kind of person does that—dragging people's pasts into their futures—whether they want that or not?"

"I only find them, Emma. They don't have to go home."

"Then you don't know Jenny." Coker was staring at the far end of the room with what could only be called a wistful look on her face.

A painting sat on the floor, its face against the wall. I stood up and walked over to it.

"You keep your hands off my fucking property, Chase. I didn't hire you to fuck around in my life."

I picked up the painting and turned it around. It was a bowl of fruit with a worm's head sticking out of an apple. The worm had a face and the face favored the guy who'd come ashore in his boat earlier this afternoon and never returned. That figured.

"Don't you listen? I told you not to touch that."

"This is Jenny Rogers' work."

"How'd you know? See her name in the corner?"

"What's it doing here?"

"None of your damned business."

I put down the painting and returned to my seat. "You want me camping out on your doorstep?"

She shrugged. "Jenny left it with me."

"Why?"

"Because I care about her work!"

"I have one, too."

"Why would Jenny leave her work with someone like you?" Her eyebrows arched. "Which one?"

I described the fiery work with its pulsating buildings and stirred-up ocean.

Coker's eyes lit up. Given more time she might've even drooled. "That's one of her first and one of her best. *Day's End.* I wish I owned it."

"It's the wrong time of the day for it to be day's end."

"And that shows how much you know about art. How'd you get your hands on it?"

I told her where I'd found it.

"Now that you've rescued it from that old bitch, why not leave it with someone who'll care for it properly?"

"I thought I might return it to Jenny."

"I'll see she gets it."

"I'd rather you tell me where she is."

"I've already told you, I don't know where she is."

"Then how can you return the painting?"

"When she returns, I mean."

"From where?"

"I don't know. I don't know where she is, Chase. I've already told you that." She glanced at the floor and cleared her throat. "If I did, I'd be with her. Now do you believe me?"

I only stared at her.

"Troublemakers," she muttered, shaking her head. "That's all detectives are."

"Sure you don't have us mixed up with art critics?"

Coker leaped out of her chair and faced me, her hands curling into small balls at her sides. "You have no right talking to me like that! You have no right coming here and bothering me. What the hell do you know about art? What the hell do you know about anything? You're nothing but a damn kid!"

Leaning back into my chair, I said, "What I do know is: Jenny's a nice girl, but she can't survive on the street without someone running interference for her. When O'Key tossed her out, she ran over here. If you don't know where she is you have a pretty good idea who she's with."

"I thought she went home to mama."

I pointed at the painting at the far end of the room. "Come on, Emma, you can do better than that."

"That means nothing. I bought it from her. Paid a pretty penny for it, too." She lit another cigarette. The first one lay smoldering at her feet. "Artists collect other artists' work." After a drag off the new smoke, she rubbed a foot across the smoldering butt, smearing a black mark across the highly polished floor. "Look, you, you don't really know Jenny or you'd understand she could make it on her own. Jenny could do what most other artists couldn't: sell her work."

"I thought Jenny had money—from home."

"Fucking little chance of that."

When I didn't add anything, she asked, "Did Jenny's mother tell you I called?"

"No."

"Well, I did, but she wouldn't let me talk to her."

"When?"

"Who knows," she said with a shrug. "A couple of weeks ago, a month ago. It's not something you keep track of."

"You would."

And the woman fixed me with a stare that sent a chill right through me. Behind those eyes I saw pure hate, not passionate hate, but the cold, calculated variety. This woman had more than a case of the hots for Jenny, she was borderline wacko. Maybe she'd already crossed the line. Or maybe it came and went with whoever she was talking to.

I asked, and without stammering, I do believe, "Someone trashed O'Key's apartment. Any idea who might've done it?"

She appeared surprised. "Is Kristy back in town?"

"Not that I know of. The cops are there now. They'll be coming here next."

"Why?"

"They have someone who'll swear you're the one who ransacked her apartment."

"And who's that? You?" She dropped her cigarette, mashing it out on the floor. "I don't have to take this shit off you. I've told you what I know. Jenny's not here, I don't know where she is, and if you think you can harass me you have another think coming." She got to her feet and went to the door. "You're wasting my time and yours, though I doubt your time is worth anywhere near what mine is."

I stood up, scanning the empty, white room. "Not if you decorated this place."

Coker snorted and threw open the door. It slammed against the wall and bounced back, hitting her hand. "Get out! And don't come back."

Instead I walked over and looked at her work in progress. The woman had to be painting from memory. There wasn't a subject in the room. Or so I thought.

A hand seized my shoulder and pulled me away,

but not before I saw what Coker had been painting.

"Get away from that! Nobody sees my work until I'm finished." Then she hurried me out the door, slamming it behind me. Maybe I even heard a small sob.

What Coker had painted was similar to Jenny's fruit bowl, but the face on her worm didn't look like anyone I recognized. That's probably why a huge red "X" had been scrawled across the worm's face.

Out on the street a tourist was staring at Coker's building as if trying to appreciate what the architect had in mind. Good luck, fella. The Grand Strand is full of such eyewash; nothing more than what people make of it, and more than one person has filled his pockets after learning that simple fact. As far as I was concerned Emma Coker was just another in a long line of self-promoters.

I crossed the street with a group of tourists, including a blond couple pushing a tandem bike, a gay couple in French-cut bathing suits, and a pack of kids looking for a place to spend their parents' money. Before I reached the other side, George Fiddler fell in step alongside me.

"Hello, Miss Chase."

Without looking at him, I asked, "Why didn't you tell the cops about Emma Coker trashing O'Key's apartment?"

"What makes you think I didn't?"

"Because they aren't crawling all over her. I had plenty of time to talk with her."

He grabbed my arm. "Did she **say** when she'd last seen Jenny?"

I shook off his arm and kept moving. "Several weeks ago."

"That's a lie!" The gay couple glanced at us as we

reached the other side of the street. "Well, it's true," he said as much to them as to me.

"How can you be sure?"

"I saw them together last week."

"Where do you think you saw them, George?"

"Where do I think I saw them? I saw them!"

"Well, then, where?"

"At the Pavilion."

The Pavilion is a huge open-air entertainment center and the heart of tourist life along the Grand Strand: video games, rock and roll, every food imaginable. Across the street are the rides and nightclubs. Emma Coker wouldn't be caught there and it must've shown on my face.

"Well, I did."

I never stopped walking and he never stopped following me.

"You don't believe me?" When I didn't respond, he said, "Emma was holding Jenny's hand, and when she wasn't, she had an arm around her waist."

Now I stopped. "Why didn't you tell me this?"

"I—er, wasn't sure when I'd last seen them—together, and when the police let me go I hurried over to catch you and I did. I saw them with my own two eyes."

"Yeah," I said, staring toward Coker's condo.

"You calling me a liar?"

"No—that wasn't the insult I had in mind."

Hmm. To knock on Emma Coker's door again or not—that was the question. You know it was just too damn hot today for me to be so indecisive.

When I looked for Fiddler again he was gone.

Chapter 4

The Golden Fleece Art Gallery is located on King's Highway but down the road from the gauche beach scene. People from Charleston have even been known to drive up and patronize the joint, but not me, and it has nothing to do with money. Paul Zidane is a groper. Take it from one who knows.

The gallery sits in a tastefully decorated strip mall with a high-end furniture store anchoring one end, a ribs place known for its long lines at the other. In between is the gallery, an expensive dress shop, and a boutique for toddlers with rich grandmas. As I came through the door a buzzer signaled my arrival and the air conditioning enveloped me as much as the heat and humidity had outside. I should've brought along a jacket. My tank top and cutoff jeans weren't enough for this deep freeze.

The shop had no second floor, and where that floor should've been, sunlight poured through a huge window in the rear of the building. That was complemented by light from a series of skylights. Sculptures filled the center of the room; on the far wall hung the abstracts.

As I walked along the wall I found one of Jenny's paintings and it had been allocated the extra space of the truly special.

The painting was definitely something to look at, as was the price tag. It depicted a normal-looking family: mom, dad, and a couple of kids making their way down a Grand Strand I recognized but with shopkeepers I couldn't place. Those hawking their wares had the bodies of snakes, rats, and wolves; hyenas, ferrets, parrots, and the occasional bear were there—all with teeth and claws.

There was movement at the far end of the room and Paul Zidane came through doors in the rear of the gallery, closed them behind his back, then glided up the aisle toward me. He was a slender, middle-aged man with thinning black hair and he wore a gray pinstriped suit, light blue shirt, and yellow silk tie. A matching handkerchief jutted out of his breast pocket, a smile was affixed to his lips, and he held his hands so you couldn't miss the cuff links studded with diamonds.

"Can we help you?"

I resisted asking who the "we" was, instead saying, "Susan Chase, Paul."

"Ah, yes," said Zidane with a practiced smile. "Harry Poinsett's young friend. How is Harry, my dear?"

"What I wanted to ask you . . . " Zidane was giving me the once-over and I just knew if he could get me behind those double doors, he'd like nothing better than to put his hands all over me. I shivered and it wasn't from the AC. "Have you seen Jenny Rogers lately?"

"No. Why? Is Harry looking for her?"

"I am."

"But why?" This time his once-over appraised my outfit. "Certainly you're not interested in—"

"Art?"

He smiled indulgently.

"Actually, Paul, I haven't seen much that's interested me since the turn of the century."

"Not . . . since the turn of the century?"

"I'm from the school that believes when the Average Joe began to appreciate art was when impression-
ism reared its ugly head—so the Joe wouldn't have a
clue as to what the contemporary artist had in mind."

A polite chuckle, followed by, "Is this something
Harry told you?"

"That's why I'm having trouble with my Rogers."

"You have a Rogers?"

"Day's End."

"Are you sure it's a Rogers? I know Jenny did a
piece by that name, but if you brought it in perhaps I
could authenticate it."

"I'll have Harry do it. What I'm more interested in
is authenticating the artist."

"Authenticating . . . the artist?"

"I'd like to know about Jenny's work. It might help
me find her."

He put his hands together, forming a small temple.
"And your client, if I might be so bold to ask?"

"Jenny's mother."

His face quickly soured and the temple fell apart.
"Then I can't say I wish you much luck. That relationship's quite toxic, though it's inspired some excellent
work." He glanced toward the front of the gallery. "Perhaps, if you'd like to get more comfortable . . . this way,
please." And he led me to the rear of the gallery, into a
nook, gliding across the floor with his funny little walk.

I took a seat in a straight-backed chair while Zidane
sat on one side of a love seat, looking a little bit disap-

pointed. He asked, "What do you know of Jenny's relationship with her mother?"

"I'm a friend of the family."

"Ah, yes," he said, as if understanding how I drummed up business in the rough-and-tumble world of private-eyeing. "Well, as you know Jenny and her mother never really got along."

"An understatement if there ever was one."

Zidane pursed his lips. "Unless Jenny was . . . how can I put this delicately?"

"It can't be done. Jenny couldn't function unless she was under her mother's thumb. That's pretty much common knowledge. What I'd like to know is how Jenny started painting. It might help me find her. The last I heard she was working at the library."

Zidane glanced toward the front again, and seeing no one else he could posture for, put an arm across the back of the love seat and concentrated on me. And me, I felt the icy grip of the air conditioning closing in.

"About three years ago Mrs. Rogers was hospitalized . . . in the psychiatric ward. The woman's quite mad, you know, and Jenny made such a nuisance of herself that the doctor ordered her to stay away. Her mother wasn't getting proper rest. Well, Jenny tried staying home but with no one to tell her what to do she was at a loss, so she returned to the hospital. The doctor said if Jenny kept this up her mother might never recover. She needed complete rest and isolation."

Zidane examined the nails on one hand before going on. "In that particular wing one can see people undergoing a variety of therapies. Some were painting. The doctor told Jenny, out of exasperation more than anything, that it wasn't healthy for her to be there all the time. She should find something to do, take up a hobby, do something."

"Like paint."

"Yes, and that's just what the poor girl needed: to be told what to do. She went out that very day and bought the necessary supplies and started to work. She even changed shifts at the library to have her days free. Obsession runs deep in that family, Miss Chase. I understand her father's success came from being on the road six to seven days a week."

"Or he didn't care to go home."

"That very well may have been. Mister Rogers was a graphic design artist, and from what I know of that business, customers come to them."

"Had Jenny ever painted before?"

"As a child," he said, as if it had been done in a former life. "Then a bit as a teenager, but her mother pooh-poohed it. Now, left to her own devices, Jenny became obsessed to the point of forgetting about her mother even when she was released from the hospital."

"I'm sure that didn't go over all that well with mom."

"Not at all," Zidane said with a soft chuckle. "It about hospitalized her again."

"Then Jenny must've had real talent," I said, shifting around. I shouldn't have sat down. I was beginning to ice over.

"Oh, Jenny had talent, my dear." He made another temple with his fingers. "Talent just waiting to be nourished by myself and others." He dismissed the "others" with a wave of the hand. "Most were penny ante artists Jenny quickly outstripped. Then she came to me—most do when their careers stall—for advice. I was the one who introduced her to Kristy O'Key."

"Was this when she moved in with O'Key?"

He seemed taken aback. "You know about that?"

"Of course. What I don't understand is why O'Key threw her out? Lovers' quarrel or what?"

"Absolutely not. Kristy's not gay."

"Then what did they fight about?"

He looked toward the front of the gallery again. "Simply put, the passion had gone out of Jenny's work. If Jenny couldn't fight with her mother, she couldn't paint. No stimulus, no work, or work of any consequence. I have several of her paintings I'd like to sell—they're in the back—but they're so lifeless, the most ordinary of work. One's even a beach scene." He tsk-tsked. "Kristy didn't have time for such hackneyed work. She's a serious artist who went a long time without recognition."

"I know the feeling, people not taking you seriously. Maybe that's what Jenny was suffering from?"

Another chuckle. "That wasn't it at all, my dear. Jenny had immediate success, Kristy's was a long time coming. Kristy comes from money—the O'Keys of the Keys as they call themselves—but doesn't receive a dime of family money. Never has, never will, and when her parents—now only her father since her mother's death—cut her off, Kristy eked out a living waiting tables until her work caught on." He smiled again. "That didn't go over well with her father. I've heard there were several scenes. When Jenny didn't demonstrate the same resolve . . . really, what could a serious artist have in common with someone who whines about lost talent? If you'd seen any of Kristy's work—"

"I have," I snapped. The weather in here was getting to me. I'd lost touch with my toes.

"Then you know Kristy works in black and white, which shows how remarkable she is, not only to draw such images out of only two colors but to have the courage to stay with her beliefs in the face of, not only lack of parental approval, but public indifference."

"Then Jenny's problem's solved, isn't it?"

"Er—what do you mean?"

"She can draw inspiration from fighting with O'Key."

Again that indulgent smile. "If Kristy would tolerate such distractions. With Jenny's mother that *was*
Jenny's life."

"When was the last time you saw her?" I wanted
out of here. I was freezing to death. "Jenny, that is."

"It's been several weeks." He thought about what
he'd just said. "But I should've seen her . . . I've sold a
few pieces of her work and Jenny wanted some quick
cash. She was quite perturbed when I wouldn't ad-
vance her a few thousand, but I really don't know where
the work's going."

"Quick cash for what?"

"Who knows? For living. For anything. Artists are
always asking for money, or leaving work with me to
be sold. I don't lend money against just any work
though—unless I think the artist has talent."

"Seems like a pretty silly reason to throw someone
out—that she couldn't paint as well as before. Shows a
real lack of compassion on O'Key's part."

Zidane only stared at me.

I said nothing, and he said nothing, and I don't
know about him, but it took one hell of an effort on my
part. My fingers were numb.

He caved first. "Well, there was some talk of drugs."

I laughed and hoped it hid the sound of my chattering teeth. "Here at the beach? You've got to be kidding."

"Now see here, Susan," he said, sitting up. "I'm not
the kind to spread gossip, especially about my clients."

*Oh, right. The only thing that would slow you down
would be that funny little walk of yours.*

Zidane sat there staring at me and I sat there staring back. After an eternity, make that an ice age, he said, "Jenny tried drugs as a last resort to revive her lost talent."

"You're telling me Jenny got into drugs when all she had to do was move back home and fight with her mother and her talent would've been revived?"

"I don't think Jenny considered that a viable alternative. She wanted Kristy's approval. Most do. When you succeed in black and white, everyone notices you, even the uninformed."

Rather than take that personally, I asked, "O'Key's not into drugs?"

He shook his head. "Couldn't afford them before, sees them as a distraction today. It's hard for the average person to understand—because of what they've seen on television—but few artists use drugs. There's no profit in it."

"If Jenny never painted again, it'd make her work much more valuable, wouldn't it?" I inclined my head toward the doors leading to the storage area. "Even the paintings you have back there that are so ordinary."

Zidane only smiled.

"Have any idea where I might find her?"

"Really, Susan, I don't think she's in town."

"Could she be traveling with O'Key?"

"Not from her condition the last time I saw her."

"Still on drugs?"

"And borrowing for more. You might try Emma Coker—another artist, albeit a hack." He smiled. "If you do, keep your pants on."

I ignored the crack. "Anyone else?"

Two old women with blue hair were admiring the painting in the window. That caught Zidane's eye, and

I found myself wishing they'd come in and buy something. By now I was openly shivering.

Zidane returned his attention to me. "There's a young man who claims to be a playwright: George Fiddler. He followed Jenny around, trying to catch her eye."

"Could he be Jenny's supplier?"

"Possibly. Fiddler's lived here for several years, but I've never heard of any of his work being performed. His family sends him money so he *won't* return home."

"Why's—why's that?" I asked, teeth chattering.

The doorbell tinkled and the two old ladies came in, one telling the other she thought this was the place. No doubt Paul Zidane would convince them of that.

He stood up, brushed down his pants, adjusted his jacket, then ran a hand across his thinning hair. "Duty calls, Susan. Do tell Harry I said 'hello.'"

I followed him up the aisle, and I have to say it was good to be moving again. My brain was saying hello to my hands, nice to feel you again. "What's this about Fiddler's family wanting him to stay at the beach?"

"Oh, he'd picked up a runaway and kept the girl at his house while his parents were out of town." Zidane glanced over his shoulder. "Locked in a closet."

"Raped?"

Zidane stopped, a discussion of rape not conducive to selling to little old ladies with blue hair. "No—it seems Fiddler only wanted to take care of her."

"Then why isn't he in jail?"

"Because, my dear, the girl disappeared before they could bring him to trial."

Chapter 5

From the Artists' House, I stood with the owner gazing out the front window at a pay phone where three black guys hung out. The guys were smoking cigarettes, catcalling the passing ladies, and generally cutting the fool. All three wore similar clothing: tight-fitting pants, shirts unbuttoned to the waists, plenty of gold jewelry, and beepers on their belts. The shopkeeper and I were discussing the whereabouts of Jenny Rogers; the guys across the street were dealing dope.

The Artists' House was situated on a side street, as selling artist supplies wasn't as profitable as selling junk to tourists traveling the King's Highway. The Grand Strand has both indoor and outdoor malls, but the ones making the real money operate out of the strip malls, catering to the most primitive impulses of the tourist trade.

"Those boys destroyed Jenny Rogers." The owner was a short man with beefy arms, a Greek who talked not only with an accent but with his large hands. "Damn those boys!" he said, shaking a fist at the dealers. "I have lost more than one customer to them. Sorry about the language, young lady, but those boys, they make me mad, especially that Kenny Mashburn, the one on the telephone. He sold Jenny Rogers the dope that ruined her life. I hate him most of all. People were just beginning to notice her work."

The shopkeeper shook his head. "They say in the colored neighborhoods the dope dealers stay away from the boys who can play basketball, but here . . . ." He gestured at the street. "Those people think the work of an artist will be . . . 'enhanced' is the word they use to make the poor beginner buy their first drugs." He turned to me. "I know what you're thinking, young lady, turn those boys in to the police. Well, I did, and the next day a brick was thrown through my window. Ruined a good easel, it did. So now they stay on their side of the street and I stay on my side."

With a shrug he added, "Anyway, what would it matter? Jail those boys and a new group will come along—because my shop is here. I know what they tell my customers: buy some paints, that new brush you need, and some cocaine to open your mind. Make your work live forever. And those boys can give you names of famous painters who have used drugs." He shook his head. "It doesn't work that way, but that's not something you can tell a beginner."

"Do you remember the last time you saw Jenny?"

"What? Oh, I can't remember, young lady, but I can tell you this: That girl was in terrible shape."

He couldn't tell me when he'd seen her, but he remembered her condition. Jenny certainly got people's attention; but could I get a line on her? Maybe I should do a line or two and open my mind to the possibilities.

The shopkeeper watched the guys across the street

trail a tourist down the sidewalk. The tourist had a
bouncy walk, and within seconds the boys had it mas-
tered, but they weren't gone long. They had to get back
to their business connection: the phone. A tourist was
using it when they returned. He took one look at them,
hung up, and hurried off down the street.

"It's getting so an honest man can't make a living,"
started the shopkeeper again. "I have a house in a good
neighborhood. A nice place. People moving in all the
time. Young people with families. Young men who are
home all day. Now I ask you, young lady, what kind of
job is it a young man can have where he is home all
day?" He shook a finger at me. "Drugs—that's what it
is. My wife and I worked hard to get what we have.
Raised our kids and raised them right, and what does
it get us? Drug dealers living next door. People think
drug dealers live like on TV: one attractive woman after another, parties night and day, fast cars . . . that's
not how it is. Most live in my neighborhood and make
business trips inland. Anyone can do it. There is a lot
of coastline along the Grand Strand. So what do today's
children learn? I'll tell you what people your age learn,
young lady, that there's an easier way to make money
than working for it."

"So there's no way you can pin down the last time
you saw Jenny? Maybe she was in making a purchase?"

He considered this, having to switch from preach-
ing to remembering, then motioned me to the rear of
the store, past shelves of paint, inverted paintbrushes
in bottles, and stacks of sketch pads and canvases.
Overlooking the store was an office: one wall filled with
sales receipts, the other covered with small pictures
by various artists. Between the walls was a desk littered with paperwork, and over that desk was installed

a two-way mirror giving the shopkeeper a view of the store—and the infamous pay phone.

He pulled down some invoices, flipped through them (each stack was held together by a metal ring), then returned that stack to the shelf. "If she bought something, young lady, I should be able to find it. I keep everything in order. Anyone can look anytime they wish. Everything is always in order."

He took another stack and flipped through it. As he did, I checked the artwork on the opposite wall. Emma Coker's painting hung between O'Key's and Rogers' and the location robbed it of any presence, turning Coker's work into something that might be found on any insurance company's calendar. As for comparing Jenny's work to O'Key's, well, it was hard to say whether Jenny got more out of colors than O'Key did from shades of black and white.

O'Key's painting depicted a narrow street, and the longer you stared at it, the more you felt the walls closing in on you. That came not only from the way the buildings leaned in, but also from the people hunched over as they moved along, all with some kind of burden on their backs—and faces. None of these painters struck me as being a particularly happy camper.

"This is it," said the storekeeper, tapping an invoice. "The sixteenth. Jenny was in a day or two before that."

"Almost a month ago—how can you be sure?"

"Because, young lady, this is Kristy's invoice and she was buying colors. I remember because I teased her about buying those colors."

"Colors?" I'm sure the surprise showed on my face.

"Yes—she said they were for Jenny." He glanced at the invoice. "I don't understand. Weren't those two on the outs?"

The drug dealer I wanted to talk with was on the phone, another was down the street selling nickel bags through the window of a hovering car. The third guy eyed me, sizing me up as a potential customer. So nice not to be considered just another pretty face, but I did wonder what he thought about the size of my legs.

"Hi ya, babe. Looking for a little action?"

I jerked a thumb at the phone. "With him."

The dealer glanced at Mashburn and held up his hands. "Okay, okay. I don'ts want to cut in on another brother's action."

As the punk strutted off, a bright red convertible trailed along behind him. When he stopped, the convertible pulled over and the driver, a blonde, called out to him.

The punk stepped over to the car. "I told you to stay away from here."

The girl said something about needing a fix, needing a fix real bad. Instead of giving her a fix he gave her the back of his hand. That didn't stop her from asking—it only changed her tone. "Please . . . ."

Another slap and the girl started crying, then pulled away. Tourists stared but only for a moment. The punk saw the looks, lifted his chin, pulled back his shoulders, and sauntered off down the street. Good thing he did. Pistol whipping the SOB would've queered my dealings with Kenny Mashburn.

Mashburn was still on the phone, one of the pedestal models where Superman would be hard pressed to change his shirt. Mashburn was assuring someone he could make it. Yeah, he'd be there. Naw, they didn't have to worry about him. He'd show, and with the shit, too. The punk's shirt was black, his slacks green, his hair slicked back and oily. Gold jewelry compensated for a lack of chest hair.

After hanging up he asked, "Yeah, babe, how can I do you?" He slid his hands into his pockets, thumbs out, and leaned against the side of the booth. On his hip was a cell phone, so the pay phone was for receiving secure calls—and posing.

"I'm looking for Jenny Rogers."

He looked me over, paying particular attention to my nose, face, and arms. "Never heard of her."

"She's one of your customers."

He stuck a toothpick in his mouth, and after running it from one end to the other, settled it in one corner. "Fucking fuzz getting younger and younger these days, I'm telling you."

"Actually I'm looking for Jenny for her mom."

"Yeah and things are tough all over."

"Then you won't help me find her?"

"Fuzz is fuzz to me, babe, and fuzz never gave me nothing but a hard time."

"Well, Kenny," I said, reaching past him to the phone, "I'm not here to set any precedents." I punched in some numbers as Mashburn continued to lean against the booth, close enough for me to smell his cologne, something with a tangy base.

The toothpick stopped at the end of his mouth again. "Who you calling, babe? And how you know my name?" He glanced across the street. "That old man send you over here?" When I didn't answer, he paid more attention to the phone call. "No way any fuzz can touch me, babe."

"You know, Kenny, most women find the expression 'babe' personally offensive."

He laughed and the toothpick almost fell out of his mouth. "Yeah and I reckon you be one of them."

Into the phone I said, "Nat Jenkins." Checking behind me, I saw the two other dealers looking our way.

"Hey, don't be on there too long. I'm expecting a call."

My hand slid onto my fanny pack. "Tough shit."

Mashburn rolled off the booth. "Oh, one of those tough bitches, huh?"

"Beyond your wildest imagination, Kenny. Beyond your wildest imagination." Into the phone, I said, "Nat? Susan Chase. Yeah. I got one for you." I gave him the location of the pay phone; the number had long ago been rubbed off. "Right. Three of them. Thanks."

I hung up and stood back, hands on hips, feet spread apart. Now the other two dealers were looking our way—and keeping their distance.

Mashburn glanced at the phone. "What that all about?"

The pay phone rang. Mashburn looked at the phone, then at me.

I said, "Thought you were expecting a call."

"Yeah." He picked up the phone. "Hello?" A puzzled expression crossed his face. "Hello? Anyone there?" He worked the cradle switch with his fingers, then listened again before saying, "Phone's dead."

"And you're out of business on this corner because you wouldn't do business with me."

"Fuck you, too, bitch." He dropped the phone the length of its cord, then slapped the one on his hip. "I still gots this."

"Yeah," I said with a cheery smile, "but for the really big deals you have to use a landline and I'm partnering with you for the rest of the day."

"That right? You just try following me."

"Don't worry. Babe. I don't expect to have any problem."

"It'll be your ass, too." He looked down the street. The other two dealers were openly staring at us. On the street vehicular and pedestrian traffic had vanished.

"Be right back," he hollered. "Gots something to take care of."

Mashburn started down the street, crossed against the light, and on the other side glanced back and saw me trailing along behind. He bumped into a tourist reading a map, slapped the map out of the way, and disappeared into an alley. When I arrived at the mouth of the alley Mashburn was halfway down, arms folded across his chest, feet apart, an easy smile on his face.

I stepped inside and a group of air conditioners created an invisible barrier between me and the street. If anything happened in here nobody would be the wiser. A rat slunk along a busted wooden skid, several dumpsters were canted to one side, and the air was charged with the smell of clogged grease traps. Charged with something. The hair on the back of my neck stood up.

From down the alley Mashburn said, "If you know what's good for you, bitch, you'll stay away from me."

I advanced on him. "And the sooner you tell me what I want to know the sooner you'll be back in business. Remember, Kenny, you have quotas to meet."

"I don'ts have to do nothing, bitch."

As I approached him Mashburn glanced behind me, then checked his backside. No one in here but us—and rats. While his head was turned I ripped away the Velcro side of my fanny pack and the snub-nose .38 fell into my hand. Never leave home without it.

Mashburn turned around. "I told you—"

I jammed the .38 into his face.

"Hey," he shouted, stumbling back. "Take it easy!"

"Jenny Rogers coming back now?"

Mashburn tripped over a box and landed on his butt. "Hey," he said, reaching behind him to hold himself up, "that thing loaded?"

"Don't know. Let's find out." I pointed the gun between the bastard's legs and cocked the hammer. I wished I'd had this little item on other occasions, one in particular. *People trying to exert control over me, men trying to exert control over me! Trying to fuck with me, trying to fuck me!*

Mashburn quickly closed his legs. "Hey! Watch where you're pointing that thing!"

A grin crossed my face, something simply beyond my control. "Kenny, when's the last time you got laid?"

A perplexed look, followed by, "What . . . what you talking about, girl?"

"When's the last time you got laid?"

"Uh, a couple," he cleared his throat, "a couple nights ago." The last part squeaked as it came out.

"Was it good, real good? Did you make her happy? Make her beg for more?"

"Er—yeah." He scooted backwards a couple of feet. "What you talking about?"

"So nice to have such memories"—I pulled back the hammer on the Smith & Wesson—"cause that's all you'll have if you don't tell me what I want to know about Jenny Rogers."

His hands came up. "Hey, wait, lady! Please!"

"I'm waiting, but I'd rather be listening."

"I'll tell you! I'll tell you! Just point that thing someplace else."

I did—at his face. "Get started, punk! You're wasting my time."

"Right! Right!" He composed himself. "Rogers only started using a few months ago. Said a friend sent her to me."

"Name, Kenny. Name."

"Emma Coker. Real tough bitch but never uses. That's how I get most of my customers. Referrals. Safest way, too." He flashed a weak smile. "They don't usually carry."

"What was Rogers buying?"

"What the hell you mean? She was buying coke. Kenny Mashburn don't deal in any of that cheap shit."

"How often did you see her?"

"Maybe once, maybe twice a week."

Aiming at his crotch again, I shouted, "Kenny!"

"Hey, she wasn't a big user. I'm telling you the truth here. That bitch was weird."

"Weird? In what way?"

"Like some kind of mad scientist."

"Mad scientist? What you talking about? I'm losing patience here."

"She wanted to know how much each hit was, and you can bet I was all over that Coker bitch, about Rogers being some kind of heat, but she vouched for her. Said Rogers was just a little flaky. A little flaky, hell, she was a lot flaky. Measuring everything and hassling me about one hit weighing more than others—maybe all the stuff not being the same quality. Am I responsible for that? I just sell the stuff." He shook his head. "I got tired of her shit. Told her to get lost, and you know what that bitch said?"

"This Rogers we're talking about here?"

"Yeah, Jenny Rogers. You listening to *me*?"

I pointed the pistol at his groin. "Sorry, Kenny, but you just don't seem to have the focus of a man about to lose his balls."

His hands gripped his crotch again. "Hey, cool it! Cool it here! She said—Rogers said I was *her* connection and she wasn't going anywhere. Well, I told her I'd give her a discount if she'd buy in quantity, then she could measure the shit and every hit would come from the same bag, weigh the same. After that I didn't see much of her."

"You take the coke to her or meet her on the street?"

He shook his head. "She didn't have no regular place. Lived with this artist, Kristy something, for a while. Supposed to be somebody special but not one of my customers. Then she went to live with that Coker bitch when this Kristy person threw her out."

"Where'd she go after leaving Coker?"

"Came by where I was doing business. Told her I'd deliver, but she said she didn't know where she'd be, that she'd stopped living with Coker."

"Seen her lately?"

Mashburn thought for a second. "Once or twice at this Fiddler dude's place. Same building as the place where this Kristy person live. He's one of mine."

I was going around in circles, all leading back to George Fiddler. "Anyone around when you were dealing with Rogers?"

"Never. She treated drugs like it was some kind of secret." He laughed. "Man, drugs ain't no secret—not on the Grand Strand."

"How long since you last saw her?"

"A week—no, that's not right. I haven't seen her in a while. Maybe it's a month."

I stuck the pistol in his face again. Beads of sweat dotted his forehead. "Hey! I'm being straight with you! The bitch was a head case but a regular customer. Now she's gone. That's too bad. I like to keep my customers."

"Sell her enough to OD?"

"Wait a minute. Wait a fucking minute here. I ain't responsible for what people do with the shit. They want to take the big bye-bye, it's not my problem." His eyes narrowed. "She dead?"

I lowered my gun. "Not as far as I know."

Mashburn dropped his hands. "As God's my witness, babe, I don't know where that bitch is."

"Any guesses?"

"Hell, could be anywhere. She was weird, but all artists are." He smiled. "And they love their coke."

I put my pistol away and walked past him, down the alley, heading for you-know-where. I was going to brace George Fiddler's young ass.

"Hey, babe," Mashburn called from behind me, "you wouldn't've really shot old Kenny, would you?"

I turned around. Mashburn was on his feet, brushing off his ass, his dignity, too.

"Who's to say you weren't trying to mug me?"

"Me for one," he said with a laugh.

"Sure, and you were going to tell the cops I was asking you about being Jenny Rogers' candy man."

I hustled back to the Mariner Hotel and raced up those four flights of steps. I was going to give George Fiddler a piece of my mind. The little jerk had only followed me over to Emma Coker's to find out if I'd learned that Jenny had been with him! *Seen them hand in hand at the Pavilion.* The fool probably imagined himself Jenny's protector and she his ward. I only hoped Jenny was still there. I was in the mood to wrap this up and quick. She'd been across the hall all along, while the little asshole had been writing his own script—and I'd gone along.

I was muttering to myself and pulling myself up the railing of that dimly lit stairwell—big chunks at a time, eyes riveted on the next step—when someone came around one of those blind corners and slammed into me.

"Out of my way!" screamed a woman, ramming me as I was about to grab another chunk of railing.

I went sailing back, out over the steps. I saw a face surrounded by dark hair—it was only a blur—next, a light without its canopy, then pain exploding at the back of my head, lights going off like fireworks. And as suddenly as those lights appeared, they were gone.

Chapter 6

The next thing I knew Paul Zidane was leaning over me, his face filled with concern. That seemed appropriate. My head ached, my back felt broken, and the corners of my vision were clipped off.

"Are you all right, Susan?" Zidane had one hand under my shoulder, another gripping an arm.

When I nodded, pain shot through my head and the blackness tried to overwhelm me. Tears formed in my eyes. Yeah. I was all right. Real all right.

There was a soft spot at the back of my head. Probably where my brains had oozed out. Check that. I didn't have any brains or I wouldn't set myself up for such a fall. There was a pun in there somewhere, but I didn't feel like going looking for it. I wiped the tears away.

I was on a landing in a darkly lit stairway with people staring at me from the top and bottom. And my tank top was above my breasts. Now that hadn't happened falling down any damned stairs.

"Could you help me to my feet?"

"Susan, I don't think . . ." Not only would he not give me a hand, but he held me down.

"Well then, I'll have to take care of this from here."

I slapped him. There wasn't much force in the blow, but it did connect. Zidane jerked back. Upstairs, someone gasped.

"Don't you ever put your hands on me again, you fucking pervert."

"But I was only trying to—"

"Yeah," I said, re-covering my boobs. "I know what you were trying to do." I scooted up against the wall and took another look around. I wasn't sure what *I* was doing here. It didn't look like an art gallery. Who were all these people?

Below us gawkers scattered and were replaced by Lt. J. D. Warden, then Sgt. Mickey DeShields. Warden saw me scrunched up on the landing.

"What are you doing here, Chase?" When I didn't reply, he stepped over me and continued upstairs. "Bring them along, DeShields." He disappeared up the stairs and around the next landing.

Mickey stood below us on the stairs, looking from me to Zidane. Mickey was one of the blackest men I have ever known—his skin had an almost blue tinge to it. High-top fade and clothes that only look good on him: black jacket, orange shirt, and dark tie with a lot of stylized "Xs," black slacks and half boots. Really, on him that stuff looks good. When Mickey pulled me to my feet, I almost puked all over his pretty shirt and politicized tie.

"What happened here, Susan?"

I didn't know, but one thing for sure, I might throw up if I didn't watch it. My stomach was really churning. "Ask . . . Zidane?"

"Mister Zidane?"

"I found Susan as I came upstairs."

"That right, Susan?"

"As far as I know."

"What do you mean—as far as you know?"

"I don't remember."

I shook my head and the pain went right to my stomach. My legs weakened. I gripped the railing to stand. Bile rose in my throat again.

"You okay?" asked Mickey.

"Sure."

"You were knocked down or you fell down?"

"I don't remember." And this time I did not shake my head.

"What are you doing here?"

I couldn't remember. Besides, nobody could think with a head like this. "I don't know. I really don't know."

"And you?" DeShields asked Zidane.

"Looking for Jenny Rogers."

"Who's that?"

"A missing person," I said, remembering. "Warden knows all about it."

"You're both looking for the same person?"

Zidane said that was correct. I busied myself by hanging onto the railing.

Zidane said, "I came over to see if I could find Ms. Rogers. She's a prominent artist."

Mickey motioned to the steps. "Let's go upstairs and talk with Lieutenant Warden."

"Really, Officer, I need to return to my gallery."

"There's a dead man upstairs, Mr. Zidane, that's why SLED's been called in. No one leaves the building until you've been released by Lieutenant Warden."

"Whose body?" I asked, holding my breath.

"A kid by the name of Fiddler—anyone you know?"

"I don't think so. Anyone with him?"

"Don't know, Susan. We just got the call."

"I called," said a black guy from the top of the stairs. "George Fiddler was a friend of mine."

We went upstairs, Mickey holding onto my arm to support me. "See anything else?" he asked.

The dude glanced at me before saying, "I was coming downstairs when I saw this man"—he pointed at Zidane—"kneeling beside the girl. The chief of police said I should show you up, but I didn't make it that far." He glanced down the landing. "George Fiddler was a friend of mine," he repeated.

"The chief of police is upstairs?" I asked.

"Yes, ma'am."

On the fourth floor we found the dead guy on the floor in the middle of his apartment, in front of an old wooden desk. He seemed vaguely familiar . . . maybe I knew him from somewhere.

The guy's desk was covered with papers, not typed but neatly scrawled and stacked in the right hand corner. Worn furniture sat in a semicircle in front of an antique console TV, paperbacks filled the bookshelves; the walls were covered with posters of Arthur Miller, several featuring the playwright with Marilyn Monroe. Beside a dresser stood an easel, and underneath it, a shoe box filled with paints and brushes. An artist's palette leaned against the dresser. One arm was flung out behind the dead guy, the other trapped under his body. He wore jeans, a sweatshirt, and sandals, and was skinny as a refugee. Light-colored hair clumped up in a pool of blood.

"I need to sit down," I said.

"Not in here." Warden knelt beside the body.

The black guy who had led us upstairs looked like he might join me in collapsing, but the chief of police only shook his head.

"Messing around where you don't belong."

"You left me on the stairs—what kind of person does that?"

"I called the paramedics, after checking to see if you were still breathing."

And maybe fondled my tits, I thought, flushing with shame and rage. Tears appeared at the corner of my eyes, but I didn't dare wipe them away. Not in front of these men.

As I stumbled out of the room, Warden said, "Don't you go anywhere, Chase. DeShields, I want to talk to Owens, then Zidane."

In the hallway Mickey turned me around and checked the lump on my head. He barely touched it, but that was enough to make my legs buckle. Zidane watched as Mickey seated me on the stairs. At the far end of the hall, the wind whipped the curtains around. It felt good against my overheated face. While I was collecting my thoughts, the paramedics arrived.

"Want them to take a look at you?" asked Mickey.

I waved him off and lay my head on my arms.

"Susan, J.D.'s going to want to know how you happen to be here."

I didn't know what to say. Everything was blank.

"Jenny's mother hired her," Zidane said.

I looked up.

"She was in my gallery this morning," added Zidane. "Susan, that is. That's when I learned Rogers was missing. Rogers is friendly with George Fiddler and Emma Coker. That must be why Susan's here."

Mickey looked at me.

I shrugged. "Works for me."

"Who knocked you downstairs?"

"If I remember I'll let you know."

"J.D. will want more than that."

The chief of police came out of Fiddler's room. "I know for a fact this is the second time Chase has been in this building today. She's also on my list of suspects who might've burgled O'Key's apartment."

I put my head down again. Why wouldn't these people go away and leave me alone? While working up a pity party I heard someone leave Fiddler's room and Mickey tell Zidane to go inside.

The chief of police stopped at the stairs, playing to the crowd, it would appear. "Stay off Pawleys until the end of the Season, young lady. I've got enough kids to baby-sit. And put on some clothes if you want to be considered a real professional."

"Okay, folks," I heard DeShields say to those gathered on the stairs, "show's over. Be about your business now. Chief, could you help us with the crowd?"

But the chief wasn't through. "I don't know what's wrong with kids these days: Dress like bums, caps worn backwards, no respect for the law . . . ." I looked up to see him tap the patch of the American flag on the shoulder of his uniform. "Lots of my friends died so you could run around and make a fool of yourself." Then, mercifully, he headed downstairs.

I put my head back down. At any moment I was going to throw up everything I hadn't eaten all day.

The black guy, the friend of the dead man, and whose name was "Owens," stopped in front of me. "I just want you to know you slapped the right guy."

I hoped he couldn't see the tears when I raised my head to thank him. Down the hall where the curtains flapped around I could see the harbor through the window. It caused me to remember something.

"Is Zidane right about why you're here?" asked Mickey. "You were coming to see George Fiddler?"

"I think . . . he was harboring Jenny Rogers."

"Harboring her? You mean like a fugitive?"

"To protect her?"

Mickey squatted in front of me. "You're asking me?"

I scooted over and leaned against the wall. "I need a cigarette."

"Susan, the only reason you smoke is to stall—or blow smoke. Was Rogers the one who knocked you on your butt?"

"That has such a nice ring to it."

He shifted his weight to his other leg, still squatting in front of me. "I say again, was Rogers the one who knocked you on your butt?"

"She didn't kill Fiddler, Mickey."

"That's not what I asked."

"Yes, Jenny Rogers could've been the one who knocked me on my butt."

Paul Zidane came out of Fiddler's room, looked like he wanted to say something, thought better of it, then hurried downstairs.

Mickey got to his feet, then helped me to mine. "Time to go see the boss."

But when I stood the hall spun around.

"You okay?" asked Mickey.

"Yes." I had to use the wall to stand.

"Need a hand?"

"No—I'm fine."

Letting go of the wall, I brushed back my hair and went into Fiddler's room. My mouth tasted like an old dishrag and probably smelled that way, too. I fumbled around in my fanny pack but couldn't find any Certs. But my gun was still there. A Smith & Wesson .38 with a shroud so the hammer doesn't snag on all the shit us girls tote around.

Inside the apartment, J.D. Warden still knelt beside the body. He had his jacket off and I could see his holstered pistol and the half moons of perspiration under his arms. J.D.'s a husky guy, slightly taller than me, but only by a few inches. He's also old enough to be my father, and acts like it from time to time.

"Why'd you let Zidane go?" I asked.

Warden stood up. "Because he's a solid citizen and he was told not to leave town. You, Chase, I may have to lock up if you don't tell me what you know."

In my current condition I could hardly resist.

Mickey copied down everything in a pocket-sized notebook. Warden asked for a description of Jenny Rogers and I gave him that. He even wanted to see my knot, and when he touched it, he had to help me stand.

"You got something?" Warden asked the technician.

I pulled away. "I'm okay, J.D."

He held me in place. "Now's not the time to prove you're a tough guy, Chase."

The tech took a small chemical packet from his bag, twisted it in half, and gave it to me. When I stuck the sucker to the back of my head I about went down for the count.

Warden gripped my arm. A smile appeared at the corners of his mouth. "Easy, Chase. Can't have you collapsing in the middle of a crime scene."

"What . . . what have you learned?"

"The landlady told us she heard footsteps—after hearing something tumble downstairs. When she opened her door she saw someone run outside, a woman." He pointed at the dead man's desk. "There's two or three hairs on that corner."

"And you figure?"

"That this woman fought with Fiddler. Fiddler fell

back and hit the desk, snapping his neck."

"A woman did all that?"

"Happens every day."

"I'd like to see the statistics."

DeShields covered his mouth with his notepad. Warden and I amused him. DeShields says it's like watching a father-daughter act.

"I'm trying to give you the poop here, Chase."

"Why's that?"

"To let you know the trouble your friend's in."

"Hardly."

"Listen to me. Someone you didn't see, or recognize, knocked you downstairs. I think it was the woman who fought with George Fiddler. A woman doesn't know if she can slip away from people, people who use their hands on them—"

"Men," I said sourly.

"Right. A woman would throw up her arms to make sure she got past. A man would simply ram through, using his shoulder to move you out of the way."

"Maybe. Maybe it was a small man, J.D."

He sighed. "I've got work to do. Cases backed up all the way into next week. I think we're looking for a woman here, maybe even your friend."

"Did you get a description of the suspect—the so-called woman who ran down the stairs?"

"Dark hair, jeans. Green or blue blouse." He shook his head. "They weren't sure of the color."

"Long hair? Short hair?" I asked, feeling my strength returning, especially in my backbone.

"But it could be your friend."

"Rogers wouldn't have the nerve. Was it a big woman? Small? Stocky? Tall?"

"Not exceptionally tall or heavy. The woman came

down the steps—they're in line with the lobby door—
and was gone."

"Rogers isn't the type to kill anyone, J.D."

"We're all the type, you just have to hit our hot
button." He looked around. "See anything that might
belong to Rogers?"

"Why would I tell you?"

His face darkened. "Because you want to keep on
playing private eye along this beach."

I pointed at the dresser. "The painting equipment
beside the dresser—that could be Rogers'."

"That's a good girl. Now take a look in the closet."
When I started to cross the room, he added, "Without
touching the knob."

I flashed him a look that would've melted butter.
DeShields saw my look and chuckled. Inside the closet
hung dresses and tops in the same washed-out colors
I'd seen Jenny wear. Beneath them were suitcases and
a couple of boxes. Fiddler's stuff was there, too, but I'd
seen enough. I headed for the door, passing Warden
and someone in a suit, the coroner for Georgetown
County, I supposed. Both men hunched down beside
the body. Warden never looked up.

"You're free to go, Chase. We'll put out an APB for
your friend. You go home and get off your feet."

At the door I stopped. "Like you said, J.D., this
doesn't look premeditated, so no armed-and-danger-
ous in that APB."

Warden looked up. "You come up with anything,
anything at all, I want to hear about it. You got that?"

"How's that? I'll be home with my feet propped up."

Chapter 7

The usual thrill seekers were hanging around: locals with nothing better to do and tourists hoping for a juicy story to take back home. Camcorders whirled, cameras clicked, and reporters were held at bay by a hastily formed police line—which used up just about every member of the Pawleys Island police force. Kids sat on parents' shoulders for a better view, an ice cream truck did a land-office business, and the piers jutting into the channel emptied of fishermen. I didn't want to leave the building that way. How many runaways could you find if your face was splashed all over the TV?

A voice behind me said, "You can sneak out the back. I do it all the time."

I turned around and saw a little girl in blue shorts and a white top. She was barefoot and had short black hair, a pallid complexion, and bright blue eyes. When I faltered she took my hand and led me to the rear of the building. There I took a seat on the back stairs. My head ached and my stomach was still in turmoil. Neither one liked the idea of going out into that heat and humidity.

The little girl disappeared into an apartment and returned with a glass of ice water.

"Thank you," I said, taking the water. I gulped it down, thanked her again, and returned the empty glass.

"It's hot today," said the little girl.

A breeze through the back door was the only thing in my face now, making me feel much better. Then again it could have been the little girl's smile. Maybe it was time to take a comp moment.

"I'm sorry that woman knocked you downstairs."

That perked me up. "Did you see her?"

"Yes," said the girl, nodding. "She was in a big hurry."

"Have you ever seen her before?"

"I thought so, but I don't think so."

"Why's that?"

"Her hair was dark."

"You mean she was . . . ."

The girl nodded. "Like you—blond."

"But you thought you had seen her before—here?" By now I was kneeling in front of her, gripping her arms.

"Upstairs—visiting Kristy."

"The artist?"

"Yes." She smiled. "Kristy taught me how to paint." The girl made a face. "Her room was a real mess. If my room was that messy I'd be sent away."

"Sent away?"

"Home to my mom."

"You're just here for the summer?"

"With my daddy." She glanced down the hall. "But I have to be real good and I can't answer the phone."

"You can't?"

"No. When Daddy's at work Mama can't know when I don't have a baby-sitter."

"I see," I said, understanding the subterfuge of a dysfunctional home. My mother had walked out on us when I was thirteen. When I was fifteen my drunken father had fallen off the family shrimp boat and drowned. Pirates boarded us, thinking they could claim *Daddy's Girl* as salvage. When they found me sleeping below, that's when things got kind of dicey.

"What's your name?"

"Victoria, but you can call me 'Vic.' Everybody does. But my mother."

"Well, Vic, if you see this woman again would you call me?" I took a card from my fanny pack and gave it to her. "And don't forget to tell me where you live or I might not remember . . . ." I stopped. "What I mean is that I meet a lot of people and you might have to jog my memory."

The girl smiled. "Because you hit your head."

I nodded and found that wasn't so bad. Maybe I could stand—even walk again. "I'm afraid I did."

"I wanted to help, but the man said to go back to my room. I wasn't supposed to be outside. Daddy's at work now."

I described Paul Zidane.

"Yes," she said, nodding. "That was the man."

"Did you see the man go upstairs?"

She shook her head. "No. I went back to my room."

"Thank you, Vic. And my name's Susan."

"I'm sorry he touched your boobies, Susan."

My face heated up as I rose to my feet. "Well," I said, after clearing my throat, "I guess now you understand why your mother wants to make sure you're safe."

As I went down the back steps of the Mariner Hotel a woman hurried by on the road that runs along the chan-

nel between the island and the mainland. She had a
squat body and short black hair and glanced over her
shoulder at the flashing lights at the front of the building. Stumbling out to the road, I watched her duck
between a couple of houses and disappear in the direction of the beach. I cut between a couple of houses
myself and spotted her down a street running parallel
to the one we'd just left. I was only a few houses away,
hobbling along, when she cut through again. Gritting
my teeth, I broke into a lope. Sweat ran down my face.
I really felt awful and thought I might throw up.

When I reached where she had cut through, I found
the woman negotiating a thicket of azaleas between
two backyards. She must've heard me coming because
she whirled around, holding her hands up in some sort
of self-defense technique. Then I remembered her—and
her attitude.

"Stay away from me, Chase. I know karate."

A cop once told me the best way to avoid a confron-
tation is to move steadily toward the perp as you chat
him up. Or her, in this case. I did, and at the same
time, my hand shot between Coker's hands, slapping
her across the face. Well, that might not've been exactly what the cop had had in mind.

"Show me a little of your technique, Emma. I'm always willing to learn." God but I felt absolutely rotten.
Hopefully I wouldn't throw up in the midst of my power
play. My legs felt weak and the headache had returned
with a vengeance.

Coker lowered her hands. "Why are you following
me, Chase? I answered all your asinine questions earlier today."

"I've got some new ones, such as why were you at
the Mariner Hotel a few minutes ago?"

She glanced behind me. "You must be mistaken. I haven't been near the place. I was out for a walk, trying to work out a problem . . . with my painting. Something you obviously wouldn't understand."

"Bullshit. Nobody can think on these streets—it's too damn hot."

Coker's nose elevated slightly. "What would you know about the creative process?"

"I'm not here to debate art theory. I want to know what you were doing at George Fiddler's."

"George Fiddler's? But I wasn't—I told you I was out . . . for a walk." Her chin trembled.

"I saw you there."

"You're crazy." She turned away, moving slowly down the row of bushes, trying to find a way to slip between the houses. "Now get away from me before I—"

I stayed right with her. "Before you what? Call the cops? Why don't we? I know where we can find a couple of good ones." Nearby, a geezer stopped clipping his hedge and stared at us. "I followed you from Fiddler's, Emma."

When she faced me again she wrung her hands. "Why are you persecuting me? Did someone hire you to disrupt my work—ruin my concentration?"

I laughed. The girl could really go on and on.

She lifted her chin. "It's impossible for someone like yourself to understand a person with my gift."

"Cut the shit, Emma, and tell me what you were doing at Fiddler's."

She bit her lip. "I was trying to find Jenny—if you have to know—before you did. She's much too delicate a person to be used by someone as crude as you."

"You said Jenny had toughened up lately."

Coker didn't have an answer for that.

"You were in the building when Fiddler was killed, weren't you, Emma?"

"No, no, I wasn't there! I didn't go in. There were too many policemen. When I saw you, I left. You're horribly distracting, Chase."

"If you're so concerned about Jenny, why didn't you go inside? She might've needed your help."

Coker stared at the ground.

"You *were* there, weren't you?"

She started away. "I have to return to my studio. I have work to do."

"Fiddler's dead," I said, following her. "But you already knew that, didn't you?"

"I—I don't know anything about that."

I moved in front of her, blocking her way. "And I think you do."

"No, no, I was just passing by."

"I thought you were looking for Jenny."

"I—I was, but I didn't see her."

"Didn't see her where? In the building? In Fiddler's room?" I softened my tone to add, "You can tell me."

Kids on their way to the beach glanced at us as they walked by, towels over shoulders or around their necks.

In a low voice, Coker said, "In Fiddler's room."

I seized her arm. "I think it's time we had a talk with those cops."

She pulled back quickly, jerking my head and causing it to ring with pain. My eyes dampened. Again my legs weakened.

"No, no," she pleaded, "don't do that. George was already dead when I got there." Her hand flew to her mouth as if she could stuff the words back in.

I might be sick, but I was also sick and tired of this

bitch. I swallowed down the bile and took her by the arm again. "Come on, we're going to see the cops."

"But I didn't see anything—really!"

"Then you don't have anything to worry about."

"Don't do this to me. It could ruin my reputation."

"Yeah—that's our primary concern here, not finding out who killed that poor kid."

Warden didn't like Coker's story any more than he liked me coming up with another suspect. It makes for more paperwork and tends to draw out the investigation. DeShields read Coker her rights and they pounded on her in the hall outside Fiddler's room. I did what I could to help.

"Earlier today Fiddler told me Coker ransacked O'Key's apartment."

"But I didn't!" She glanced in the dead man's room. "George would say anything to keep me away from Jenny."

"Chase," Warden said, "would you go over there and sit down. Your face is white."

I did, but I didn't like it. Okay, okay, I liked being off my feet.

"Chase's question's still a good one," Warden said, "so explain what you meant."

"George likes to have a girl all to himself. In Charlotte, he locked one in a closet. Check with the police up there. They know all about him. He's some kind of pervert."

"The time you saw Rogers with Fiddler was Rogers restrained in any way?"

"Yes!"

Warden got in her face. "I want the truth, lady. I'm going to check out Fiddler with the Charlotte police, then run *you* through the computer."

"Me? Why?"

"Because you're a suspect in a murder investigation."

"But, I—"

"And I ask you again—was Rogers restrained in any way when you saw her with Fiddler?"

Coker looked as if she'd bitten into something she didn't like. "No," she spit out.

"Then why'd you ransack O'Key's apartment?" asked DeShields.

"It wasn't me," she said, turning on Mickey. "I don't know who did it, but it wasn't me."

"Chase," asked Warden, "is this the woman who knocked you downstairs?"

"You'd take her word against mine?" asked Coker. "Chase hates me. Fiddler, too."

"Don't forget O'Key," I called out from the stairs.

"That's right," Coker said, nodding. "They're all jealous of my talent. It's something every artist learns to live with."

"Yeah," I said, "like O'Key had to learn about you."

Coker glared at me.

Warden said he was still waiting for an answer.

Grudgingly, Coker said, "Yes—Jenny could've killed George while trying to get away from him."

"When I locate Jenny I'll let her know you were willing to give her up."

"You're not her friend. I am."

"Do you know where Rogers is?" asked DeShields.

Coker shook her head. "I haven't seen her in weeks. I've looked all over, but she's gone."

"Could she be with O'Key?"

"I hope not."

"Why?" asked Warden.

"O'Key thinks she's the Great Goddess Painter, but

her work's nothing. Ask any critic. She works in black and white. No one works in black and white. There's no texture."

"I thought that's why she did it."

Again she turned on me. "You little fool! What do you know about art? What do you know about anything?" To Warden and DeShields, she said, "Chase forced her way into my apartment this afternoon. And wouldn't leave. You don't know what it's like dealing with her."

A smile crept across Warden's face. "I think we have a fairly good idea. Would you care to press charges against Miss Chase?"

She glanced at me. "I guess not. No harm's been done."

Lt. Warden hadn't been put off by Coker's trip around Robin Hood's barn. "Chase, is this the woman who knocked you down the steps?"

Coker uttered a small sound of disgust, mostly through her nose.

I had to admit I couldn't be sure. For all I knew it could've been Jenny Rogers. But I didn't say that.

"Listen, Lieutenant," Coker said, "I admit I was here looking for Jenny, but that's all I'm admitting." She nodded toward Fiddler's room. "The little worm was already dead when I arrived."

Warden turned to DeShields. "Take her to Myrtle. Finish questioning her there."

"But I never go to Myrtle Beach."

I laughed. Truly, this woman's elevator didn't run all the way to the top.

When DeShields took Coker's arm she threatened SLED with a lawsuit, spouting the name of one of the most prestigious firms along the Grand Strand. "He buys my work, I'll have you know."

"Is that supposed to be some kind of reference?" I asked, getting to my feet.

That caused Coker to explode in a flurry of curses as she was led away, and as far as I could tell, she never once repeated herself. Warden watched her go, then looked at me. "Now will you go home and leave this to us?"

"Whatever you say."

But Warden only shook his head as he returned to Fiddler's room.

People don't just disappear. So, skipping the obligatory trip to have my head examined, I drove up King's Highway to the Myrtle Beach Library—the last place Jenny had worked. It must've looked funny, me driving along, ice pack held to the back of my head. Assholes waved and shouted as they whipped by; assholes, as opposed to dumb-asses who let themselves get knocked down a flight of stairs.

I'm not a big fan of the library in the normal sense of the word. You can learn a lot more, and a lot faster by watching TV; still, it can be a good place to gather your thoughts. I wasn't headed there to gather my thoughts but to question Doris Moffitt. Doris and I had once worked at Food Lion together. Doris loved working at Food Lion until her doctor told her she had to lose some weight. She took a job at the library, and as far as I know, no one has caught her munching on any of the cookbooks.

In the reference section Doris told a pimple-faced girl she'd be taking a break in the courtyard behind the library.

"Haven't you already had your break today?" asked the girl.

"Then this'll be my first one for tomorrow."

"I don't think it's fair, you getting two breaks in the same afternoon."

The pimple-faced girl thought *she* had a problem. I didn't want to go back outside, not with this headache. On the way up King's Highway I'd taken several aspirins, but nothing seemed to help. And my back still ached from my fall downstairs.

"Why don't we talk inside?" I suggested.

"Oh, we can't do that, Susan. People would see us and know I wasn't working."

"And that's just what you'll be doing," taunted the girl from behind the counter.

Doris steered me away.

"What about the employee lounge?" It'd be cooler and I'd have my own trash can to throw up in.

"Oh, no, you couldn't go in there. That's just for employees."

It was hot as hell out there in that courtyard, and if you're wondering how I can guard the beach all day, I usually have an umbrella and don't work the day after I've been knocked down a flight of stairs.

Doris scanned the courtyard before taking a seat. What was she worried about? There was no one out here, no one that stupid and that was Doris' problem; my problem now.

"I don't know if I should be seen talking with you, Susan."

"Why not?"

"Because the girls heard you ask about Jenny."

"So? They know she's taken a leave of absence."

Doris shook her head. "No—the library won't let Jenny come back to work."

"Why not?"

She shifted around on her rock perch. "Jenny was selling drugs. Right here at the library."

"Before or after her leave of absence?"

"Both."

"How many customers did she have—at the library?"

"I really couldn't say."

"Did you actually see her selling drugs?"

Doris shook her head.

"Then what proof do you have?"

"Robin Young was fired for using drugs."

"Using them at work?"

"Yes."

"So?"

"He said he bought them from Jenny."

"Young told you that."

"Oh, no, it's all over the library. Everyone knows. Mrs. Rae took down his confession before they let him go." Doris leaned forward, conspiratorially. "You know the kind of life these artists lead."

"No, Doris. Do tell."

"Well, first Jenny ran away from home, then she took up with this artist, Kristy O'Key, who travels all the time. Jenny was gone a lot with her. Later, she moved in with this, er—dyke, then she lived with that playwright, George Fiddler. The last I heard, she was about to do some traveling of her own."

"Where was she going?"

Doris' face lit up like a child who's been given a new toy—or several donuts. "I'm sure it was some place exotic. Traveling with Kristy O'Key gave Jenny the itch to paint just like Kristy did."

"In black and white?"

"Oh, no. Painting the world as she saw it. It sounds *soo* exciting—traveling without a care in the world. I wouldn't have the nerve, but Jenny did."

"When did she leave?"

"Oh, I don't know. Last time I saw her was when she came by my place to borrow some money."

"Money? How much?"

"Five hundred dollars. Enough to tide her over until her next check comes in. You know, that money she gets from her trust fund every month."

"Has she paid you back?"

"Oh, no, Susan, I haven't seen Jenny since she borrowed the money."

"No cards or letters? Phone calls?" My hopes were really sinking now.

"No," Doris said in a puzzled voice.

"When did you last see her?"

"A couple of weeks ago. But there's plenty of time to pay back the money. Jenny's annuity check wouldn't have arrived until now, and she'd have to send a money order if she's overseas."

"Doris, if Jenny's selling drugs, why'd she need to borrow five hundred dollars? People in that line of business are usually rolling in money."

"Gosh, I don't know. I never thought of that."

Chapter 8

The O'Key family made their pile as shipbuilders, then, when no one wanted wooden ships any longer, they replanted their land with pines, which could be cut for pulpwood. This means the O'Keys have more money than several families in Charleston, and that has ticked off more than one blue-blooded family living along the Battery; the O'Keys' preference for not living there.

The O'Key mansion was in the country, a huge stone thing with turrets—if you can believe that—surrounded by acres and acres of grassland and a wall to keep the riffraff out. When I stopped at the gate, a guard stepped out of the kiosk and used a light to compare my face with my ID. The guy was solid-built with little neck. He also wanted to see my PI's license—when I told him why I was there.

"Sorry, Miss, but the O'Keys want to know who's who."

I rolled my eyes and turned over my license. A call to the house brought more bad news.

"Sorry," he said, returning the license, "but they're not interested."

"Are they interested in news about their daughter?"

"Kristy?"

"That's the one."

"What's happened?"

With a sweet smile, I said, "That's for me to know and for the O'Keys to find out."

He stepped toward my jeep. "You know, kid, I could shake it out of you."

I slapped my fanny pack and quickly the gun was in my hand, the barrel in his face. He stepped back and held up his hands, phone and all.

"Now, instead of playing macho man, why don't you get back on the phone and tell the O'Keys I have some important information about their daughter?"

He did and got the reply I wanted. Now it was his turn to smile. "But you'll have to leave your pistol here."

I drove through acres and acres of grassland cluttered with palm trees and clumps of flowering bushes: oleanders, hibiscus, poinsettias, gardenias, camellias, and azaleas, all highlighted by golden begonias and bougainvilleas. The property had once been a swamp, the house built on the high ground, then the adjoining land drained and the gardens assembled around it. Lights reflected off ponds, fish broke the surface, and streams bubbled under more light than any moon could provide.

The doors of the house were huge wooden barriers, twice as tall as me, and the fellow who answered one of those humongous doors was a skinny old bird in a dark suit and bow tie. He said to follow him, that Madam would meet me in the study. Really, I don't think I would've seen the inside of this place if I hadn't stopped at a service station and pulled on a pair of slacks, flats,

and a blouse—which I keep in a footlocker welded to
the floorboard of the Jeep in lieu of a backseat. Earrings and other jewelry I keep in the glove compartment. Uppers and downers are in a magnetized box
affixed to the undercarriage.

In the vestibule, dual staircases curved along opposite walls, joining at the top and leading to the living
quarters. Draped over the second story banisters were
flags of various ships, worn by the weather; somewhere
in the stratosphere, a crystal chandelier provided infe-
rior light. The hallway featured furniture heavy on
wood, thin on padding; none of it looked like much fun
to sit in. Paintings of men with too much facial hair
and women who appeared to have inherited all the
brains in the family hung on the walls.

I was shown into a room with overstuffed furniture, floor-to-ceiling drapes, and bookcases on all four
walls. I burned my way through several cigarettes and
leafed my way through a few books—most with their
pages stuck together—until Mrs. O'Key finally graced
me with her presence. She caught me thumbing
through a copy of a book I'd seen on Dads' schooner.

"Do you read, Miss Chase?"

"Only when the TV's on the blink." I slid the volume
back into its slot, then brushed off my hands.

She surveyed the stacks. "I've meant to read some
of these myself but never seem to have the time."

"Well, it would cramp your social life."

She stared at me. "That was supposed to be a joke,
wasn't it?"

"It didn't have to be."

She gave me a reluctant smile, then gestured at a
chesterfield across the room. Angeline O'Key was the
perfect trophy wife: blond, blue-eyed, with a figure that

should be outlawed. And she was also about the same age as her stepdaughter.

After sitting down she spread her dressing gown around her, patting down the folds. "I've never met a real detective before." When I said nothing, she asked, "You have news of Kristy?"

"Why? Did you think she was missing?"

The woman didn't seem to understand the question.

"Your stepdaughter—is she missing?"

"I thought . . ." she started, then her eyes became very hard. "Just why are you here? Are you trying to extort this family?"

"Why would you think so?"

"Well, my husband does have a good bit of money. Perhaps I should call Lambert."

I reached over and patted her knee. "Oh, I'm sure us girls can work this out."

She drew back. "But they said you had a gun."

"I'm licensed to carry. Or did all they tell you was that there was someone with a gun to see you?"

"No, it's just that . . . ." She straightened up. "I thought you had news of my stepdaughter."

"I'm looking for a missing person. Jenny Rogers. Have you seen her?"

"Jenny Rogers? I don't know why I would have."

"I thought her mother called you."

"Oh, yes," she said, nodding. "Now I remember. That Jenny Rogers."

"I think Jenny might be traveling with your stepdaughter."

"I hardly think so."

After counting to ten, okay, I made it as far as four, I filled her in on Jenny's predicament, leaving out only that she was wanted for questioning in a murder investigation. All in all not much to leave out. "After Jenny left home she moved in with your stepdaughter."

"I didn't know that."

"Yes—it seems Kristy was Jenny's mentor."

"How interesting." O'Key found a place where her dressing gown didn't quite lay smooth against the chesterfield and patted it down.

"So I wondered if Kristy might've mentioned anything to you?"

"Oh, no, she wouldn't have." When I said nothing, she added, "We don't see much of Kristy. She runs in different circles."

I just sat there.

"Perhaps if I explained Kristy's relationship to the rest of the family you'd understand why we wouldn't know anything about this Rogers person."

Before she could, a real hunk strolled into the room. The man was absolutely gorgeous: tanned, blond hair, blue eyes, and shoulders a girl could call home. He looked to be in his late thirties and he was dressed for the club, or a day on the family yacht: deck pants and a pullover, loafers without socks. In his hand was a glass of yellow-red liquid. But up close the hunk lost all his charm. Up close you saw the bloodshot eyes, circles under those eyes, and the grainy flesh under the solid tan.

"Robbie, this is Susan Chase. She's a detective."

"Really?" he asked, and the word practically sneered at me as it came out.

The former hunk took a seat in a low-slung piece of furniture, a fragile-looking thing, Louis the First, Fourteenth, or Fifteenth, I really don't know. He put finger and thumb to the bridge of his nose, using them to

squeeze himself awake, then stared at me, not bothering to undress me with his eyes. I was beneath him
and never would be—pun intended.

"Yes," Mrs. O'Key said, "she's looking for a missing
person. Jenny Rogers. She used to know Kristy."

"Used to know?" I asked.

Mrs. O'Key looked at me. "You said she used to live
with Kristy, didn't you?"

"Yes," I said with a smile, "and you were about to
explain Kristy's relationship to the rest of the family."

"There isn't any." Robbie finished his drink with an
angry swallow and clunked the glass on the coffee table.
"But why my stepmother would be telling you that I
have no idea. How did you get in here, Chase?"

"The door was most useful."

"Don't give me any lip. Just answer the question."

"The gate called the house and I was admitted."

"Why?"

"Someone in here wanted to talk about what your
sister was up to."

He looked me over. "Aren't you a little young for
this sort of thing?"

"Depends on what you had in mind."

Robbie sighed, got to his feet, and crossed the room,
where he pulled on a velvet cord.

"Really, Robbie, I think we can help Miss Chase—"

"I'll have Lambert show her out of here."

"If I were you," I said, "I'd ask the mug at the gate to
give you a hand."

O'Key returned to stand on the other side of the
coffee table. "Oh, you think you can claim damages
against this family if we give you the boot?"

"I was thinking, after all is said and done, you might
be the one putting in for damages."

"Please, please," Mrs. O'Key said. "I don't want any bickering. Robbie, if you're not interested in helping Miss Chase, please have the courtesy to leave."

"I'll have Chuck come up here and throw her out."

"You'll do no such thing. Chuck's to stay at the gate." To me, she said, "People try to sneak in all the time. They ignore the signs, and when they hurt themselves on the property, well, it's a real mess."

The skinny bird who had met me at the door arrived with a drink. Robbie snatched it off the tray and returned to his chair.

"Would there be anything else, Master Robbie?"

"No!" He took a quick swallow of the drink. "And I'm staying to hear what you say to this girl, Angie."

"I don't think that's necessary."

"I'm staying." He punctuated the remark with another angry swallow.

Gee, if this guy drank every time he got mad he must be a real souse.

Mrs. O'Key said, "Very well."

The butler asked, "Anything for you or your guest?"

"Would you like something, Miss Chase?"

I pointed at Robbie. "Whatever he's having."

The former hunk stopped in mid-drink.

"One scotch, neat. A double," added the butler as if warning me of what I was getting myself into.

I nodded and all conversation ceased until the butler left the room.

"As I was saying, Kristy has almost no contact with this family." O'Key glanced at her stepson. "Maybe I'm not the one who should be telling you this—"

"Probably not," groused Robbie, "but you want this girl to like you."

"It's just that . . . my husband's not at all well."

"He's dying," said Robbie.

"Well, yes, and Robert spends most of his time on the family key."

"A tiny island," explained Robbie.

For a guy who wasn't all that interested, Robbie sure held up his end of the conversation.

"There isn't any relationship," he said, "so there's no reason to waste your time or ours. Kristy severed her ties with the family long ago. We hardly see her."

Mrs. O'Key's chin fluttered. "Not even for holidays."

"And we don't mention this around my father. It tends to upset him."

"But Kristy keeps in touch," added her stepmother.

"To make sure she's not completely disinherited."

"Kristy stays in touch by telegram. One arrived a week ago."

"The seventeenth to be exact," said her stepson. "The last time we heard from my dearly departed sister."

"Dearly departed?" I asked.

"Yes—she's painting South America."

His stepmother explained. "The telegram said something about painting *more* than one South American city and not to worry about her."

"Like we would."

"We should, Robbie. She's family."

"Not even as much as you are, Angie."

"Well, that's enough for me."

"Then you aren't much of an O'Key." Robbie looked at me, but I found it more interesting *not* to be included in the conversation. "Kristy only sends those telegrams to show the family she's getting along, and quite well, without any assistance from the family."

"Where'd the last one come from?"

He was about to take another swallow from his glass.

"What? Oh, from Rio—I think."

The butler returned with my drink—which turned out to be absolutely top of the line.

Robbie studied me as his stepmother said, "Kristy's last telegram, Lambert, it was from Rio, wasn't it?"

"Yes, Madam. Rio de Janeiro. Will there be anything else?"

"No—that will be all."

"Yes, Madam." The butler glanced at me before leaving the room.

"What if an emergency came up?" I asked, pulling myself away from the scotch.

"There *is* an emergency. Our father's dying, but Kristy still ran off."

"Robbie, please."

He was staring at my glass. "Something wrong with your drink, Miss Chase?"

In reply I downed the drink in one long swallow and thumped the glass on the coffee table. Mrs. O'Key looked there first, then at her stepson.

"Another?" asked Robbie with the smile of a competitor.

"Only if you're having one." The liquor hit bottom and sent a pleasant tingle all the way to my toes.

Robbie stood up, crossed the room, and tugged on the velvet rope again. Returning to his seat, he said, "Now, is there anything else we can do for you, Miss Chase, before you empty our liquor cabinet?"

"Robbie!"

"Then you have no idea where Kristy's staying?"

He shook his head. "And that's just the way Kristy wants it."

"Have the police informed you that her apartment was burgled?"

Mrs. O'Key was plainly shocked, but her stepson only shrugged. "What can you expect—look where she lives?"

"The young man living across the hall was killed this afternoon."

"Nooo!" moaned Mrs. O'Key.

Robbie shrugged again.

I told them about George Fiddler, trying to warm them up as much as their scotch had warmed me. Mrs. O'Key nodded as if reassuring herself that death couldn't touch her in this big, old house. After all, there was a guard at the gate and floodlights all around.

Lambert arrived with our drinks. He smiled as he put mine on the coffee table.

After the butler left, Robbie said, "Another Bohemian dead and gone. No great loss."

This time the stepmother said nothing, but she did look worried, and I didn't think it was about her missing stepdaughter. I downed my drink in another long pull. Soon I'd regret skipping supper, but I had to admit my headache was gone.

When I put down the glass, it clunked somewhere off in the distance. "One woman's disappeared, a young man's been murdered, an apartment burgled—all in the same building. Cops don't like coincidences. SLED will be paying you a call."

"Anyone wishing to speak to us can speak to our attorney, as you can in the future, Miss Chase." From his shirt pocket he drew a card and passed it across the table to me.

Having your attorney's business card in a pocket of your sport clothes—what did that tell you? I took his card and fumbled around in my purse for one of my own. "If Kristy gets in touch, have her give me a call."

Instead of passing the card over to Robbie I put it on the coffee table. I might've lost my balance reaching any farther. When I stood up the room moved around me.

Mrs. O'Key studied the card as she got to her feet. "Kristy wouldn't know anything about this. She was out of town."

"Personally," said Robbie, failing to stand as a lady crawled out of the room, "I'm more concerned about all the drugs coming ashore around here."

I looked down at him. He seemed to be moving, but that couldn't be right. It had to be me. Or the room.

"Going to finish your drink?" I asked.

"I will. Later."

"Sure you will," I said with a grin.

I left the room, and I'm proud to say, under my own steam, or the steam of half a bottle of good scotch. Those hadn't been small glasses we'd been drinking out of.

"Stay in touch, Susan," said Mrs. O'Key at one of those humongous front doors.

Caught between the lure of good whiskey inside and heat and humidity outside I wavered.

"But if you ask me," continued O'Key, "I think Jenny Rogers *is* the reason Kristy left town."

I focused on her and it took quite an effort. I didn't know how I was going to get home. I *was* the designated driver. "What do you mean, Mrs. O'Key?"

"'Angeline,' please," she said with another smile.

"'Angeline' it is." It was hard not to like this woman, even if she was every man's dream.

"You said the Rogers girl attached herself to Kristy, didn't you?"

"Yes."

She glanced at the butler, who took the hint and

drifted off down the hallway. "If Kristy thinks someone distracts her from her work she'll break off the relationship, any relationship, no matter how close that relationship might be. If that doesn't work, she'll leave town. She left town after Robert and I returned from our honeymoon. Her work comes before anything, even those who love her." She smiled. "Even those who try to love her. And, as you've seen, it's terribly frustrating for Robbie."

"What's his problem? He's left with all the money."

Angeline shook her head. "Robbie is my husband's nephew, not his son. Robert adopted the boy when his parents disappeared. Their boat was never found. They tell me it was quite a storm."

Gee, maybe there were worse things than being orphaned and having no one to turn to. "And how do you handle the relationship between your husband and his daughter, Angeline?"

She flashed another perfect smile. "Like all smart stepmothers, Susan. I stay out of the line of fire."

Chapter 9

The next thing I knew I was in bed—and someone was in bed with me! And he wasn't being very friendly about it. The guy held a knife to my throat, threatening to give me another smile, a bit lower than the one I wasn't wearing. Despite his warning, I twisted and turned—until he tested the blade against my throat. I stopped moving, but now my hands were free.

He couldn't do his business unless I opened up to him, and that's where I have a problem. I've had problems with men before. Harry says I'm traumatized. No shit. Try finding an unwanted member in *your* bed.

"Lie still," he hissed. "And be quiet."

There was some kind of accent there, one I couldn't place. Maybe his prick had broken my concentration.

He put a knee between my legs and forced them apart, knife still across my throat. The edge bit in as he shifted around, and I wondered why I hadn't turned on the damn alarm before going to bed.

Because I'd been drunk—too drunk to even take off my clothes. And now I was going to pay—like this. It wasn't fair! Not fair at all! I fumbled around, trying to find the panic button.

The button wasn't there!

Or I couldn't find it.

Where was the son of a bitch? All it took was one good push and I'd be covered up with people. Harry had insisted I install the thing because of the number of guys who show up unannounced where any single woman lives.

Knife against my throat, knee between my legs, the bastard ripped my blouse off, then fought with the sports bra, finally wrestling it over my head. That distracted me, but only for a moment, then I was fumbling for the button again.

Sometimes the damn thing slips between the bed and the wall. Sometimes I can't find it unless I make up the bed, and that hadn't happened in a while. The bastard felt me up, and I shrank back, as far as a girl can shrink against a headboard with someone straddling her.

"This is gonna be fun." There was that accent again, but I couldn't place it. Not Northie, not redneck—what?

He grabbed my pants, popping off the button and ripping apart the zipper, then pulling them down with one hand, and having trouble because I'm a little hippy; all the time the fucking knife held me in place. I didn't know how much more of this I could take.

And I didn't have to. I'd found the button.

I jammed down hard and the siren screamed, a noisy thing mounted on the mast. On a clear night it could be heard almost two miles up and down the Waterway. Now all I had to do was get away from that knife.

"What?" the sumbitch asked, raising up on his knees.

When the knife came away from my throat I pulled back with my feet—knees at my head—and kicked him off the bed. He landed on his butt, then cursed and scrambled after me. But I was gone, rolling off the bed and into the darkness.

Where was my damn gun! Shit, I didn't even know where I'd left my fucking purse.

"Bitch!" came out of the darkness.

I thought he was still after me until a form dashed across the cabin and knocked the screened door out of the way. In the lights from the dock I got a glimpse of a dark figure wearing dark clothing, then he was gone, no flashes in the night, no glint off a blade. And nothing hit the water. Only the thumping of feet as he raced down the pier. Then the sound of a shot and more thumping feet, this time coming in my direction, and shouts of "Susan!"

I fumbled to my feet, pulling my blouse around me, then flipped on a lamp. Overhead the siren continued to scream. Harry came through the broken screened door, ajar.

"Susan, are you all right?" He wore a robe over pj's and carried a .45 left over from his days in Saigon.

"I'm—I'm okay."

He found me at the spigot and counter that serves as a bar. When I turned my back on him, he gripped my shoulders. I was shaking so hard I couldn't even pour a drink. But something else was pouring. Big, fat, juicy tears ran down my cheeks and they wouldn't stop.

"Anything happen, Princess?" he asked over the siren. More people leaped from the pier to the deck of *Daddy's Girl.*

I shook my head, but the tears continued to flow.

"Did you—did you get him?"

"I fired over his head, but he didn't stop. Someone went after him, but I was more worried about you."

"I wish . . . I wish you'd gone after him."

Still holding my shoulders, Harry faced the people at the door. "Susan woke up to find a prowler going through the cabin and set off the alarm. She'll be fine."

There were sounds of sympathy I didn't acknowledge. How could I? I was *sooo* embarrassed. I just wanted them to go away—so I could pour a damn drink. But at the moment I was doing more damage to the lip of the glass than to its bottom.

"How do you turn off the siren?" asked someone who probably had to get up in a few hours.

Harry left me to turn off the siren. When he returned he took the bottle out of my hand and ushered me over to a chair. "I'll fix this." But he had to find another glass. The one I held was too chipped around the edges.

By then the guy who'd chased my "prowler" down the road was back, out of breath and without his quarry. Harry thanked him, then closed the door so the AC could do its job. The drink he handed me I downed in one swallow. Bending back my head to throw down the drink reminded me of the fall I'd taken earlier in the day. That, plus half a quart of scotch and very little food sent me running for the toilet. I kicked the door shut, fell to the floor, and knelt over the bowl, hot from embarrassment, pain racking my head. It was easy to puke my guts out.

"Susan?" asked Harry from the other side of the door. "Anything I can do?"

"Go . . . away. Please."

"Do you want me to call the police?"

"He didn't . . . he didn't do anything but tear my clothes. Dads. Honest."

"Okay, but I'm setting the alarm before I leave."

Then he was gone, leaving me more alone than I cared to be. But I didn't know that until I'd used up all the hot water.

I came out of the shower and stood in front of the mirror. I slapped my hips, my face, most all of my body, then I took another shower. It didn't help. I felt dirty, dirty, dirty. Worse, everyone knew it—that's why they always picked on me.

Nothing helped—until I worked my way through a couple of cigarettes, pulled on some clothes, and wandered over to Harry's. Stumbling down the pier, I saw my jeep parked—if you call "parked" pushing over a post until it kissed the ground. I was lucky to be alive—and unsoiled. Well, relatively unsoiled.

When I knocked, Harry told me to come on down. I found him in the galley, robe still on, hair askew, stubble beginning to show. "Going to have some soup. How about you?"

I said "no" but changed my mind by the time he brought the stuff to a boil. Harry filled two bowls and started without me. For a while I sat in the booth across from him, clanking my spoon against the side of my bowl and watching him eat, then dug in myself.

Finished, he washed out his bowl and returned for mine. I scooted farther into the booth and pulled my legs up against me. "Soup in the middle of the night?"

"Couldn't sleep. Neighbors making too much noise."

And with that I broke down, sobbing onto his shoulder once he slid into the booth beside me. After a moment I wiped my eyes and turned away. There was a silence between us I didn't understand, and when I looked again, Harry was holding out a warm cloth. I don't know where it came from. I never heard the spigot turn on. He took a seat across from me as I washed my face.

"So what happened?"

I told him about O'Key's apartment being ransacked, being knocked downstairs, apprehending Emma Coker, and my trip to Georgetown. It took about a half-hour to get around to the guy with the knife.

"Thank heavens for the panic button," he said.

"Yeah, and don't say it. I should've activated the alarm before going to bed."

His eyes twinkled. "Well, this should cure you."

I looked around for something to throw at him, but the table was bare. "I'd been drinking."

"I see."

"Don't look down your nose at me."

"Then don't tell me you were drunk."

"Who else would I tell?"

"I don't want to hear it, Susan."

"Hey," I said, dropping the cloth to the table and pulling my legs up under me again. "I'm not the one who drinks over lost loves."

Harry said nothing.

"Sorry. I forgot. Some things are off-limits. My drinking and your social security benefits."

Now Harry smiled. Having friends is tough, keeping them's even harder.

He asked, "The alarm's warning whistle didn't alert you to set the security system when you arrived home last night?"

"Er—I don't think I set the alarm when I left this morning. I was kinda in a hurry."

"Because?"

"I was late for work."

He stared at me, waiting for an explanation.

"I'd been out the night before."

"Drinking."

"Dancing, too. Which means I shouldn't go dancing."

"Did I say that?"

"No—you have other ways of making a point."

"Was he anyone you recognized?"

"In the dark—you've got to be kidding."

Harry said nothing, but the question did make me think. "He was a good-sized fellow and I don't mean the way you're thinking."

"Anything else?"

"He had an accent and he was black."

"Black?"

"Yeah—he was real dark running out my door."

"It's dark, Susan. Not many lights here. I should speak to the manager about that."

"Okay—he was white."

"Was he?"

"Of course not—I know what a Bubba smells like: There's the chaw and they don't usually change clothes before coming over to rape you."

"Susan, there's no way a black man would come in a yacht basin. They're more guns on boats than in any subdivision."

"I still think he was black."

"But no one you knew?"

I ran a mental inventory of all the black guys I knew. Junior Brooks repaired engines at the next landing, but his wife said he wasn't very threatening even when led on. Handy Adams ran a floating crap game, but he was in jail. There was Mickey DeShields, but it couldn't've been Mickey. Then, there was that damn

Kenny Mashburn, but I really didn't think he had the balls.

"Why you?" asked Harry.

"I'm a woman—if you haven't noticed."

"But tracking you down, then coming in here and attacking you—we're off the road. People don't think of the Waterway when they think of the beach."

"He was black," I said with a yawn, then touching the place where the knife had creased me, "and he had a very sharp knife."

Harry stood up. "I'll walk you back to your boat."

"'Preciate that."

He followed me up the ladder and out the hatch. "You still have that gun I gave you?"

"In my purse."

"I doubt he'll return, but I'd keep the pistol by your bed for the rest of the night."

"The rest of my life, you mean."

At *Daddy's Girl* I punched in my mother's birthday to deactivate the security system. Nobody knew my mom. She hadn't been seen around these parts in years.

"You'll find her tomorrow," said Harry, meaning Jenny, not my mother.

"I will. Where?"

"There's only one possibility left."

"Dads, I don't have the money to fly to Rio."

"Then prove Rogers can't be there."

I thought about that. "That'd be a different way of doing it."

"Have you told Marvin you might not be in tomorrow?"

"Dads, I don't need a baby-sitter."

He pointed to the phone and wouldn't leave until I told Marvin's machine I might not be in tomorrow. By the time I finished Harry was at the rolltop desk I'd acquired after Hugo blew through. I don't know if the desk was actually being thrown away, but the poor thing sat beside the road so Pick and I laid it on a trailer and brought it home.

"Written anything lately?" he asked, flipping through my journal.

"It's there," I said, holding my breath.

"May I look?"

"Of course. Why do you ask?"

Harry makes me write every day and I do—usually. He found the last entry.

THE LADY

Legs tired,
shoulders slumped,
her world
in those bags.

Big coat,
old coat,
brown shoes,
worn shoes,
red scarf
some color.

The grate
her bed,
the night
her cover,
the stars—
failed to
come out.

"This is good, Susan. Maybe your best. Have you sent it out?"

"It's not that good."

"How do you know if you don't send it out?"

"I'll think about it," I said, yawning and basking in

the warmth of his compliment.

Harry gave me a peck on the cheek, and before leaving worked the action of the screened door. "I'll have Pick look at this tomorrow. Come over for breakfast when you feel like it."

"It's a date."

"And Susan?"

"Yes?"

"That dog that hangs around?" Harry was referring to a black Lab who mooched off those moored at the landing. "Maybe you shouldn't be so eager to run him off next time he shows up."

WHO AM I?
An essay by Susan Chase, Esq.

I was born in Key West, Florida. My father fished there until the Gulf was fished out, in other words, until people wouldn't extend him any more credit. So up the coast we went: mother, father, and me, and the brother—until he got killed in Daytona. The sister had OD'd in Savannah, and finally my mother went out for a pack of cigarettes and never came back. Only the strong survive and the smart ones get out early.

One night Daddy got drunk enough to fall overboard and drown. Pirates boarded us, thinking they owned the boat as salvage. They didn't know about me below. Their "Ahoy theres" woke me up. I was lucky there were only two of them. The first one I stabbed in the back with a galley knife when he turned around to tell the other guy they were in luck—there was a young thing below—and once they had their fill, I knew it'd be over the side with me. All the time I kept wondering where was my daddy?

When the guy with the knife in his back stumbled topside, the other guy came below to carve out a piece of his own. He was smoking a cigar and bragging he was bigger than any cigar. Come on out and get what you've got coming, girlie, and if you're real nice, I'll make it quick and easy. He wasn't talking about the rape.

I turned on the propane and went out the forward hatch—those were the days when I wasn't so hippy. The bastard blew himself up the ladder and into the pilothouse. Only the strong survive and the smart ones know how propane reacts to a lit cigar.

I don't know what happened to the bastards and I really don't care. I was too busy getting the hell out of there. Now, if I could only find Mama, I could tell her it was safe to come home.

Chapter 10

The next morning I went over to Harry's for breakfast, more likely brunch by the position of the
sun. I didn't know if Marvin had called about me
not showing up for work. I'd cut off both the phone
and the machine before going to bed, and yes, I set the
damn alarm. Harry saw me coming down the ladder.
He also saw my ivory slacks and navy blue blouse. I
even wore jewelry.

"I didn't know such an attractive young lady would
be joining me for breakfast."

"What you cooking?" I peered at the Mixmaster on
the counter behind him. "Pancakes?"

He flicked on the machine and a yellow foam in-
stantly whipped up. "Omelet. How would you like
yours?"

"With hot peppers."

"Are you sure? You were really ill last night."

"That was last night."

He made a face. "Young stomachs . . . . How's the
head?"

"It'll be okay."

"That's no answer."

"A little sore. I took some aspirin."

"Maybe you should see a doctor."

"Dads, I tried to remember what I learned from watching Oprah; it's not me the rapist is after—it's any body."

"When you land on your head, Princess, a therapist isn't the first person you need to see." He shifted the bowl around under the beaters.

The coffee was ready and smelled great. I poured a cup, then refilled Harry's mug, one of those where Kirk, Spock, and Bones are in the transporter; when the cup heats up, all three disappear, when the cup cools down, the figures reappear. A gift from one of his children. Harry never understood the attraction of *Star Trek*—that generation or any other.

Over the whine of the Mixmaster, he asked, "Bring along your passport?"

"I've got it," I said, sipping my coffee. "I just don't want to use it."

"Pack a bag?"

"In the jeep—if I need it."

"Where you headed first?"

"Warden's office, then to Mrs. Rogers'—if I can stand it. I may go there first—to get it over with."

"I'll follow you into Myrtle."

"You don't have to, Dads. I can handle this."

"I'm not going with you. I've been to Rio before. I'm having some pictures made."

"For who—your grandchildren?"

He glanced at me. "You'd be surprised how many women my age are looking for beaus."

"And you, you beast, you're leading them on."

"I rather think they're leading themselves on."

"Pictures of who?"

Harry turned on the gas, put an iron skillet on the eye, and poured some oil in the pan, then tilted the pan, greasing the bottom. "O'Key and Rogers. You have a picture of Jenny?"

"Yeah, but not one of O'Key."

"I'll get that from the library. What's your friend's name again?"

"Doris Moffitt—just don't ask her to go on break with you."

"Why's that?"

"Private joke."

"Oh. I'll meet you at the airport. You can catch a flight into Miami, then one to Rio."

"Dads, I don't have the money for this."

"Ask Mrs. Rogers. She's got plenty."

"She didn't look like it. I didn't even see a TV at her place."

"You know that check you showed me last night?"

"Yes?"

"I called a friend at Coastal Federal this morning. That account has less than a hundred dollars in it."

Coffee slurped over the edge of my cup and burned my hand. "Ouch!" I put down the cup and reached for a cloth. "That bitch."

"Please, Susan, watch your language."

Harry turned off the Mixmaster, raised the beaters, and removed the stainless steel bowl. "Three years ago that same account had over twenty-two thousand dollars in it. Now, for all practical purposes, it's empty. That happened less than a week after Mr. Rogers passed away. My friend remembered the withdrawal because he was there when Mrs. Rogers hauled, and I do believe the proper word is 'hauled,' all that money out the door. She wouldn't take a check."

Emptying the whipped egg from the bowl to the skillet, he added, "Money—in its absence we are coarse; in its presence we are vulgar. Even stupid." He began fighting to keep the fluffy stuff from overrunning the boundaries of the skillet. "Where you think that money is now?"

"It's in the house! It's in the damn house. No wonder the old bitch keeps the place locked up so tight. That kind of money would fill more than one mattress."

Harry sighed, then said, "Actually, if the bills were in hundred dollar increments and a mattress is approximately twenty cubic feet, twenty-two thousand dollars—"

"Okay, okay, I get the idea. We both agree she's completely nuts. That's why Jenny's father set up the trust fund. He knew his wife wouldn't spend a dime . . . but I wonder if he thought she'd be fool enough to keep the money at home. George Fiddler was wrong. Mrs. Rogers doesn't want the money—she wants control of her daughter."

"Isn't that what Emma Coker told you?"

"Yes—and there's not a dime's worth of difference between the two."

I was setting Harry's breakfast table when someone called my name topside. As I went up the ladder, Harry said, "This won't keep forever, Susan."

It was a young woman in a red skirt, a white sleeveless blouse, and pumps with a matching belt and too much lipstick. She held an envelope purse, strap drooping toward the pier, as well it should. She was squeezing the life out of that sucker.

"Miss Chase?"

"Yes?"

"He told me"—she gestured at Pick, who was hosing out a boat—"that you were here. I just had to see you."

"What can I do for you?"

"I need you to find someone."

Well, well, looks like I didn't have to fly down to Rio after all. "I'm working on a case right now."

"Really?" The young woman looked distraught.

"Yes."

"But you've got to help me find Eddie." She squeezed the purse again.

"Really, I'd like to help you, but I can't work two cases at once—how old is Eddie?"

"Sixteen, and if you found him, I could talk him into coming home." Her lower lip quivered and she squeezed the purse again. "My folks are really worried."

"How long's he been gone?" *Stop this, Chase, stop it right now. You can't possibly work two cases at the same time, no matter how desperate this woman looks.*

"A couple of weeks," she said, staring at the pier.

Gee, maybe Eddie left town with Kristy O'Key. "Why'd he leave?"

"He fought with my parents. They're always fighting."

"Over what?"

She shrugged. Down the pier Pick stopped swabbing out the boat and stared at us. "What kids always fight about, anything and everything."

"How're things at home now?"

"Er—fine," she said, looking up.

"Miss, I can't possibly help if you don't tell me the truth."

From below Harry hollered, "Soup's on!"

"I'm sorry," I said, moving toward the hatch, "but there's nothing I can do."

She stepped to the side of the schooner. "I have pictures. A list of friends. Places he hung out."

"Like I said, I'm tied up at the moment, and if it's not a good idea for Eddie to go home, then we have to talk that out, too. Possibly with Child Protective Services."

"But they told me . . . ."

At the hatch I stopped. "Who told you?"

"People."

"What people?"

"The people who said you'd help me find him."

"Come back in a few days. I'm going out of town right now." On a frigging wild goose chase.

"But a few days might be too late."

"Too late for what?"

"I mean it might be too late." She started away, moving quickly for a woman in heels across a dock. "You should've helped me, Miss Chase. Now I'm in real trouble."

I left the hatch and followed her as far as the stern. "What kind of trouble? Are you pregnant?"

Without answering she finished the pier and opened the door of a red convertible. A Mazda Miata. The door closed at the same time the engine cranked, tires spit gravel as she wheeled around, and she was gone, out of the parking lot and down the road. I shook my head and gestured helplessly to Pick who was still watching me, then went below for breakfast.

"Who was that?" asked Harry from where he'd already started on his meal.

"Somebody who expects one hell of a lot from a private detective."

His fork stopped at his mouth. "Pardon?"

"And in that she's no different from Mrs. Rogers. If Eddie doesn't want to be a father, there's nothing I can do about it. And I can't make Jenny come home—even if I find her."

"My dear, I don't have a clue what you're talking about, but at least you've made up your mind about going to Rio."

"Nope," I said, shaking my head, "there's still some-one I need to talk to. May I use your phone?"

"After breakfast, Susan. I didn't just whip up this omelet. I labored over it. I even put in peppers."

Lois Wyman's name was on the brochure I'd found lodged behind Kristy O'Key's refrigerator. Wyman booked all of O'Key's trips, I quickly learned.

"She's one of our most valued clients."

"Do you also make her hotel reservations?"

"Only for the first night."

"The first night? Why's that?"

"After that Ms. O'Key makes her own arrangements."

"Kristy doesn't let you help her much, does she?"

"We respect her privacy, Ms. Chase. Something other agencies didn't. We don't push trips on her or other-wise bother her while she's working."

"What can you tell me about her latest trip, the one to Rio?"

"Nothing at all. Our relationship with our clients is strictly confidential."

"You'd rather talk with the police?"

From the sink Harry frowned. He hates it when I run a game on someone. What the hell, they deserve it, acting like big shots.

"The police?" repeated the woman on the other end of the line.

"I value client confidentiality as much as the next fella, but when the police tell me to assist them in a murder investigation, you can bet your ass I do."

"Murder investigation?"

"You see, I don't want to be hassled when my license comes up for renewal. Either cooperate with me, Ms. Wyman, or you'll spend the afternoon explaining why you couldn't answer a few simple questions over the phone."

"Ms. O'Key, she's not . . . in any trouble, is she?"

"Not as far as we know. We just want to ask her some questions, but we have to know where she is."

I heard the phone being put down, then a door shut. That was followed by the rattling of a keyboard and Wyman read off the date and time of O'Key's flight and the hotel: the Premiero. For one night only. She gave me the number of O'Key's open-ended ticket.

"Other flights could be booked against this ticket and I wouldn't know anything about it."

"Is it possible Jenny Rogers is traveling with her?"

"It's possible, but when Kristy booked the flight it was for one. She paid in cash and the ticket was delivered to her apartment."

"Is that normal?"

"The cash is normal. Usually she gives me several days' notice, but you know how these artists are, when the spirit moves them . . . ."

I fidgeted on my stool. I was getting a little tired of artists and their moods. It wasn't something you could count on—or figure. "You handled the transaction yourself?"

"I wasn't here. The part-time girl did and the ticket was delivered by courier to Ms. O'Key's apartment."

"Anything else you can tell me?"

"I only wish there was. I just finished an IRS audit

and the damn thing wasted a whole week of my time.
I'm so backed up on my work I don't know when I'll
catch up. If it were anyone other than Kristy I could
tell you more, but nobody butts into her business.
That's why she broke with the last two agencies. And I
don't ask a lot of questions—just give her the facts."

"So there's no way you can help me find her."

"Not that I know of. The day after she arrives she
disappears into the city."

"Why does she do that? Besides being an artist, I
mean." I wanted to shortstop that bullshit before it
started.

"I can't be sure, but someone once told me her family meddles in her affairs, her father in particular."

Never even met the man and already didn't like him.

"You've got your work cut out for you, Ms. Chase.
Rio's one of the largest cities in South America."

I think I knew that and maybe that's what was bug-
ging me. It wasn't anywhere near that time of the month.
"Just give me a ring if she calls." I gave her my number
but with little enthusiasm. I had the feeling I wasn't
going to be around. I'd be in fucking Rio de Janeiro. I
put down the phone, fuming.

"You want to use some of that heat on these dishes?"
Harry was in soapy water up to his elbows.

"This isn't going to be fun, Dads."

"Neither is washing dishes."

"One more call if you don't mind."

Harry shook his head. "Some people have no sense
of responsibility to their fellow man."

"'Woman,' please."

"A woman would've already had these dishes done."

I was about to comment on his blatant sexism, then
remembered who'd cooked breakfast.

My next call was to the Golden Fleece Art Gallery. "Mr. Zidane, Harry Poinsett would like to know if anyone in Rio handles Kristy O'Key's work?"

From the sink Harry made another face, but I wanted to keep Paul Zidane at arm's length, or even farther, maybe with a ten-foot pole.

"My dear, Latinos wouldn't buy anything in black and white. It doesn't look expensive enough."

"Heard anything about O'Key switching to colors?"

At the sound of his chuckle my chest grew tight. I had to concentrate on what the bastard was saying. ". . . colors? Impossible, my dear. It would ruin her reputation. By the way, how did you make out with Emma Coker?"

"I kept my fucking pants on!"

"In that case perhaps we can do lunch sometime."

"I doubt it. I keep my pants on then, too." And I slammed down the phone.

Warden's office is located in the rear of the Law Enforcement Center. Passing through the squad room, I got stares from people I didn't know, catcalls from those I did. I acknowledged their attention with excessive curtsies or obscene gestures, depending on the target of my affection. What was wrong with these guys? Hadn't they ever seen me in slacks before? Hmmm. Probably not.

DeShields was with Warden—they shared an office— and today Mickey wore a brown sport coat, brown shirt, and orange tie. His slacks were tan, so were his half boots. Warden couldn't compete with such a clotheshorse; he wore a gray business suit. Mickey said hello and complimented me on the way I looked, but Warden only grunted. It sounded like one of his better days.

Warden's desk was littered with paperwork, the in/out trays full.

Taking a seat in one of the chairs in front of Warden's desk, I asked, "Get anything out of Emma Coker I can use to find Jenny Rogers?"

"Chase, you must really be desperate, coming to us for help."

I looked to Mickey, then back at Warden. "Okay, okay, how much of a beating do I have to take before you start answering my questions?"

"And why would we want to help you?" asked Warden.

With a sweet smile, I said, "So next time I catch one of the bad guys I'll turn her over to you and not the local authorities. Do that enough and the legislature might think you're redundant down here."

Mickey chuckled, but Warden frowned. He said, "Coker knows nothing or she'd be using it to cut a deal."

"But," Mickey said, "she's threatened us with that high-priced legal talent—"

"Who at this very moment is talking to one of his golfing buddies," said Warden, "who happens to be a judge and he's making plans to spring her."

"Murder's not a bailable offense."

Both men looked at me as if I had a lot to learn.

"Susan," Mickey said, "your missing person had no bank account but the one controlled by her mother. I talked with that old lady. She's a real piece of work. I got the impression she doesn't quite approve of you."

"Of anyone."

Warden asked, "How do you keep your clients, Chase, when you inspire so little confidence?"

"With my charming personality—necessary ingredients for anyone without a government job. Where's the money her father left her being sent, the thousand a month?"

Mickey was surprised. "You know about that? I got the impression Rogers didn't tell you about her daughter's annuity."

"She didn't."

"Uh-huh. Well, the insurance company mailed the last check General Delivery, Pawleys Island; before that, to O'Key's address; before that, her mother's."

"But there's a change of address," added Warden.

"For George Fiddler's apartment."

Both men nodded.

"Jenny still on your list of suspects?"

Warden smiled. "Number one since she disappeared."

"You don't know that she's disappeared, J.D. I don't know that myself."

"And that in itself is amazing, Chase, that you'd admit you didn't know something."

"Susan, you didn't do your client any favors by not identifying Coker as the one who shoved you downstairs."

"Been able to locate O'Key?" I asked.

When Warden said nothing I looked to Mickey again. "She flew out on the fifteenth of last month."

That crossed-checked with what Robbie O'Key had said last night. The O'Keys had received their telegram the following day. "Anything else?"

"Anything else—what?" asked Warden. "Beyond that we don't have any interest in O'Key."

"You should lean on your counterparts in Rio, J.D. They might be able to tell you something."

Warden shook his head. "When the State of South Carolina wants something out of those people I don't want SLED owing them a damn thing." He wrinkled his nose when I took out my smokes and pointed at a sign on the wall. It said: "Thank you for not smoking." I glanced at the cigarette before putting it away.

"You could always fly down to Rio and ask O'Key yourself."

"If someone would pay my way."

"What about Jenny's mom?" asked Mickey. "Won't she spring for it? She's willing to hire a private cop, she ought to be willing to send that cop down there to make sure there're no loose ends."

"I talked with her before coming over and she said I'd learned nothing that pointed to her daughter's being in South America, so she won't foot the bill." What I didn't tell these guys—because it was too damn embarrassing—was that Rogers would only talk with me through that frigging little door of hers—while the neighbors looked on. "Kristy O'Key's stepmother told me Kristy left town to get away from Jenny."

Warden sat up. "Christ, Chase, do you bother just anyone or only the ones who can kick up a fuss?"

Mickey slumped in his chair. "I can feel a meeting with the director coming on." He looked at his boss. "Am I too young to put in for early retirement?"

"Sorry, guys, but I can't put a case on hold, move on to another, and wait for a break in the one I've left simmering. I've got a living to make. What do you know about this Fiddler kid?"

Warden was still fuming, so Mickey said, "Oh, he was just some kid who tried to do a good turn."

"He didn't strike me as heroic."

"No man could be heroic enough for you, Chase."

"I heard Fiddler kept a girl in Charlotte locked up in a closet."

After glancing at Warden, Mickey explained, "Fiddler's parents were out of town when he took the girl in. She was fourteen and living on the streets. Fiddler was lucky he wasn't jailed for kidnapping. The girl could've called it either way. She could've owned that family."

"Maybe that's why she disappeared?"

Warden smiled. "For a girl from the streets, she wasn't very smart."

"Have any idea where she is today?"

"She's dead, Susan."

"She was a doper, Chase. What'd you expect?"

"OD'd?"

Warden nodded.

"No suspicion of foul play?"

"Nothing the people in Charlotte could find."

"Was the DA planning on taking Fiddler to trial?"

Warden leaned forward on his desk. "He was a fool, Chase, not a seducer. God, but you women wear me out. You think everyone wearing pants is after you."

When we got down to name-calling, Warden and I were usually through, but I made sure he saw I was wearing pants, brushing off my bottom as I left his office. As everyone had pointed out there was only one rock left to turn over and I couldn't ignore that rock— not if I considered myself to be Jenny Rogers' friend.

Chapter 11

It's nine hours to Rio—from Miami—and approaching South America I ignored the pilot's wake-up call, that is, until the oohing and aahing began. I'm not sure anything can compare with the sparkling green water of Guanabara Bay, the vegetation climbing the cliffs above it, or the loaf-shaped mountains surrounding the city of Rio. It was enough to make you forget about the long flight down. Almost. Waiting for me at the gate was a giant of a man, as wide as a beer truck and almost as tall. He had a hatchet for a nose, ears pasted against his head, and slicked-back hair.

"*Senhorita* Chase?"

"Yes?" I said, pulling on my jacket. It was damn chilly down here.

"Harry Poinsett asked me to meet you with a car." This was said in the brand of Portuguese that can only be found in Brazil. It's a bit too fast for me and he had to switch to English.

When he did, I said, "That was not necessary."

The huge man smiled, revealing several missing

teeth. "It is a great honor to show you around Rio, *Senhorita*. When I was a young man, I worked for *Senhor* Poinsett when your President Nixon visited South America."

The beer truck was Affonso, my escort—actually my bodyguard, as a woman walking the streets of Rio made about as much sense as a white man strolling through Watts or Liberty City. Affonso had a taxi waiting, and after fetching my bag, we headed for the hotel where Kristy O'Key had spent at least one night a month ago.

It was a wild ride, lurching in and out of traffic. We were run off the road twice. The pedestrians were not amused. The Premiero had an elaborate lobby, high ceilings, and spacious hallways. A white-gloved operator used an antique elevator to lift me to my room, which included a well-stocked fridge, a color TV, and a phone. The room had its own bath with a tub large enough to stretch out in. I could see why Lois Wyman had booked O'Key into this place. It had character. An artist would like that. I know I did.

I could've gone to the police and been told it was impossible to find someone in a city the size of Rio. I got a dose of that when I asked about O'Key at the front desk. They told me Kristy had been there, didn't know where she had gone, and that she was traveling alone. That much I'd gotten over the phone before flying down. Out on the street I began looking for the people who know how to do this kind of job.

Once word spread that the *gringo* lady was offering a reward, kids poured out of alleyways, left the stoops where they made their beds, and gave up their own scams. I passed out photographs of O'Key and Rogers, saying the first kid to find either one would receive a hundred dollars and showing them the money. After

they scurried off, Affonso and I made the rounds of the
art supply houses, eventually branching out farther
and farther from the hotel. Anyone who painted in black
and white had to stand out. Or so I thought.

By nightfall I knew I was in the wrong part of town.
Tomorrow I'd move up to Santa Teresa, a local haven
for artists. Up there the streets were more picturesque,
made of cobblestone, and damn little traffic—important to anyone who'd been dodging lunatic drivers all
day. Back at the hotel we found a kid waiting for us.
He had located O'Key, or so he thought.

Where, I asked.

Painting in a plaza. The boy glanced at Affonso and
became more specific. The woman was painting Christ
the Redeemer, not from Hogback Mountain, but from
another of Rio's loaf-shaped hills. We had to hurry,
though, as the light was going and artists didn't work
after dark, they went off, got drunk, and sang loud
songs.

I told Affonso I doubted this was the woman, but
we had to make sure. He said he'd go fetch her, but I
smiled and said I didn't work that way. So we took a
cab into the hills, and after a twisting and turning ride
confirmed the woman wasn't O'Key. She didn't even
have the right color hair. Maybe I was offering too much
money. But I had gotten results.

The kid was plainly disappointed. I told him to try
again and left him staring at the woman, who was pack-
ing up her gear, probably to go off, get drunk, and sing
loud songs. By the time we returned to the hotel, another kid was waiting for us.

Another dead end, but before I knew for sure we
had to walk several blocks. I hammered on a door until a woman answered. She wasn't O'Key and not the

only one disappointed. A burly man came to the door and threatened me with bodily harm if I didn't leave them alone. I left, muttering curses in Portuguese. The guy followed me into the street, where Affonso materialized out of the darkness. After a short exchange between the two, Affonso and I headed back to the hotel and the burly man back to his place, probably to kick the cat and his woman.

Upstairs I mixed a drink and stripped off my clothes, letting them fall where they may, then collapsed into a tub of hot water. God, did that feel good. Maybe I'd sleep here—then I remembered my drink. For that I had to return to the bedroom—where a light blinked on the phone. I called the switchboard and they connected me with the night manager.

"*Senhorita* Chase, I do not wish to trouble you, but there is someone here who would like to see you."

I glanced at my clothes strewn across the floor. "Can you send him up? Say—in about ten minutes?"

The night manager cleared his throat. "We are certainly pleased you chose our hotel for your visit to Rio, and certainly would not want anything to spoil your stay, but the person who wants to see you is a small boy." He cleared his throat again. "A small boy who my hotel detective says is—er, how do I say this?"

"Not someone you'd like to have wandering around your hotel."

"Ah, yes. But that is my problem. Certainly not yours."

"Tell the boy it'll be at least five minutes, and don't let him get away."

I pulled on my clothes and went downstairs. This could take all night—and wear out my welcome with the hotel staff.

The night manager was waiting for me, as was an older
man with suspicious eyes and gray hair: the hotel dick.
From behind the front desk three young men eyed me,
wondering who was this *gringa* who openly consorted
with beggars and thieves.

"Ah, yes, *Senhorita* Chase," said the night manager.
"I just wanted to make sure all was in order. You see
there are a great many of these children and sometimes they lure the uninitiated into the streets."

I showed him my ID. "I'm working with the South
Carolina State Law Enforcement Division. We're looking for a missing person who might be in your city."

The hotel dick gave me the once-over that wasn't
your usual once-over.

"But," said the manager, "Brazil is such a large country—Rio, itself, has millions of people. How will you do
this?"

"I'll manage. Where's the boy?"

He gestured toward the door. "With one of the door-
men. If he was important I wanted to make sure he did
not slip away."

I didn't think I needed both of them to show me to
the door, but they had the reputation of their hotel to
protect—from a woman who openly consorted with
beggars and thieves.

The boy sat on the steps with an old black man
who wore the maroon uniform of the hotel. The boy
sprang to his feet, but the old man took longer. And
this guy was going to keep the kid from running away?

"Miss, I have found the lady," the boy said in Portuguese. "The one who paints."

"Where?" I asked in the same tongue, which surprised them.

The boy glanced at the manager. "I will take you to her."

"*Senhorita* Chase," said the hotel manager, "I cannot allow you to go with this boy, nor should you go out at night alone." Gesturing at the old man, he added, "I insist Carlos accompany you."

Affonso came up from behind him and put a hand on the manager's shoulder. "That will not be necessary."

The manager stepped back as a sedan with a red stripe pulled to a stop at the curb. I grabbed the boy and dragged him down the steps and into the taxi. Affonso got in with us and the cabbie's mouth fell open as he watched my bodyguard fit himself into the front seat.

The night manager followed us to the car. "Do be careful, *Senhorita*." He glanced at Affonso, then tapped the top of the car, signaling us to be off.

The building was in the hills and not anywhere close to Santa Teresa. So much for *this* woman's intuition.

"She is here," said the boy, noticing my long face. "I have seen her."

Somehow I managed a smile, but my mind was on the hotel's supply of hot water. Then again, if I was going to be charging around the countryside all night I wouldn't need more than the occasional cold shower.

I woke up when Affonso said, "This is it."

We were beneath an old adobe building that rose five floors against one of Rio's loaf-shaped hills. Lights were on in most of the rooms and from several came the sound of small parties. It was the weekend no matter which side of the equator you were on.

I told Affonso to wait with the cab while the kid and I went upstairs—to the fifth floor where four doors opened onto a hallway. A man and woman came out of an apartment, stopped, and stared, not at us, but at the door across the hall.

Inside, a female shrieked, "You silly bitch! I don't know why I put up with you!"

The man said someone should call the police.

I flashed my ID, dropping the flap and tossing it up like I'd seen done on TV. "I'll take care of this," I said in my very best Portuguese.

The woman nodded grimly, but the man muttered it was about time. I didn't know what I was about to take care of, but I followed my basic rule: the less fuzz around, the less bother. When I rapped on the door my young guide disappeared downstairs, but the shrieking stopped and the door opened.

Another misfire. It wasn't O'Key. A woman in a purple top and green skirt, barefoot, with red hair down in her face, stood before me. With her free hand she brushed back her unruly hair.

"Yes? What do you want?" She coughed in my face without making any attempt to cover her mouth.

What I wanted was to find my Baker Street Irregular and wring the kid's frigging neck—until another face with doe eyes and granny glasses appeared at the door.

Jenny! Sometimes I even surprise myself.

"Susan!" she said in a hoarse whisper.

"May I come in?" I asked in English.

Jenny glanced at the red-haired woman. "Er—no, Susan. This isn't a good time."

"What're you talking about? I fly all the way down here and you won't even invite me in?"

Jenny's companion snarled at me in Portuguese.

"Go away from here, you—whoever you are."

In the same tongue, I asked, "What gives you the right to tell me what to do?"

She stood tall. "Because this is my home."

"You live here with Jenny and Kristy?"

"What do you mean? There is no one here named Kristy."

While I was trying to figure that one out she blew smoke in my face.

"Leave," said the woman. "You have no business with me or my woman."

"Even if I say 'please'?"

She pointed her cigarette at my face. "You will leave and you will leave now."

I jabbed back—with my fingers in her throat. The bitch stumbled back and dropped her cigarette when she sat down hard on the parquet floor. As she did, Jenny disappeared into the rear of the flat.

Pulling the woman to her feet, I frog-marched her down the hall. She didn't resist. She was too busy trying to remember how to breathe. On the stairs we ran into Affonso and I turned her over to him, telling him to make sure the bitch kept her distance. I know, I know. It's a tough way to make new friends in a foreign land, but I was a little self-conscious about having a bodyguard along.

I returned to the apartment and began checking out the place: rattan furniture with green pads for cushions, a coffee table littered with sketches in pencil, dried flowers sprouting from wide-mouthed vases. On a wall I saw my face in a mirror. Another reason not to let me inside. Next to the mirror I found a hallway ending in a closet; on one side was the bedroom, and across from that, a kitchenette. A balcony overlooked the street, its

furniture a couple of chairs with cane bottoms and a
wooden box serving as a table.

Below me, under a streetlight, Affonso steered
Jenny's friend across the street as the cabbie and my
Baker Street Irregular leaned against the taxi, watching. When Affonso looked up I gave him a thumbs up.
The woman shot me the bird before I stepped back
inside the apartment—where I found Jenny standing,
shoulders slumped, a resigned look on her face.

"Did you know your mother's looking for you?"

Jenny only stared at the floor. It was then I noticed
she'd cut her hair and colored it black.

"Jenny, your mother's worried about you."

She looked at me with those doe eyes. Jenny was
the kind of person who'd always need a man, or mother
around. What good would it do to drag her back to the
States? She wouldn't change. But leave her with the
bitch I'd run off? I don't think so.

"Jenny, we've never had trouble talking before."

"You mean you've never had any trouble talking."

I didn't know what to say to that.

"Did Mama really send you?"

"Yes. She's worried about you." Come on, Chase.
Why're you trying to patch this up? That's a job for
professionals, not someone who comes from an equally
dysfunctional background.

"I can't go home, Susan." She wrung her hands. "I
just can't."

"Yes, you can—if you want to."

"Then I don't want to," she said, a sudden firmness
coming into her voice. "I have a new life down here."

"And new friends."

She flushed. "I mean painting. Oh, that's right, you
don't know about my painting."

"I know all about your painting. Your mother told me about it when she hired me to find you. From what I've seen, some of it's quite good."

"Mama paid you to find me?"

"Yes."

"I never would've thought—"

"Maybe she cares about you more than you think."

"I—I don't know about that, but she won't let me paint. She insists I go back to my job at the library."

"Jenny, you don't have to live at home. You've already proved that. And you don't have to go back to work at the library. You have your annuity."

She shook her head. "It wouldn't work." And she fell into a silence I didn't understand.

Okay, okay. If the girl had to put some distance between her and her mother, fine. I'd only been paid to find her, and I'd done that. To cool off I walked down the hall and into the bedroom. Jenny's suitcase stood against the wall, under one of those racks usually found in hotels. Her purse lay on the bed. The bath and kitchenette were as empty as the bedroom. The woman I'd thrown out didn't live here. Matter of fact, it didn't look like anyone lived here.

"Where's Kristy?" I asked, returning to the living room.

Jenny was on the couch now. Tears rolled down her cheeks. "She's dead."

"What!"

Quickly I took a seat beside her. "When? How?"

"I killed her."

I felt myself recoil. "Are you serious?"

"No."

"When? How?" And hadn't I just asked those questions?

"I don't remember. I just know I killed her."

"Then where's the body?"

"I—I really don't know."

"What do you mean you don't know? When you kill someone you ought to remember something."

"I was high on cocaine. I don't remember anything. If George hadn't helped me I never would've gotten away."

It was good I was sitting down. "Are you saying you killed O'Key back in the States?"

"Why, yes, Susan, so you don't have to keep up the pretense of Mama wanting me to come home. I know she didn't send you down here. Mama wouldn't spend the money. The police sent you, didn't they?"

"For what?"

"To sign the extradition papers . . . so I'd come home and stand trial."

I took her hands again. "Jenny, you've got this all wrong. The police didn't send me down here, and if they wanted you extradited, Brazil wouldn't hesitate. The only people they don't extradite are embezzlers. Brazil considers that part of American foreign aid."

"I—I don't understand."

"What part of this do you think *I* understand?" I told myself to calm down, to take a breath. "Let's start at the beginning. Why'd you kill O'Key?"

She looked at the floor. "We fought."

"Over what?"

"My work."

"Were you two lovers?"

Her head jerked up. "Of course not. I'm not like that."

"Then what was wrong with your work?"

"It was bad."

"And you killed O'Key over that? That makes about

as much sense as O'Key throwing you out because your
work didn't measure up."

"It didn't."

"I don't give a damn about that! I want to know
about this murder you think you've committed, where
you killed O'Key, and how George Fiddler fits into all
this."

Jenny nodded in small jerks. "Okay, okay, I'll tell
you." She forced a smile. "You're always in such a hurry
. . . ."

I bit my lip instead of screaming. "Just tell me what
happened!"

She did and it was something about killing O'Key
in the country. Where, she didn't know, but it was only
a matter of time before the police found the body. That's
why Jenny thought I was there. The police had found
O'Key's body and asked me to talk her into coming
home. It was enough to make my head spin, but now
wasn't the time to wig out.

"And you have no idea where you killed her?"

"Like I said, I was high. I don't remember anything. All
I remember was George finding me in Kristy's apartment."

"So you're the one who tore up that place?"

"Yes," she said softly.

"And you told Fiddler you'd killed O'Key?"

Another nod. "George helped me pack, found Kristy's
passport, and made me look like her. Dyed my hair.
Cut it. They hardly looked at me when I came through
customs, and I wasn't wearing my glasses."

"The checks you get from your father—Fiddler was
going to forward them to you?"

She nodded.

"And you planned to hide out here the rest of your
life?"

"I'd have to. I'm wanted for murder."

"Not by any police I know."

She stared at me. "I'm not?"

"No."

"You're just saying that to get me to come home."

No, sirree, kiddo, but if I really wanted to take the wind out of your sails I'd tell you that George Fiddler's dead. Murdered. And I've seen that body. "Have I ever lied to you before?"

She gazed through the archway to the balcony. "Then they must not've found the body . . . ."

"No—but they'll start looking for one if you keep talking like this."

There was a knock at the door.

Jenny sprang to her feet and looked at the door. "They're here! You brought the police with you."

"Don't be silly, Jenny." I stood up, reaching for her.

"Don't come near me!" She backed away.

I followed her across the room. "Jenny . . . ?"

"Stay away from me!" She backed onto the balcony. "I'm not going back."

"I only want to help you."

Reaching the wooden railing, she put a hand on it. "I'll jump! I will. I promise you I will."

From the other side of the door Affonso asked, "*Senhorita* Chase, do you need any assistance?"

"You see, it's only the man who helped me find you."

Jenny wasn't so sure. She didn't speak the lingo. "Susan, go away. I promise I'll jump."

"*Senhorita* Chase, the driver would like to know if he should leave or not?"

"The cabbie wants to know if he should wait or not, that's all."

"Don't have him wait. Leave. now."

When she glanced behind her, I took the opportunity to step toward the balcony. Jenny saw me coming and held up a hand.

"Don't come any closer, Susan. I promise you I'll jump. I don't have anything to live for." She put a foot up over the railing.

"Don't be silly," I said, continuing toward her. "That isn't the police and you aren't wanted for murder."

"You're lying."

When she hoisted herself up on the railing I faltered. It was the wrong move and I knew it. But the little fool had her ass hanging over the railing.

"Okay," I said, raising my hands in surrender, "go ahead and jump, but you're going to feel like a fool when you get to hell and learn O'Key's not there." I turned away, returning to the sofa where I picked up my purse and opened it. "I don't seem to have any change . . . ."

"Leave, Susan!"

"No way. I'm staying—to see you through this."

"I don't need your help."

I walked toward the bedroom. "Do you have any change? I saw your purse in here."

"Go away, Susan. My life is none of your business."

I slipped off my jacket and dropped it on the bed. "You've got plenty of *cruzados*. What's the exchange rate? How much should I tip him?"

"You've got to leave." Her voice sounded closer now. She was probably standing in the archway.

From the hallway Affonso asked, "*Senhorita* Chase? Please answer me."

"Jenny," I called from the bedroom, "tell the cabbie I'll be there in a second." I stepped out of my shoes and raced out of the bedroom.

Jenny stood in the archway, looking at the door. When she saw me coming she bolted for the balcony. Slipping on the tile, she fell to her knees. As I raced across the room she scrambled to her feet and leaped for the railing. It was going to be awfully close. All she had to do was slip over the side, whereas I had to grab her and pull her back.

I missed her torso but got my arms around her legs and we slammed into the railing with a thud and a yelp. One of my arms went numb from shoulder to fingers so I was one-arming myself on top of her as Affonso opened the door.

"*Senhorita* Chase!"

Jenny screamed bloody murder and clawed onto the railing, which had been knocked loose by our fall. Reaching for the top, she pushed the railing over. Below, I saw the cabbie and the kid who'd led us here. Their mouths hung open as they stared up at us.

Affonso rushed over. "*Senhorita*, let me help you."

"Yes—please."

The huge man snatched us up, then pulled us back onto the balcony. Using my numb arm I didn't feel a thing. He looked from me to Jenny and back at me again. Jenny fought, cursed, and threw in an occasional scream from time to time.

"This is the young lady for whom you are searching?"

I nodded, rubbing my arm to get the feeling back.

"What is wrong with her? Is she on drugs?"

"Nope. She just hears her mother calling her to come home."

Chapter 12

ith the help of Affonso I packed up Jenny and her luggage—after exchanging our tickets—and we flew out that night for Mexico City. From there we took a bus north and crossed back into the States. After hitching through Texas we were dropped off on a two-lane outside Memphis where I flagged down a Greyhound heading east. A couple of days later we were back on the Grand Strand. I didn't believe for a minute Jenny had killed O'Key, but I wasn't taking any chances. After all, O'Key *was* missing; but no one knew that—yet.

Leaving Rio the strangest thing happened. While I waited to board the plane, I felt someone staring at me. It's not all that unusual, being blond and taller than most women, but the man staring at me, well, his look chilled me. Emma Coker wasn't even in this guy's league. The guy was black, of average height and weight, and stared at me across the rope separating the passengers from those being left behind. My legs weakened and I put down my suitcase.

"Is there something wrong, *Senhorita?*" Affonso held

onto Jenny with one hand, the other gripped my arm.

"No—I'm okay."

When I looked again the guy was gone.

If I hadn't been so tired I would've made the connection. As it was, I had the distinct feeling I never wanted to see that face again. During the trip I tried to catch up on my sleep while Jenny slept, cuffing our hands together when I couldn't keep my eyes open any longer. But the man's face appeared in my sleep and wouldn't go away. Then I understood why: A black man *had* tried to rape me and my body knew it better than my mind ever would—or wanted to.

In Alabama I reached Pick and asked if Harry was around. When Pick replied in the affirmative, I said I'd call back in a few minutes—at the marina's pay phone. It was more like a half-hour. We were laying over in Birmingham and a couple of guys had pegged me and Jenny for their next good time. They promised Jenny some exceptionally good crack cocaine and she looked interested—until I flashed my ID.

"She's with me, fellows, and if you don't want to be, you'll move along."

After the two guys moved along, Jenny slumped into her chair and stared at her feet. "I don't know why you're doing this, Susan."

"And you make me wonder if you've ever had a friend before. Or was your mom all you ever needed?"

That didn't even rate a glare; more's the pity.

In Charleston, Harry met us and drove us to a rehab clinic in my jeep. The clinic is run by doctors who, after becoming hooked on drugs, lost their licenses, their families, and finally their self-respect. Now they operate on the other side of town, but their waiting room's still full. You take a seat in a school desk nailed to the floor and wait for your name to be called by a young woman behind a piece of bulletproof glass. Addicts have sometimes gotten their wires crossed, thinking this is a place to get drugs, not get off them.

McGinnis came out and gave me a hug, then shook hands with Harry. I don't let many men hug me, but for some reason Mac's hard to resist. A string bean of a man with eyes that miss nothing, Mac wears the simple uniform of a lab tech.

"Good to see you again, Susan. How you been?"

"Could use some sleep."

"No beds at this inn. A casualty of the war on drugs. We lost that one, too, if you're keeping score." He looked at Jenny. "Who's your friend?"

Jenny stood beside me, head hanging. Her hair was a mess, her blouse and pants dirty. And somewhere between here and Birmingham she'd lost one of her shoes.

"Jenny Rogers. Got someone who can give her a physical?"

"Rachel's free."

"Jenny, this is McGinnis. 'Mac' for short. He's a stand-up guy. You can trust him."

McGinnis put an arm around the girl, but Jenny balked at going with him.

I put a hand on her shoulder. "It's okay, Jenny. You're safe here."

She nodded reluctantly, then let Mac walk her over to the door. As soon as Mac opened the door you could hear the voices, frantic people looking for a way out.

McGinnis raised his voice over the din. "Don't let them frighten you. We've got all kinds of people in here and we try to help each and every one of them."

Harry watched the door close behind them. "Why are you doing this, Susan?"

"Jenny needs some time to get her act together."

"Then why do I have the feeling you've crossed a line here?"

"Probably because I have."

When Mac returned I was asleep at a broken-down desk picked for its backward tilt. I sat up and looked around. While I'd been sleeping the reception room had filled up with concerned adults and nervous teenagers. Harry sat in the chair beside me, studying their faces.

"We've lost a whole generation here."

I sat up. "Yeah—mine. And we know whose fault that was."

Mac pulled me to my feet, then we followed him through the door. "Rough night?" he asked.

"Last few nights."

"Living on the edge again, are you?"

"It's cheaper than dope."

We went through a set of doors and turned down a hallway. On my right a man shouted that they'd better let him out of there and if they knew what was good for them they'd be quick about it. In the next room a girl cried for her mother. Beyond that was Mac's office. Closing the door to the office blocked out most of the noise, but I could still hear the girl. She was under the impression she'd been abandoned and she just might be right. It'd happened before. The strange thing about this place was that no one was here against their will; they could leave anytime they wanted and that was probably the reason for the fervor of complaints.

Mac watched me fumble my way into a chair on the

other side of his desk. "Want to talk about your condition or Jenny's?"

My head snapped up. "Mine? What do you mean—mine?"

Harry took my hand and gave it a little squeeze. I glanced at him, then brushed back my hair. My clothes were dirty from three days and nights on the road. "Is Jenny on anything?"

"There's a trace of a sedative in her urine and her right wrist's irritated, but not from shooting up. You do that?"

"With sleeping pills and handcuffs."

He tsk-tsked. "Practicing medicine without a license."

"How long's she been off the stuff?"

"Two or three weeks."

"Something scared her straight."

"Should I ask what's going on?"

Harry interjected, "You don't want to know."

"Anyone looking for her?" asked Mac.

"Uh-huh," was all I said.

"Would that include the police?"

"She's on a short list of murder suspects."

"Jenny doesn't look the type."

"I had a cop tell me we're all the type, you just have to hit our hot button."

"Lock them up and throw away the key," Mac said with a snort. "That's all cops know."

"In her condition Jenny'll admit to anything, especially if the cops get their hands on her."

"So you're looking for a place to stash her."

"For a few days."

"I don't know, Susan. While being examined, Jenny told Rachel she'd come home to take her medicine. It's only a matter of time before she confesses about whatever she thinks she's done, and I don't have to remind you that this clinic operates more on motivation than it does money. Anyone might turn her in, including me. If I didn't, it'd undermine the morale of the whole staff."

"Mac, I need to see some people and I don't need to be dragging Jenny along."

Mac looked at Dads. "What about Harry?"

"He hasn't got your training."

"Or the inclination." McGinnis had once dried out one of Harry's grandsons. Then, one day the kid fell off the wagon, tore up Harry's schooner, and ran off into the swamp, never to be seen again.

Mac said, "Jenny'll sleep the rest of the day. When she wakes up we'll see if she'll bathe herself, then take it from there. I can probably get Ronnie and Rachel to go along with some sort of observation period."

"Good."

As I got to my feet I caught a glimpse of myself in the mirror on the back of the office door. My hair was a disaster and my face gave a clue to what I'd look like ten years from now. I brushed back my hair. How long had I looked like this?

"Would you like to take a nap?" McGinnis glanced at Dads. "Harry and I might have a little talk."

"Sorry, but I've got someone to see—don't I?"

Harry was more than happy to agree.

"Besides, without me around you can tell the cops Jenny walked in on her own."

"So who's your client?"

"Her mother."

"She paid with a bad check," added Harry.

Mac smiled. "Well, it's the thought that counts. Want me to inform the mother as to the whereabouts of her daughter?"

"I'm hiding Jenny from her, too."

McGinnis got to his feet. "Not telling your client you've found her daughter? You do play by your own rules, don't you?"

"You mean there's another set?"

I dropped Harry off in Georgetown where he could catch the bus back to the landing. Along the way I filled him in on my trip to Rio.

"You don't really think Jenny killed O'Key?"

"No more than I thought she'd left town."

"With such confidence perhaps it's time you turned this whole thing over to Lieutenant Warden."

"And have him think Jenny killed not only Fiddler but O'Key as well?"

"Er—just watch the road, Susan."

I looked. Nothing coming but a couple of eighteen wheelers. I easily returned to my side of the road.

"I don't like your being involved in murder and neither will Lieutenant Warden."

"If it is murder."

"If it is murder you're supposed to go to the authorities. This is way beyond looking for runaways."

"Did you set up the appointment with Robert O'Key?" I asked, clumsily changing the subject.

"Robert will see you."

"What did you tell him?"

"Only that you had some information about his daughter."

"What'd he say?"

"'What's she done now?'"

"Sounds like he really cares."

"Robert gave me any number of reasons why he shouldn't, but it's all a front. I handled some business for the family when his son was caught smoking dope in Mexico."

"Robbie?"

"Yes—they only have the two children."

"Maybe only one if Jenny's right."

"That's what I don't understand—how could you not know if you'd killed someone?"

"Ask any drunk driver." I turned into Georgetown, a city at the southernmost end of the Strand. "What'd you do for O'Key?"

"Robert called the embassy and asked for our assistance. And I can tell you, Susan, he was very interested in what might happen to his son."

"I thought Robbie was a nephew, adopted."

"Adopted? I didn't know that."

"I heard his parents died at sea—in a storm—then Robert and his wife adopted him."

Harry shook his head. "Must've happened while I was overseas. I don't know anything about it."

"What was the story about Robbie in Old Mexico?"

"Nothing. The police looking for a little squeeze."

With a small smile I asked, "And O'Key reimbursed you?"

"Susan, I wouldn't've asked."

"And O'Key didn't offer." I clapped him across the back. "No one lives by your code anymore, Dads. Nowadays, it's every man for himself; women, too, if they want a share."

"Then why are you doing this for Rogers?"

"Jenny has money of her own."

"I believe that as much as I believe you flew down to Rio for her mother."

"Then you never should've lent me the money."

The bus terminal loomed ahead.

"Would you like to hear your messages?"

"Please."

"Doris Moffitt called to see if you'd found Jenny, then called me. Is Doris a close friend of Jenny's?"

"I've never known Doris to have much interest in anyone but her big fat self."

"Marvin was angry when you didn't show up for work. He's had more than one lifeguard out the last few days. Another reason to drop this, Susan, before you run out of job opportunities."

"It's the only way I have to recoup my expenses."

As I turned into the drop-off zone Harry took out his wallet and pulled out a bill. "Then let me give you some money."

"You don't have to."

"You have to have walking-around money."

I took the fifty. "Okay, but I'm paying you back."

"You won't be able to—if you continue to take cases without any hope of remuneration. Jenny Rogers doesn't have to pay you a damn thing, and she might not pay you if you embarrass her mother." Harry stepped down from the jeep and put his wallet away. "And Mickey DeShields called. He wanted to know if you'd learned anything in Rio."

"I didn't tell him I was going—how'd he know?"

Behind us a minivan honked.

"He knows you, Susan, he knows you. And a young man called."

"Dads, you are bad, saving the best for last. Who?"

"Chad Rivers."

"Do I know him?"

"He said he's the young man you chewed out for bringing his boat ashore among the bathers. He said he was unable to get back to you and now he wants to make it up to you. Maybe dinner sometime."

"I thought he had a girlfriend."

"I wouldn't know anything about that, my dear. And I had Paul Zidane come by and pick up *Day's End* to have the painting authenticated."

I had lifted my foot off the brake. Now I jammed the brake against the floorboard. When I did the minivan honked again. "Get it back, Dads!"

"Don't worry, Susan. It's in good hands."

"What do you know about Zidane's hands? Get it back. Please." I leaned across the seat. "Dads, I appreciate everything you've done, but if you really want to help me, get that painting back."

"Susan, I don't know why you're acting this way. Paul said he'd have some prices when you returned from South America, if it's really a Rogers."

I sat back in my seat. No amount of money was worth losing my best friend. "Then do me a favor, would you? Call Zidane and tell him Jenny's back and ready to start painting again."

"Wouldn't that be a lie, my dear?"

"But one that might help Jenny. She'd have something to look forward to."

Chapter 13

Along the coast of Carolina is a smattering of islands, and ferrying me out to the farthest one was an antique wooden Chris Craft with a shiny coat of varnish and an old codger at the helm. The marina was located in a cove—a shack where you bought bait and tackle after parking in the crushed-shell parking lot. At the pier several aluminum skiffs were moored, but the Chris Craft, now that was something special, and the boat had its own little house set away from the others.

"Down here, Missy."

My captain had the weatherbeaten face of an old salt and wore a nautical cap, one with an anchor patch that looked like it'd been sewn on as an afterthought. Once I was aboard, he shoved off with his foot, which made the boat dip rather savagely, then learned I had the sea legs to cope with his clever maneuver. Flashing a smile, I took a seat on a cushion in the stern, patting my dress down around me.

In honor of Robert O'Key I wore a floral print, a pair of woven flats, and some accessories bought at a yard sale. But my smartest move had been to stop by Super Cuts and have my hair washed and styled. In their rest room I'd taken a sponge bath and, I'm afraid, left the place worse for wear. All in all I was about an hour behind schedule.

My captain was studying me. "Going out to see Mr. Big Shot, are you?"

I answered with another smile.

He laughed, showing a good number of teeth, most of them yellowed. "Then we'd best hurry, Missy. O'Key won't be around much longer. Won't be around to play the role of the big shot. No, sirree, not much longer."

I stared at him, and after he'd had his fill of staring back, he hit the throttle and the Chris Craft roared out of the cove. We broke through the outgoing tide and headed in the direction of an island that had been sculpted into its current form. From a rock-strewn shore-line grass grew like carpet up to a beach home with an observatory cupola. The structure was supported by poles lifting the deck higher than the hundred-year flood line, and trumpet creepers hid its bracing. There was nothing at the rear of the house, not so much as a window, but as we rounded the seaward side, a screened-in porch came into view, a deck above it, then a smaller one, higher still, off the cupola. A man sat in a chair on the highest deck, and on the pier, a younger one waited. I couldn't make out the man on the uppermost deck, but the one on the pier appeared to be a real hunk, at least from a distance. It was Robbie O'Key.

We were approaching the dock much too fast, but my captain knew his business, cutting the power so the Chris Craft slid in alongside another boat: a fiber-glass beauty with twin engines and skiing gear stowed in the stern.

After giving me a hand ashore, my captain glanced at Robbie. "They know how to reach me, Missy." And with a flick of the wrist and a touch of the throttle he was gone.

To my right an artificial beach was set off by royal palms, and behind the palms, a tennis court enclosed by chain-link fence. Inside that fence Angeline O'Key practiced her serve, but Robbie just stood on the pier, drink in hand, black hate in his face.

"Look, Chase, I didn't invite you here." He moved so I couldn't pass.

"No—your father did. Now if you don't mind . . . ." I tried to go around him, but he shifted left and right, getting in my way. "Robbie, I enjoy dancing as much as the next girl, but if you don't want your ass kicked off this pier you'd better let me pass."

Startled, he stepped back and I took the opportunity to slip by.

"Listen," he said, trailing me up the walkway. "I don't know what you think you're doing, but that's one sick old man up there and he doesn't need to be bothered."

At the steps leading to the porch I stopped and waved. From the tennis court Angeline waved back, then tossed a ball overhead and hit it, slamming it into the net. Several balls lay on her side and now this one joined them.

From behind me, Robbie said, "Angeline won't say anything, but I will."

I said nothing, but remained standing at the steps leading to a screened door attached to two pillars anchoring the house to the subterranean floor. With a snort Robbie opened the door and I followed him across the porch, into the house, and down a hallway. To the right a couple of doors led to bedrooms, between them a grandfather clock signaled how late I was, and to the left an archway framed a living room/dining room combination. Through the archway I caught a glimpse of rough-and-ready furniture, a black marble fireplace, and artwork in black and white. We climbed a set of stairs where pine-trimmed windows lit up the stairway. On the next floor Robbie motioned me up a wrought-iron spiral staircase leading through the ceiling.

Oh, well, nothing says you have to sit just anywhere while waiting for the Grim Reaper to come collect you. So up the spiral staircase I went, sticking my head through the hole in the floor.

"What are your rates, young lady?" That had come from the deck of the cupola.

"Sorry, but I never discuss my fees while hanging from a ladder."

A snort from the deck, then, "Harry Poinsett said you were somewhat of a smart aleck."

Little I could say to that so I pulled myself up the last few steps, and rather quickly, too, suddenly remembering that I wasn't dressed for climbing and Robbie O'Key stood below me.

The glassed-in room had a telescope on a tripod and a trash-can-sized machine plugged into the wall; under the circular windows stretched cabinets of white pine where magazines flapped in the breeze like spoiled children begging for attention. I walked out on deck and took in the view. And quite a view it was. At the edge of the island the water was light blue, clear enough to see the bottom, but farther out it darkened, blending in with the sky. Small puffs of clouds drifted by; overhead a jet left a trail across the sky; the wind snapped at me, tossing the hem of my skirt around.

"Nice view."

"Yes—if you like nothing."

I scanned the view again. Perhaps I'd missed something.

"This is nothing compared to where my first wife and I honeymooned. This is one big . . . nothing, but that place was special and in the heart of the wetlands, plants and animal life at your door. It's owned by the government now. If my father hadn't owned these islands I would've been left with nothing."

Well, nothing to him would've been plenty for me.

"You plan and plan and nothing turns out the way you wish. If the government doesn't get you something else does. In my case, emphysema."

Two rockers flanked the door and I took a seat in the empty one. Robert O'Key was a rugged-looking fellow with shoulders filling out a shirt that had forgotten its color halfway down, changing from royal blue to burnt orange. His shirt was tucked into khakis and on his head sat a baseball cap. A thin, plastic tube ran from his nose and was held in place by a strap around the back of his head. Oxygen sucked from the air by the trash-can-sized machine—a concentrator—fed O'Key through the tube. Emphysema usually goes hand in hand with cancer and most of that cancer is caused by smoking. Seeing O'Key strapped to his machine made me swear off cigarettes once again.

From here I could see Angeline and Robbie on the tennis court. Angeline was wiping sweat away with a towel and listening to Robbie as he gestured in our direction. After hearing him out, Angeline shook her head and returned to attacking the practice board, a huge green wall with a white line across it. Soon the air was filled with the *thump-thump-thump* of balls but no more than three or four thumps in a row. Though an eager student, the woman had trouble keeping the ball in play: She was always out of place, the ball jamming her or flying just out of her reach. Robbie glanced up at us, then stalked off the court. His stepmother didn't appear to notice.

O'Key sighed. "That was all wrong, wasn't it?"

"Pardon?"

"My ungentlemanly manner."

"To tell you the truth I hardly noticed."

He chuckled. "You do reply in kind, don't you? Sorry I was such an ass, Miss Chase. I thought I was over the anger stage of dying but . . . I should be able to handle death with more dignity. My father would've, his father, too."

"You were there when they both died?"

O'Key looked at me long enough to make me wonder how long it'd been since anyone had stood up to him.

"I asked about your rates, thinking someday I might throw a little business your way."

"In what regard?"

"To get the goods on Robbie's next wife."

"I'm not that kind of detective. I locate runaways."

"Then you'd be perfect. Robbie's always running away from responsibility." He looked out to sea. "But I won't be around to bail him out next time, will I?"

I didn't know what to say to that.

In a moment O'Key said, "I appreciate your not patronizing a dying man."

That didn't seem to require a response so we sat there communing with nature, the wind tossing around my hair and the hem of my dress.

"Hell of a note, isn't it? All this air and all I can use is what comes through this damn tube."

More silence while we watched more balls hit the

practice wall. There seemed to be a level of proficiency Angeline simply couldn't surpass; four out of five licks against the wall, then the ball was out of reach or fouled off, sometimes into the ocean. But she remained calm, never once becoming upset. In that she was just as consistent.

"Susan Chase," said her husband. "Orphaned at fifteen, dropped out of school about the same time, lives on a fishing boat left by her father when he fell overboard and drowned. Probably drunk again. Girl's mother walked out on the family several years earlier." He turned to me. "Now, is that why you look for runaways? Are you searching for your missing parents?"

My neck did more than heat up. It burned. "For the sake of accuracy I'm a woman."

"Oh, one of those, are you?"

"Consider it a character flaw: wanting to be treated with the proper respect."

O'Key smiled, then continued. "The woman"—he rolled the word around on his tongue as if trying it on for size—"has a reputation as someone who can keep her mouth shut. You know, Miss Chase, with that kind of reputation, you could make a great deal of money in my circle. All sorts of disgusting things go on, I'm sorry to say. You know about my daughter's Bohemian lifestyle, my first wife drank too much, and when she did, she ran down people in her automobile. It's all I can do to keep Robbie in line. You watch yourself around him."

"I'd be interested in something a little more substantial."

O'Key's snort turned into a laugh. "The money Robbie can throw at a girl *can* be substantial." He twisted around in his seat and rang a buzzer on the wall. "How about a drink? Sounds like you're old enough for one."

"Well, all I can say is, it's about time."

He laughed, and below us, Angeline stopped and looked up. The woman was plainly confused. She had just returned a ball for the ninth or tenth time, probably setting a new personal best.

"Well done!" shouted her husband, then to me, "No matter how much I drink, my liver's sure to outlast my lungs."

We watched Angeline work the practice board until Lambert climbed the ladder and poured drinks from a cabinet in the cupola. The butler wore his usual suit and shirt but no tie. Evidently the tie was optional when at the beach.

"A scotch," Lambert said, serving me from a tray and with another smile. "A double. Neat—if I remember correctly, Miss Chase."

"It'll certainly do," I said, returning the smile.

Then, after asking if there would be anything else, and receiving a reply in the negative, the butler disappeared down the ladder.

"I take it you two have met," O'Key said.

"At your place in Georgetown—when Robbie challenged me to a drinking contest."

"Which you lost."

"I don't know. Robbie seemed to lose interest before I did."

"Only because he'd been drinking all day and planned to continue into the night."

I took a swallow and rolled the liquid around in my mouth before sending it down. When the scotch hit bottom it radiated throughout my body and turned the wind into a cooling breeze.

"Up to your usual standards?"

I licked my lips. "More so."

So we sat there, enjoying the liquor and the view, which in a short time began to soften around the edges; O'Key, too.

"My daughter's a lot like you, Miss Chase. I realized that when Harry Poinsett phoned: a mind of her own and she never backs down. I have to apologize. I was toying with you, trying to bring back old memories."

"Not a problem."

As he gazed at the tennis court a serene look crossed his face. Angeline was still at it, whacking the ball against the practice wall. *Thump-thump-thump* the balls went, but her game didn't improve. What did it matter? That wasn't her game.

"I seem to be doing a good bit of that these days: apologizing, especially to my daughter. Kristy can't understand that a father might know what's best for his daughter. She could have as much money as she wants but won't take a dime. She insists on making her own way in the world, which is absolutely ridiculous. You only live once and any way you can make it easier . . . and she paints in black and white just to get my goat—which shows how much she knows about art. I've paid more than one critic to tell me her work is practically worthless."

My only answer was to enjoy another swallow of his whiskey. It made more sense than his logic.

"I told Kristy if she'd put a dab of color in those cityscapes—cityscapes is what she paints—she might make a name for herself." He shook his head. "Imagine an O'Key working for a living. It's been a long time since anyone in this family's ever done that. But no, Kristy has to do everything her way—so she lives in a run-

down apartment on a gaudy part of the beach with odd
people drifting in and out at all hours. My friends still
ask when she's going to grow up and come home."

"Sounds like she's won you over to some degree."

O'Key was in the middle of a swallow. "What—what?"
he coughed, wiped his mouth, and coughed again.
When he couldn't stop I reached over and thumped
him across the back a couple of times.

On the tennis court Angeline stopped and looked
up. Her husband waved her off with an angry motion.
"What do . . . you mean?" he finally got out. The old
man's face was flushed and not only from the liquor
going down the wrong way.

"You began by not approving of your daughter's
work; now you argue over the direction that work should
take."

"Miss Chase, I don't need anyone telling me how to
handle my children."

So for the next few minutes we watched the gulls
hit the water like kamikazes. Finally I asked, "I'd hoped
you might know something that could help me find
someone I'm looking for—Jenny Rogers."

"Can't help you there. Rogers is just the kind of
person I'd rather Kristy not be associated with." He
pulled a yellow sheet from a pocket of his shirt and
handed it to me. "This is the girl I'm concerned about."

The telegram read: IN RIO STOP MAY PAINT MORE
THAN ONE SOUTH AMERICAN CITY STOP NOT TO
WORRY STOP KRISTY.

I returned the telegram. If Jenny Rogers had sent
the telegram, then where the hell was Kristy O'Key?

Her father refolded the paper and stuffed it into his
pocket. "That's all I've got left of my daughter. We had
another fight before she left."

"About what?"

"Oh, the usual: wanting her to come home and live with me." He glanced at the court where Angeline was policing up her gear. "With us. Sometimes I forget about Angeline. I don't think Kristy ever does."

"She knew about your condition and still left the country?"

He sighed. "She's run off before—after prep school when I had other plans for her. That time I had to hire Pinkertons to find her."

"Where was she?"

"Enrolled in some art school in New York City. God knows how she found out about it. I wanted her to attend Agnes Scott where her mother went. Kristy ran off again after her mother died."

"Your wife says Kristy can't cope with distractions and that's why she leaves."

O'Key glanced at the tennis court, empty now, Angeline and her equipment gone. "Not can't. Won't. I told Kristy it wasn't appropriate to move out so soon after her mother's death, but she did anyway. I lost a good hostess when Kristy left. She certainly knew her way around my friends. I hired a detective to find her that time, too." He turned to me. "I've had quite a few dealings with people in your profession. To protect one's family from others, and themselves, you have to keep tabs on everyone. I even had Angeline checked out. She's from New Orleans, actually Baton Rouge. We met doing charity work, but with all the sharpies there are, one has to stay on his toes. My wife might've been another gold digger."

Rather than burst his bubble, I asked, "So a trip to South America's not all that unusual?"

"Not at all. Kristy takes a room in the worst part of town—she did that in both London and Paris—to catch the essence of the city, whatever the hell that means. I never pretended to understand. When you paint in black and white one section of town's as good as any other." He paused. "Is it true what Harry Poinsett said about you being able to keep your mouth shut?"

"It has been so far."

He considered the idea. "Odd to find someone like you in this day and age. Everyone seems to want to kiss and tell—and be paid for it. Be paid quite handsomely for it, I might add. How would you go about finding my daughter, if I wanted you to?"

"I'd have to fly down to Rio. At best it'd be a long shot. That's an awfully big city."

"That's what I thought," he said, looking out to sea.

"Would you happen to have a key to her apartment?"

He looked at me. "I thought you'd already searched her apartment. The police said you were inside when they arrived."

"I might've missed something."

O'Key stared at me, and I stared at him, and we sat there until he finally pulled a card from the same pocket that held the telegram. He gave it to me. Printed on one side was his name; scrawled across the back: Please extend the bearer every courtesy. Robert O'Key.

"Will there be anything else, Miss Chase?"

"If there is I'll get back to you."

After a final swallow of my drink I got to my feet, stepped through the cupola, and climbed back down the ladder. I wasn't sure what had gone on up there, but the whiskey had been damn good.

Chapter 14

They were waiting for me in the living room when I came downstairs. Through the screened-in porch I saw a single boat at the pier: the fiberglass beauty, not my captain's. Robbie sat beside Angeline, drink in one hand, the other across the love seat behind her, feet propped up on the coffee table.

"How do I get ashore?" I asked.

"You swim."

"Robbie, don't be that way."

Angeline still wore her tennis outfit, a short thing allowing for the maximum exposure of leg. I had to admit the woman had a marvelous tan, and after her husband was gone she'd have no end of men volunteering to help her with her game, not to mention her tennis. She turned to the serving window. Through it you could see pots, pans, and cooking utensils hanging from an overhead rack.

"Lambert?"

The butler pushed his way through the swinging door. "Yes, Madam?"

"Call Tip. Miss Chase is ready to go ashore."

"Yes, Madam."

"And bring Miss Chase another drink."

"Certainly, Madam." Lambert smiled at me again. "One double scotch. Neat. Coming up."

"I don't know about that . . . ." I was still trying to understand what had happened upstairs and for that I'd need a clear head.

"Certainly you have time for a drink, Susan."

Hearing Angeline use my first name, Robbie wrinkled his nose.

"I think I exceeded my limit upstairs."

Angeline glanced toward the roof. "Yes—Robert's been drinking more than usual these days."

Robbie snorted as he pulled his feet off the coffee table. "Whatever's normal for a man who's dying." He got to his feet.

"Robbie, don't be so morbid."

"And you, Chase, I never thought I'd see the day you'd turn down a drink."

"Robbie!"

He crossed the room, brushing past me on his way to the door. "I'm going out, Angie, since you evidently want to talk with this creature."

"Please don't. You know how I feel about drinking and driving."

At the archway he stopped. "I don't need a mother, Stepmother." And he stormed out of the house and down the walkway.

Since Robbie wasn't going to give me a ride I took a seat across from Angeline on the sofa. The living room/dining room was filled with the heavy wood and thick-fabric furniture I'd seen when I'd first entered the house. Walls were floor-to-ceiling shelves cluttered with bric-a-brac and small pieces of sculpture. To my right stood a bar, to my left, a black marble fireplace flanked by a couple of chairs. Over those chairs hung O'Key's work. I didn't have to see her signature to know her work.

An engine started near the pier, then a boat raced away, the engine being wound out.

Angeline shook her head. "I do hope he comes back. I have some shopping to do. I'm going to Waccamaw. I love that place. Do you shop there?" Waccamaw Pottery was a ten-acre mall featuring everything from everywhere, mostly manufactured in South Korea, Taiwan, or China.

"I really don't do that much shopping."

"Yes, yes, I know. Too many tourists. You can hardly find a parking space. I take Lambert along and he drops me off. Otherwise it would take all day."

"Well, that's what shopping's for."

She studied me and the remark, knowing by now to look for any hidden meaning. With a smile that erased all thought, she asked, "How are you coming with your investigation?"

"Pardon?"

"You know, finding Mrs. Rogers' daughter."

"It's coming along."

"I want you to tell Kristy we need her at home."

"You think they're together?"

"I didn't—not until you came to see us." She smiled brightly and patted down her tennis outfit, what little of it there was to pat down. "But you'll tell her if you see her, won't you?"

"Tell Kristy . . . ?"

"That we need her at home."

"I think you already asked me to do that when I was at your place in Georgetown."

"Oh, I'm sure I did." She glanced toward the cupola

again. "That was probably for Robert. But flying down to Rio, won't that cost a great deal of money?"

Thankfully, Lambert chose that moment to come through the door with my drink—on a tray. Maybe that's why he hadn't poured my drink from the wet bar. He needed a tray to tote it. Hell, there could be any number of reasons why anything might be done in this house, all beyond me. I took a sip. But there was one thing you could always count on: The liquor would be first class.

"Anything for you, Mrs. O'Key?"

"No, thank you, Lambert."

He nodded to her, smiled at me, and disappeared into the kitchen again.

"I know how it feels, Susan, having to watch your money. I wasn't born to this wealth." She gestured at the love seat. "Why, after playing tennis I feel I should cover this thing before sitting on it. But that's silly. If the cushions became soiled I could have them cleaned. Or replaced." She glanced upstairs. "I try so hard for Robert. I've only known him a short while and soon he'll be gone and you know what people will say—that I'm cashing in on his death."

"Well, you are, but what can you do about it?"

"I know, I know, but people can be so cruel. When I'm on Robert's arm I receive a great deal of attention. Alone I don't think I'll have the same kind of clout."

"Oh, I don't know, people seem to respond to money no matter whose hands it's in."

"Do you, Susan?"

"Do I what?"

"Respond to money?"

"I like it as well as the next gal."

"I envy your independence."

"You're already independent. You have money."

She waved off the notion. "Oh, there are so many responsibilities that come with money, even more so when Robert's gone. I'm just learning, but one thing I know: When you're responsible for that much money there's no such thing as independence. I'll even be responsible for Robbie's share. There's no way he could handle money; Kristy either, though I doubt she'd want it." She paused. "You hear how I talk."

"Pardon?" I was in the middle of another sip.

"Like 'there are so many responsibilities that come with money.' Did you hear the way I said that? It sounds so phony." She tucked her legs up underneath her on the love seat. "No lady would ever sit like this." She glanced toward the kitchen. "I have to be on my toes to make sure Lambert doesn't catch me."

"Catch you doing what—not being a lady?"

She leaned over conspiratorially. "That's why Lambert's always around—to make sure I play my role."

Dishes rattled in the kitchen and Angeline sat up and straightened her legs. "Why I didn't know how to play tennis when I first met Robert, but he so loved the game I just had to learn. Now I play every day no matter the weather and for what? Robert's never going to play again, but he loves to watch. So I have one of the boys over"—another glance at the window again—"from a socially acceptable family and we play."

"Well, soon that'll all be over and you can take charge of your life." I listened hard for the Chris Craft. What was keeping my captain?

"Oh, but it won't end with Robert's death. There's a circuit I'm expected to travel, charitable events I'm expected to attend and so many parties. That doesn't end with the death of one's spouse." She sighed. "It used to be such fun, doing charitable work, but now it's become a chore. I hate to say it, but Robert's illness has been a blessing in disguise. We don't go out as often." Her voice twanged and she smiled. "Why I'm just a good old girl from Baton Rouge, actually East Feliciana Parish. So you see I really do envy your independence."

A horn sounded from the water.

"Time to go," I said, standing up.

Angeline came after me, taking my arm. "But you've barely touched your drink."

"Sorry, but Tip's here."

"Oh, don't worry about him." She held my arm as we walked toward the door. "He's on some kind of retainer or some such thing. I'm sure I'll learn all about it when Robert's gone. I'd really hoped you'd stay and tell me about some of your adventures."

For that, my dear, I would truly have to be drunk. "I have to work—to stay independent."

As we entered the hallway she glanced upstairs once again. "Oh, yes, what did Robert want to see you about?"

"Sorry, but I can't say."

She patted my arm. "It's all right. I'm his wife."

I really didn't want any drawn-out good-bye so I said, "The ethics of my profession don't allow me to discuss a case with anyone but my client."

"Not even his wife? Our attorney tells me everything."

I really doubt that. "Sorry, Angeline." Then I had a wicked thought, and said conspiratorially, "Unless murder's been committed. That dissolves all client confidentiality."

"I see," she said, considering what I'd said. "You don't think we've had anything like that, do you?"

"Who knows? This is the beach. Bodies can surface anywhere."

The thought appeared to immobilize her and I had to open the screened door myself. As I hustled down the slate walkway she called after me.

"Don't forget to come back and tell me all about it."

Yeah. Right. Sure.

My captain watched me seat myself in the stern of the Chris Craft again. "Enjoy yourself, Missy?"

"About as much as you thought I would."

"Well, come back anytime, but you'd better hurry. Mr. Big Shot doesn't have much time left." With a practiced hand he wheeled the boat away from the dock.

Approaching the marina, he throttled back and I could be heard over the engine. "Why do you call O'Key that, Tip?"

"Well, he thinks he's a big shot, doesn't he?" My captain brought his craft alongside the dock. "Acting like he owns the whole damn world. Well, he don't."

"What did Robert O'Key ever do to you?"

"Nothing, Missy. Nothing at all."

He stepped out of the boat and threw a line around a piling. Before he finished with the bow I was out of the boat and tying up the stern with a rolling hitch—easy to tie, easier to loosen.

He examined the knot. "I think you've done this before."

"I was raised on the water." I slipped off my flats and stretched my feet, wiggled my toes. "Have to look right for Mr. Big Shot. Now, what'd he do?"

My captain spit between the boat and the pier, a pretty good shot considering. "Not me. My family." He pointed at the island. "Took my family's place—not him, it were his pa. We didn't have any money and my ma was sick. Well, what could my pa do? He had to sell;

so Pa died in a nursing home, not on the water. That boy of his is the worst—thinks everybody works for his daddy."

"Works for his daddy, not for him?"

"Yeah," Tip said with a grin, "kind of tells you something about the kid, don't it?"

"How do you get along with Mrs. O'Key?"

"Okay, I guess. First wife was a lush. Killed herself up on King's Highway and the family paid to hush it up. She run into a carload of kids. Put them all in the hospital. One's still there and it's been six years. Young girl who ain't gonna get no older." He spit between the boat and pier again. "You can see why Mr. Big Shot married that empty-headed gal. She don't worry about nothing could drive a person to drink." He grinned. "But the new Mrs. O'Key has lots of young men over to play tennis. I guess she gets lonely out there."

Driving up King's Highway I stopped near Pawleys Island for gas. Filling up, I watched the traffic fly by, including a Jag convertible with Robbie O'Key at the wheel, arm draped across the seat, blond hair flying. He stole a look at me. Poor bastard. Absolutely clueless as to how to play the new hand life had dealt him. Or perhaps this was the way his life would have played out even if his parents had survived their boating trip. A few minutes later I drove past another station with Robbie's Jag at the pumps. I didn't see him, but he could've been paying for his gas or buying a couple of beers.

Ten minutes later I was in his sister's apartment and ready to go over the place with the proverbial fine-toothed comb. Unfortunately, the apartment had already been cleaned: books were in their shelves, dresser

and couch put back together, and most of the paint
scrubbed off the floor. Murphy bed tucked in the wall,
artist gear stacked in a corner, the kitchen absolutely
spotless.

While I stood there, muttering a curse or two, someone spoke behind me. I whirled around, hand auto-
matically going for my purse. It was one of the dudes
I'd seen the first time I'd been in the building: leather
top, gold chains, earrings.

"What you doing in here? This door's supposed to
be locked."

"Maybe I'm the cleaning lady."

"No way. They were in here yesterday."

"Is that so?"

"Yeah, with Mrs. O'Key."

Angeline didn't tell me that. I showed the guy my
key. "You certainly have more than the usual amount
of interest in this place," I said. "Why's that?"

"We watch out for each other 'round here. The cops
won't do it 'cause we're not tourists."

"Then why didn't you report the break-in? The apartment sat here, ransacked, for weeks."

"Sorry, lady, but I've been out of town, my buddy,
too. We were down at Hilton Head taking photographs."
He gestured at Fiddler's room with its crime scene tape
still across the door. "Anyway that was up to George."

"He didn't do such a good job, did he?"

"Hey, that's not nice. George is dead." He squinted
at me. "You're the woman who fell downstairs."

"Yes—made it all the way to the top this time." And
it took a trip to Rio to lose the headache.

"We used to have a nice, quiet place here . . . ." The
guy shook his head. "For sure they gonna be kicking
us out. People come to Pawleys don't want this shit.

They already packed up the little girl and sent her home."

"Victoria—the one they call 'Vic'?"

He nodded. "Her mama saw them taking George's body out the hotel on TV. Called her ex and told him to put the kid on the next plane home."

"Have you seen Kristy around?"

"She's out of town. Gonna be gone a while. They towed her van yesterday."

"Who towed it?"

"Some wrecker company."

"How do you know this?"

"Kristy has the space next to mine."

"Did you get the name of the company?"

"No. Why?"

"I want to know where they took it."

"Same place they always take it: Georgetown." He was puzzled. "Why you want to know?"

"You're telling me they towed Kristy's van to the O'Key house?" I ran the address by him.

"That's it," he said with a nod. "Big sucker with a wall around it and a guard out front. You want to know where Kristy is? Check with her old man. He tows her van every time she leaves town. That way Kristy has to see him when she comes home. They play games like that all the time."

And what game was Robert O'Key playing with me?

He left but only after reminding me to lock up. The guy was right. They had a nice place here—until things started going to hell. Maybe they should hire a private detective to figure out what was going on around here.

I opened both windows and turned on the AC. The room reeked of disinfectant and was hot as hell. Sticking my head out the window, I stared at the parking lot. Had there been a van parked there when I'd been here before? I didn't remember.

Paul Zidane's letter lay on the kitchen counter, but the brochure touting Rio was gone. I scanned the room again, then I bit my lip. The place was just too damn clean and it didn't appear to have been done to drive me crazy. The bathroom had been sanitized, the apartment floor vacuumed, Kristy's silverware washed, dried, and neatly laid out in one of the drawers, and the mirror over the sink shone. Next to the phone was a pad with a number on it: the O'Keys'.

I took out my brush and repaired the damage done while driving up King's Highway. I was in the mood to look like a real private eye. I wanted to know where the hell Kristy O'Key was. My eyes needed a bit of work so I sharpened my eyeliner by rubbing the side of the pencil over the scratch pad.

In a moment the top sheet revealed its previous message: *3 pm. Huntington Beach State Park.* Now that might be a clue. I ripped off the sheet, stuffed it in my purse, and turned around—to find Robbie O'Key standing just inside the door.

"I should call the police."

I held up the key given to me by the landlady. "Wrong."

He swayed back and forth, finally finding a handhold on the back of the couch. "You found it after breaking in."

"And you're drunk," I said, trying to pass him.

He grabbed me and turned me around. "Now listen here, you, you're going to tell me what you're up to. I answered *your* questions."

"I don't have to explain myself to a damn drunk."

"I'm not drunk. I'm drinking. There's a difference."

"Not that I can see." I could smell the liquor on his breath.

He squeezed my shoulders. "Listen you, I want to know what you're up to."

"I told you before: I'm trying to locate Jenny Rogers. Now take your hands off me."

He glanced at his hands, surprised. Women probably let this jerk put his hands anywhere he wanted because of all his money.

"Then why bother my father? What could he tell you? What *did* he tell you?"

"Actually, he had more questions than answers."

"Questions about what? Who? Were you talking about me?"

"Yes, Robbie, we were discussing your paranoia."

"Why you . . . ."

He raised his hand and I stepped back, feet sliding apart, and my shoulders tightened. Slowly he lowered his hand. I would've thought more of the boy if he'd taken a swing at me.

"Listen, Chase, I want to know why my father hired you."

"Who says he did?"

"I know he did. I saw the check."

Well, hello there. Tell me more. "In what amount?"

"A thousand dollars."

"Then where is it?"

"Lambert's putting it in the mail."

I laughed. "You're full of it, Robbie."

"I'm telling you the truth, Chase."

"And I'm telling you the same thing I told your stepmother. I don't discuss my cases with anyone."

"Wait a minute. Angie asked what you and my father talked about?"

This family was a real circus, three rings and all. "You got it."

"But I didn't think . . . ." He walked into the kitchen area where he reached under the sink and pulled out a bottle. I'll say one thing for the boy, he knew where his next drink was coming from.

Robbie took down a pair of glasses from the cabinet and looked around. "Cleanest I've ever seen this place."

"Your stepmother had it done."

He harrumphed. "It still won't make Kristy like her. Join me for a drink?" Robbie filled a glass and looked at me.

"I don't drink on the job."

"You drank with my father." He poured a drink for me and put down the bottle.

"That was different."

"How?" He took a swallow, then made a face. "Jeez! How can Kristy drink this stuff?"

"Easy. She doesn't have your money."

He coughed, then cleared his throat. "She could if she wanted. My father would do anything for her. She was always his favorite." Robbie forced himself to take another drink, then made another face. "How was it different, drinking with my father?"

"I was pumping him for information."

He almost choked. "God, but you are a bitch." He put down the glass and crossed the room. "Maybe you need a real man to straighten you out."

"Yeah, right," I said, turning on my heel and heading for the door. "Call me when you find one."

I was surprised he didn't follow me downstairs; then I realized he hadn't finished his drink. But he did stumble into the lobby while I was picking the lock on his sister's mailbox.

"Now what the hell do you think you're doing?"

"Picking this lock. You don't happen to have the key, do you?"

"You don't think I'd give it to you if I did?"

"You never know until you ask."

Robbie tried to wedge a shoulder between me and the wall, but before he could get his shoulder set, the box popped open. I grabbed at the mail as it fluttered to the floor and Robbie grabbed me.

"I think it's time someone fixed you, bitch."

"I wondered when we'd get around to that."

I dropped the mail and brought up my arms, knocking his hands off my shoulders. When he stepped back, I kicked him between the legs, snapping my leg and getting the heel of my shoe into the blow, and he went down groaning. Brushing down my dress, I said, "I'll be the one making all the lame jokes around here."

I snatched up Kristy's mail as Robbie rolled around on the floor and moaned how he was going to report me to his father, the cops, and the postmaster general.

The landlady stuck her head out the door and eyeballed Robbie holding onto his crotch. "Got a problem out here?"

I tossed her the key. "Guy tried to grope me and I kicked him in the balls."

The landlady fielded the key. "Good for you, honey." And she disappeared into her unit, slamming the door behind her.

"I'll get you for this, Chase," squeaked Robbie from the floor as I stepped around him.

"I doubt that, but it does make me feel sorry for the next girl. She might not know how much you enjoy the really rough stuff."

Chapter 15

I threw O'Key's mail on the floorboard of my jeep and slid behind the wheel. At the lights I went through the usual bills—some stamped "past due"—several pieces of junk mail, an art catalog, and a letter from her stepmother detailing her father's condition, including a plea for Kristy to drop by more often and see him.

A letter from Paul Zidane asked to see O'Key's latest piece of work; one from a guy named "Carl" who was in a bind and needed a few hundred to tide him over until the end of the month; a form letter asking O'Key to donate a painting to the Children's Hospital auction; a reprimand for renting a house from an employee of Francis Marion National Forest. This last letter went on to scold Kristy for circumventing governmental policy by subleasing government property from the original leaseholder.

Now what the hell was that—besides governmental gobbledygook? I used my cell phone and was connected with the woman who'd written the letter. Her name was Looney, which she was—and much more.

"Ye land sakes! (She really said that.) I can't have you people calling me all the time. I've got work to do. The only people allowed to rent those houses are employees of the federal government."

"What houses?"

"Why the houses in the national forest. What was it you called about, young lady?"

"I'm calling about the house . . . I'm calling regarding your letter to Kristy O'Key, dated the twenty-eighth of last month. In it you say . . . ." And the letter was snatched away in the breeze over the windshield. Oh well. I should keep at least one hand on the wheel.

"I know what the letter says, young lady, it's my second and I'm still waiting for a reply from Miss O'Key. I'm telling you it's the policy of the federal government to rent those houses only to people who work for the National Park Service."

"What did Ms. O'Key do?"

"Why she went behind our backs. She got the Rideouts to lease their house to her. Disgraceful what they did. They up and took off—for a whole week. Yes, yes, I know, they had vacation time coming, but it still wasn't right."

"Where's the house located?"

She sniffed. "Only because it's my job." She gave me directions into Francis Marion National Forest by way of South Carolina Highway 45 out of McClellanville, a town that had once been submerged by Hurricane Hugo. "You may need a boat to get there."

"A boat . . . to reach the house?"

"Yes. It's awfully marshy in that part of the forest and we plan to keep it that way. With all the clear-cutting that's gone on, the government's making sure Francis Marion stays the way the good Lord intended it. I'm sure the Rideouts will miss living there, but they should've obeyed the rules. Why there's a plantation in the middle of the forest and I hear the employees leasing it act like its *their* plantation. I declare, I don't know what the world's coming to. I'm sorry Hugo didn't destroy all those houses."

Tell that to the folks in McClellanville. "Why did O'Key want that particular house?"

"Why to paint, of course. Kristy O'Key's a painter. Didn't you know that?"

"Yes, yes, I know. But why would O'Key want to work in a national forest? She only paints cityscapes."

"Citywhaaat?"

"Paintings of cities, like New York and L.A. In black and white."

"All I know is I told her what the government's policy is and she said that wouldn't do. Imagine that. Talking to a government employee like that. I know we're supposed to be your servants, but we don't have to take any lip. Next thing I know there's an outboard motor and a couple of lawn chairs missing—things belonging on the property—and I'll have you know the Rideouts had to pay for them. Their last paycheck was docked before termination," she added rather proudly.

"Any other damage to the house?"

"No."

"No wild parties resulting in broken furniture or dishes?"

"Er—no. Are you suggesting the federal government got off lightly, Miss Chase?"

"Well, you know how these artists are—there could've been blood all over the floor for all I know."

"Blood all over the floor?"

"I was only joking, Ms. Looney." Evidently Jenny

Rogers hadn't killed Kristy O'Key in Francis Marion National Forest.

Looney laughed nervously. "Well, there wasn't any other damage but for the missing motor and those two chairs. I do hope you won't tell anyone what I've told you. Evidently Miss O'Key did. I've already had another call and I had to explain the government's policy to her, too."

"Who called?"

"That artist friend of hers. Emma something-or-other."

"Emma Coker?"

"Yes," Looney said brightly. "I couldn't remember her last name, but I remember the first. I had an old maid aunt by that name. Emma Randolph."

"When did Coker call?"

"What? Oh, I don't remember exactly, a few weeks ago."

"And you told her where the house was?"

"I'm a government employee. I have to—even if I don't want to."

"Thanks for your help, Ms. Looney."

"You're welcome, and I don't want to hear of you being involved in any shenanigans like Miss O'Key."

I told her she didn't have to worry about me, that I was a good girl. Well, at least the latter half was right.

I made my next call to the Myrtle Beach Police Department, where a friend told me Emma Coker had been sprung, that some fast-talking lawyer had done the job. "That girl is well-connected, Susan."

After that I called Heartie Eubanks, who works the society page of the Charleston *News and Courier.* Heartie and I go way back to the day I dragged her out of the water when she was trying to learn how to surf. Heartie tells everyone she was rescued by a real private eye.

Heartie said, "I feel a free meal coming on!"

"Tell me what you know about Angeline O'Key."

"Do you have any dirt?" Heartie's voice was like a vulture's, poised and ready to strike.

"Why?"

"Oh, nothing personal."

"With you, Heartie, everything's personal—that's what the society page is all about."

"These days it's called the Lifestyle Section."

"Whatever."

"Well, if you haven't noticed, men fall all over Angeline."

"Who cares, as long as it's not *your* man."

Silence at the other end, then, "If you have to know, I introduced her to Winston and the next thing I know he's ogling her. I mean right across the table and even after I kicked him a couple of times."

"Angeline seemed kind of dumb and sappy to me."

"I figured her for the same, wondering what Robert saw in her besides being a younger woman, but Angeline radiates this innocent sexuality. I couldn't see how such vulnerability could be so desirable. I mean, I know a come-on when I see one, but Angeline doesn't come on. She's just being herself and Winston ate it up. All the men did. It made me sick! When Winston took me home I didn't let him come inside. He could go home and play with himself for all I cared. And Robert O'Key's in seventh heaven, squiring around this beauty with no brains. I don't know if Angeline cheats on him; Robert would probably cut her off like he did Kristy if she did. Robert's always used his money to keep the family in line."

"It didn't work with Kristy."

"No—and that really pisses him off. Kristy's *Numero Uno* in his book. Robert thinks she hung the moon."

"Seen her lately—Kristy, I mean?"

"Susan, that's hardly possible. We don't run in the same circles."

At a light I stopped and fumbled around for a water bottle. "What do you know about Angeline?"

"Not much. She graduated from some podunk high school—"

"East Feliciana High?"

"Er—yes. You're not testing me, are you, Susan?"

After a swig of water, I said, "Not yet."

"Okay. Well, she married a developer from Baton Rouge and he killed himself when the real estate market turned around on him. There weren't any children."

"How'd he die?"

"With a pistol—ugh!—and Angeline used the insurance money to move here. Said she wanted to live on the coast but had too many bad memories of the Gulf area. A year later she married Robert."

"She could've gone to Florida."

"Girlfriend, there is no Charleston in Florida, no matter what those people might tell you."

"Any other family?"

"Ones Angeline doesn't talk about. Most from the country—people who wouldn't fit into her new life. None attended the wedding. Seemed by mutual agreement. Maybe Robert paid them to stay away."

"How did she and O'Key meet?"

"At a wildlife conservation meeting."

"Robert O'Key's into that?"

"Of course, my dear. It was *his* father who did the clear-cutting. You know how it is with each generation: what one does, the next does just the opposite."

"Then what's Robbie doing?"

"Why that's simple, Susan, spending all that money Robert's trying to hold onto."

After another swig, I asked, "Wasn't Robbie adopted?"

"I think you know more than you're letting on."

"What's Angeline do with her time?"

"Well, she and Robert used to go to quite a number of parties and benefits, but that's slowed down due to his cancer. Anyway, she came over here from New Orleans, set her hat for a rich man, and bagged Robert O'Key. It makes me sick to think about it. Nobody expected Robert to pick a younger woman—he's such a prig—but he seemed to go into heat. I could've had Robert myself if I'd listened to Dodo McGee. Dodo says if they've got a pulse they're eligible. She should know. Dodo's buried three of them."

"Heard any talk about Angeline sleeping around?"

"Hmm. Be hard to do with that butler of theirs."

"What about Robbie?" The light changed before I had a chance to put the water bottle away. I tossed it on the floorboard where it rolled around, dampening the pleas contained in O'Key's mail.

Heartie laughed. "Robbie's been grouchy as hell lately. Of course it could be all those gambling debts he's piled up."

"Robbie's a gambler?"

"The boy's an absolute fool when it comes to money. Why Robert had to set up a trust fund for him to make sure he never ran out of money. He's limited to a thousand a week. Do you know what I could do with that kind of money?"

"Still dating?"

"Absolutely. A girl has to stay in shape in case Mr.

Right comes along."

"Not you, Heartie, Robbie. Is *he* available?"

"Are you thinking of taking him on? If so, you should know he's got a terrible temper. Put Frances Flagler in the hospital when he hit her."

"You're kidding—Robbie O'Key?"

"Honey, all I'm saying is you want to be around Robbie when he's either tight or comatose, but never when he's really drunk."

My last call was to McGinnis.

"Jenny's fine. It's the rest of us who are worried. She's confessed to murder. Says she killed her best friend, and Rachel and Ronnie are worried we'll be closed down if the cops learn we're harboring a fugitive."

No sense in waiting for the other shoe to drop. "What are you going to do, Mac?"

"I'm getting a lot of flack, but I'll stick it out for twenty-four hours. If anyone needs our help it's Jenny. I don't think I've ever met anyone with such low self-esteem."

"Forty-eight hours, Mac. I really need to find someone."

"Forty-eight hours, then *I'm* calling the cops."

"Not you. Me. You never know when Jenny'll need a friend. I'll take her to the cops."

"I know how loyal you are to your friends, Susan. Are you sure Jenny will get there?"

"She'll get there."

"Promise?"

"Promise." Which put me in a hell of a bind. Now I had to find O'Key and find her quick. You turn Jenny over to J.D. Warden and you eliminate the possibility of rehabilitation.

"Mac, what if Jenny recants before I pick her up?"

"Susan! You promised!"

While I'd been on the phone, I'd been on my way to Huntington Beach State Park to see if my secret decoder eyeliner pencil worked. Huntington Beach used to be a pocket of natural beauty until Hugo blew through—even the red-cockaded woodpeckers were left homeless, over half the birds killed. Hugo topped the older trees at the cavities where the woodpeckers made their homes. After the storm was over, rangers hustled around the park boring holes for the survivors. There was plenty of money to rebuild the Grand Strand, but a flock of rare woodpeckers doesn't generate enough cash flow to warrant much attention. But if you wanted a great view of the ocean, with few tourists underfoot, you couldn't pick a better spot. Still, it didn't seem like the kind of place Kristy O'Key would've chosen to work.

"Why, she came here to paint, of course," said a barefoot young woman with a ponytail. The woman wore jeans and a tank top and she was skinny enough to be pitied. A bottle of wine sat in a cooler at the foot of her easel, as did another painting similar to the one she was working on. "I never thought I'd live to see the day when the Queen would stoop to working with nature."

"The Queen?" Part of the fun of being a private eye appeared to be the opportunity to go around asking a lot of dumb questions.

The young woman continued to paint and quite vigorously, too, her eyes never leaving the canvas. The wind off the ocean picked up the hem of my dress and tossed it around. Occasionally I had to hold it in place.

"Kristy thought she was better than everyone—

working with cityscapes, never with nature, and painting in black and white. Personally, I never understood
why her work sold. You can see a city anytime—just
walk outside. But nature, now that's something special." She gestured at the panorama before us: an ocean
peppered with gulls, back-dropped by a sky where small
clouds had been set free by a breeze. "*This* is special."

"O'Key wasn't working with colors?"

"That'll be the day. Kristy wants to be remembered
as a great painter, but she painted herself into a corner with those black-and-whites." She laughed at her
own joke, then went back to painting furiously.

I studied her work: a beach scene that could grace
the walls of any Wal-Mart. "What time of day was she
here?"

"Oh, the afternoon. We get our best colors then."

"But that wouldn't interest Kristy, would it?"

"No. . . I guess not."

"Anyone with her?"

She looked at me. "What?"

"See anyone hanging around when O'Key was painting? Anyone out of the ordinary?"

"Not that I remember." She moved her brush quickly
across the scene, dabbing at it here and there. "What's
it to you?"

"Not me—what's it to the person who saw O'Key
with someone other than a tourist? It's worth fifty bucks
to that person."

The brush stopped. "Fifty dollars?"

"For the correct answer—yes." Thanks to Dads I
had the cash.

"Cash or check?"

"Cash, of course."

"But she only spoke with the tourists. Black and

white still draws its share of gawkers."

So I drifted away, trying my offer on others. Everyone was eager to help except for a guy who didn't care much for money. I didn't think he'd been at this painting game long. A black kid selling soft drinks trailed along behind me but didn't ask me to buy. I smiled and he returned the smile. I wondered if he had any beer in that cooler.

The skinny and barefoot artist approached me while I was smoking a cigarette and leaning against a pine, watching the fishermen reel in their catch. "I remember there was this black guy who stopped by a couple of times. I remember because he drove a yellow Cadillac. I saw him getting into his car when I went to the rest room."

"What'd he look like?"

From the description she gave me he could've been anyone. And this woman was supposed to be an artist, an observer of life.

"Got a name?"

"No."

"Then you don't get the fifty bucks."

"Bitch!" she muttered and returned to her work. She spent the next few minutes trying to think of something, anything to squeeze that fifty bucks out of me and about blew a gasket doing it. Later she told me the black guy had bought one of Kristy's paintings and spent a good deal of time with her. The woman would've died if I hadn't given her something, so I gave her ten bucks from the money I'd found in Jenny's purse and told her to get lost.

By that time everyone knew what I was looking for, but unfortunately few had anything to offer. So, I fetched a rod and reel from the footlocker in the rear of

my jeep. Not that surf fishing's done all that well in a
dress—you get soaked to the knees, but I waded right
in and the funny looks stopped after my first bite—
which I always throw back unless it's supper. Later,
while watching the artists knock down their easels and
wondering if I should return the following day, the black
kid who sold soft drinks approached me. All the artists
seemed to know he was there—the fishermen, too—
but the kid ducked into the trees if a ranger came along.

"Want to buy a drink, lady?"

"How much?"

"Two dollars."

"I can do better at a drink machine."

"Most of the time the machines don't work. They
get all kinds of shit stuck in them."

"And I'm sure you have something to do with that."

"Listen, lady, are you really going to give someone
fifty bucks to tell you who was talking with the lady
painter?"

"Sure."

"Can I see the fifty?"

"You've never seen a fifty-dollar bill before?"

"Sure—I've got six of them at home, but I'd like to
see yours before I tell you who was with the lady."

I showed the kid the fifty bucks.

"You'll give that to me?"

"If you know who the lady was talking to."

"I know," he said with confidence.

"So tell me."

"Fast Bennie Lawson."

"You've got to be kidding." Fast Bennie Lawson is a
lieutenant of Markey Nichols, and Markey Nichols runs
a gambling operation every cop will tell you doesn't
exist, not only because they can't shut it down, but

because they can't even find it. It's said the games move
from place to place, but any high roller can find some
action by going into a bar and complaining about the
limits of video poker.

"I knew it was a trick!" shrieked the boy. "You aren't
going to give me the money."

"No, no, no! But why would Kristy O'Key be talking
with some gangsta?"

"I have to know that to get the fifty bucks?"

"You're right," I said with a laugh. "That's my job.
Okay, prove it."

"What do you mean?"

"Tell me what you saw. Make me believe Fast Bennie
was talking with the lady painter."

The gangsta—whose name came from his lack of
sexual control—had been there twice and never bought
a single painting or a soft drink. I shot a nasty look at
the skinny woman, still painting away like mad, probably to make up for lost time and the forty bucks she
imagined I owed her. Fast Bennie never showed any
interest in O'Key's work. He'd stood by the easel, talking, and whatever he'd said had not made the lady
painter very happy. After Bennie's second visit O'Key
hadn't returned. Neither had Fast Bennie.

"What kind of car does he drive?"

"A Cadillac."

"What color?"

"Yellow."

I gave the kid the fifty bucks and he said he thought
he might knock off early. I saw the envious looks from
painters and fishermen up and down the beach.

"Yeah—guess you should come back tomorrow."

The kid saw those same looks. "Next week might
be even better."

The Atlantic Towers is a seven-story building with no more than four units per floor. That made it as exclusive as the devil. You don't build units that size on that few square feet, especially on the beach. Miniature shrubbery had been planted around the base, a fenced-in area with a key code led to underground parking, and a guard sat in the lobby watching monitors. He could see all sides of the building and several places in the garage. When I walked by he was working a cross-word puzzle.

"Who you here to see?" he asked.

"Fast Bennie," I said, crossing the lobby to punch the button for the elevator.

"Nobody here by that name."

"Check again, Jack. He's in the penthouse."

The bell rang, signaling the arrival of the elevator, but the doors never opened. Behind me the guard returned to his crossword.

"Tell Bennie I'm here. It's business."

The guard glanced at me. "Sure it is, kid."

"Okay, Jack," I said, walking past him and heading for the door, "I'll tell Markey his boy wouldn't play ball and your name will be mentioned prominently in my report."

Before I reached the door the guard said, "I'll call upstairs."

"Susan Chase is the name."

"Yeah, and mine's not Jack."

The guard gave the folks upstairs my name, and when he had the same trouble selling me to them as I'd had selling myself to him, he invoked Nichols' name. The name worked wonders again. He hung up the phone and jerked a thumb toward an elevator that was already opening. I crossed the lobby and stepped inside. When I reached the penthouse two mugs got aboard. I tried to squeeze past them, but it was no go.

"Hey, guys, this is my floor."

The doors closed and we went back down.

"Really, fellows, that *was* my floor."

"Shut up!" The ugly one had a pockmarked face and wore a beard to conceal it. Both were black guys who worked out regularly—in a gym or on someone's face. Loud shirts hung over louder pants; under those shirttails were their fanny packs. At the beach that's where you tote your shooting iron.

When we reached the basement they lifted me off my feet and carried me out of the elevator, then across the garage. The whole thing would've been comical if I'd known their intentions were honorable.

"Hey, I can walk by myself. It's something I learned early on."

"Shut up," said the ugly one again.

"You're bruising my arms." Girls are allowed to whine like that. It's expected.

"I'll bruise your face if you don't shut up."

Then again, maybe not.

They forced me into the back seat of a Caddy, the ugly one climbing in right behind me before I could reach my pistol. The driver slid behind the wheel as a voice came over the radio.

"The computer says Chase carries."

The ugly guy snatched my purse and dug around inside but couldn't come up with my pistol. "Shit! She'd be better off hitting them with the fucking purse than trying to get at her piece."

"Like to be shown how it's done?" I asked.

He glared at me, then harrumphed when he finally

came out with the Smith & Wesson. "And I thought she was just another of Bennie's whores." He pocketed my weapon.

"That's why they have a computer to do your thinking."

The driver laughed, but the man next to me wasn't amused. "Listen, bitch, I'm taking you to see Markey, but he didn't say what condition you were to be in when you arrived, so you'd better shut your fucking mouth and just sit there."

So I shut my fucking mouth and just sat there. It seemed like the thing to do.

Chapter 16

e drove out of town, out of the county and into the country, to an old, abandoned, red-brick schoolhouse with a rusty hurricane fence and weeds around it. The car stopped at the gate and the ugly mug got out and unlocked the gate, then relocked it after the Caddy had passed through—long enough for me to notice a sign announcing a singing to be held in the auditorium this Sunday evening. A revival would be held later in the summer.

The building had cameras under the eaves and bars across the windows; the windows had been painted a rather sick brown color that clashed with the brick, but at the moment that didn't seem all that important. We drove around to the rear of the building where a wooden fence shielded the school from a series of houses. On the porches of those houses sat several old black people, folks who didn't seem overly concerned about what was happening to me.

Once we were on the dock I hollered and waved to the people on those porches. For my trouble I was grabbed by the arm and dragged inside the school. I was pulled through what had once been the kitchen, now stacked high with liquor boxes and mixers, then down a short hall. On one side of the hallway a coatroom separated two rest rooms; to the right, and through a pair of open doors, I caught a glimpse of an auditorium with its stage, piano, and risers. If this was the lobby, there should be another hallway running perpendicular to this one.

But the hallway hadn't been large enough for what the gambling lord had in mind, so the classroom walls had been torn out, the building's support beams hidden by mirrors, and its floors covered with wall-to-wall carpeting. The wide and low room now had a ceiling dotted with tiny chandeliers, and where the three R's once had been taught, roulette wheels, blackjack, and craps tables stood. On a small stage a house band and singer practiced the evening's entertainment. The singer was the young woman who'd begged me to find her boyfriend the morning after I'd almost been raped. Today she wore jeans, sandals, and a blouse tied at the waist. When she saw me being pulled through the gaming tables, her voice quivered, then failed her. One by one the other musicians stopped, the last being the piano player who was really into the number, eyes closed and unaware until he found himself playing solo.

I was hustled through a doorway painted to look like part of the wall, then into a narrow room where a gorgeous black man sat behind a table, reading a copy of *Time*. A MAC-10 lay on the table, along with several other magazines and clips. My two companions laid their pieces, mine, and my purse on the table.

The gorgeous guy opened my purse, glanced through the contents, and returned the purse, then motioned us through a door-sized metal detector on the far side of the room. When a buzzer sounded I was made to follow the ugly mug through the detector, another door, and into a room where a white woman did paperwork.

"Susan Chase to see Markey Nichols," I said, brushing back my hair and conjuring a smile. "I'm expected."

The woman frowned, nodded at the mugs, and then the driver opened still another door so the ugly mug could shove me into the next room. He did it with such gusto I had to grab something to keep from running into a black marble desk.

Markey Nichols worked in a room without windows studying a computer screen. Printouts littered his desk; more paperwork was bound and stacked across a credenza behind him. What I'd grabbed to come to a stop was one of three chrome chairs with woven cane bottoms that sat in front of his desk. Without looking up, he gestured at the chairs.

"Have a seat, Miss Chase. I'll be right with you."

Someone grabbed me from behind and tried to maneuver me into one of those chairs. I jabbed back with an elbow, really leaning into the blow. It took the breath, and the tough guy, right out of him—for all of about two seconds, then the ugly mug came at me and not in the best of humor.

"Bitch! I warned you!"

I grabbed one of the chairs and stepped back to take my best shot.

"Delbert!" shouted Nichols.

The pockmarked guy stopped and glared at me. Behind him the driver leaned against the door, looking amused and slightly aroused. I turned my back on both of them and took a seat in the remaining chair, brushed back my hair again, and arranged the hem of my dress across the top of my knees.

Markey Nichols was a tiny, middle-aged guy with thinning hair tinged with gray. He had light-colored skin, almost yellow, and wore a navy blue suit, white shirt, and maroon tie.

"Drink, Miss Chase?"

"Whiskey—if you've got it."

With the touch of a button a wall slid back, revealing a bar large enough to host a Super Bowl party.

"Delbert," asked Nichols, "would you do the honors?"

The ugly mug moved to the bar and mixed my drink, slamming ice into a glass as he did. A woman's voice came over the intercom on the black marble desk.

"Don't forget your three o'clock, Mr. Nichols."

Markey leaned forward and touched a button on the machine. "Thank you, Rose. Well, Miss Chase, as you can see I don't have much time . . . ."

I hoped I did and I took out my cigarettes to make just that point.

"Sorry, Miss Chase, but you're in the no smoking section of this building."

"How would I know?" I put my cigarettes away, missing my purse and having to retrieve them from the floor. "It's the first time I've been here."

"On your income I doubt you could afford it."

"Not to mention the tax on my conscience."

Delbert handed me the drink.

I shook my head. "I didn't ask for ice."

The mug didn't like it, but he repaired the drink.

When it was right, Nichols asked, "Now, Miss Chase, are you comfortable?"

"You've got to be kidding," I said, crossing my legs. "You won't let me smoke."

"You wanted to see Bennie Lawson—why is that?"

"I'd rather discuss that with Fast Bennie."

"He really doesn't like that nickname."

"I can imagine."

"Let's just say I'm taking his calls today."

"Sorry, Markey, but I respect my confidences."

Behind me one of the mugs snorted, Delbert for sure.

"Do the best you can, Miss Chase."

Would staying mum help Jenny Rogers? Probably not. "Usually I locate runaways, but this time I'm looking for a missing person."

"Who?"

"Kristy O'Key."

"The painter?"

"Yes."

"And your client is?"

"You won't believe it, but I don't have one."

A small smile crept across the gambling lord's face. "On the contrary, I was briefed about your work habits. If you took on a few more paying customers you might be able to afford a night or two in my place."

"Presuming I wanted to."

He shrugged. "If you allow your Calvinist upbringing to come between you and a good time . . . well, that's none of my business. I've heard nothing about Ms. O'Key being missing. There's been nothing on the news."

"No one knows."

"But you."

"Right."

Another smile. "Tell me, Miss Chase, how would some lifeguard know the Grand Strand's most famous painter is missing—when no one else does?"

"Everyone thinks she's out of town."

"But she's not?" he asked, playing along.

"She's not."

"Out of town could be a lot of places."

"I narrowed it down with the help of her family."

"And yet they are not your clients?"

"They don't know that they should be."

"Perhaps if you told them what you know there would be some money in it for you?"

"And then maybe I wouldn't find her."

Nichols was puzzled.

"It's too complicated to explain."

He smiled like a barracuda eyeing its next meal. "Give it a try. The O'Keys of the Keys would certainly want to know if their daughter was missing. If she's really missing."

"It has nothing to do with your deal, Markey."

Nichols looked over my head and Delbert put a hand on my shoulder—and dug in.

"A person in my business pays attention to more than just *his* business, otherwise he won't have any business. Now, back to why you want to see Bennie Lawson . . . ."

I tried to twist away, but the hand followed me, making sure I'd wear a cover-up the next couple of weeks. Tears came to my eyes, but I refused to wipe them away. "Come on, Markey . . . can't you trust Bennie?"

"Stop tap dancing around the issue. I want to know why you went to see Bennie and I want to know now."

I forced a smile. Quite a job with those fingers digging in to me. "And I'd like to know what I keep bumping into."

Nichols sat up. "What are you talking about, girl? Make sense and be quick about it."

"Not until this asshole takes his hand off me."

Nichols' eyes flickered overhead and the hand was taken away. It took every ounce of willpower for me not to rub the hole that he'd dug into my shoulder.

After clearing my throat, I was able to say, "I started out looking for a missing person, not O'Key, and during my search your singer out there"—I gestured in the direction of the gaming tables—"asks me to find her missing boyfriend, someone by the name of 'Eddie.' Then I'm told O'Key's been seen with one of your guys and when I try to get in to see Fast Bennie I'm shanghaied out here. I'm the one who should be asking the questions."

Nichols' eyes flickered overhead again.

Delbert said, "I warned you, boss."

"Get her out of here!" Nichols brushed the paperwork off his desk, found his intercom, and punched a button. "Cancel my three o'clock, Rose."

I didn't hear her reply. I was being hustled out of the room, past the woman and her paperwork, past the gorgeous guy with the MAC-10—where the mugs picked up their guns and mine—through another door and across the gaming room. The singer had disappeared, but the band was still there, working on its sets.

"Was it something I said?"

"Shut up, bitch! Markey's not here to protect you anymore."

We were in the same positions as before: the driver in the front, Delbert to my left in the back seat. The driver was the first to go, his window shattering into a zillion pieces and his head exploding like a ripe melon falling off the back of a produce truck. He fell across the front seat without making a sound. I heard someone

scream—realized it was me—and screamed again when
Delbert took a similar hit. Blood and glass sprayed all
over me as I scrunched down, hands over my face, eyes
closed, opening them only after Delbert's body slid down
behind me. Visions of Jackie Kennedy flashed through
my head, then I heard crunchy sounds coming from
the right side of the car.

We were running off the road!

I remember this open space. When we first crossed
it I'd wondered if the creek was where they planned to
dump me after my interrogation. I reached over the
seat and grabbed the wheel and brought the car back
on the road—as the sniper put a bullet through the
rear window, barely missing my ear. Least that's what
it sounded like. I ducked back down. Running off into
the creek was looking better and better.

More bullets thudded into the car, and because
Delbert lay behind me, the poor bastard took a couple
meant for me. Then the sniper went to work on the
tires. The car sagged on its rims but continued moving
forward—with the driver's foot still on the gas. I glanced
over the top of the seat in time to see us miss the bridge
and plunge into the water.

Chapter 17

Because I was snug against the seat I felt little of the impact. I tried to remember where they'd put my gun. I was going to need that sucker—if I ever got out of here. It was under the driver, and what was left of his brains was sprayed across the passenger seat and window. His skull had a gray, ragged edge and the sight caused my stomach to turn over. I forced down the bile, then grabbed the pistol, jammed it in my purse, and looped my purse over my head as the car settled into the water. These guys might not care where they spent eternity, but I was cursing the slow descent of the electric window. The only frigging window left and I had to go out that way. Uh-huh, crawl over the headless driver and go out that way. Yeah, right, you first.

Water covered the floorboards, reaching for the seat, then rushed in through the back window. When the water hit me, I screamed, then told myself to get a grip. All I had to do was wait until the car filled up and I'd be able to swim out. Still, I almost lost it—water rising around me and dead men bobbing to the surface.

When the car was almost filled, I took a breath, let out some air, and pulled myself through the window. Outside I put my feet against the side and pushed off, losing my shoes as I swam for the far side of the swamp. My purse filled with water and became an albatross around my neck. The muck that gathers on the surface of the swamp fouled the top of my dress.

It took less than a minute to cross that little bit of water, sometimes swimming, sometimes wading, sometimes tripping over stumps, but finally I crawled ashore, gasping for breath. I rolled over behind some bushes and looked back at the creek.

Son of a bitch if the car wasn't gone! That was some fucking creek! But I was safe! Or was I?

A green sports car slid to a stop on the far side and a black man leaped out. In his hands was a high-powered rifle with a scope. He ran to the edge of the water and stared at the rectangularly shaped spot in the muck where the car had gone down. When he cursed, I joined him. The bastard wore slacks, a pullover, and a ski mask.

Then I knew the bastard! I'd seen those eyes before, and the color of the skin around them, in Rio. I pulled myself into a tight little ball, held my breath, and prayed for any sort of traffic to come along. No telling how long my floral print and wet-dog look would blend into the background.

My prayers were answered. Down the road came something approaching from my side of the creek and making a lot of noise. With another glance at the creek, the sniper leaped in his car and roared off. Then came the flip side of my prayers: the noise was a truck and the big old thing lumbered by before I could flag it down. I stood there, but only for a moment, then I ducked back into the swamp. Maybe the sniper was gone. Maybe he'd never return. Maybe I was actually safe. And maybe, somewhere, Prince Charming actually existed.

I straightened my underwear, wiped the slime off the front of my dress, and tied back my hair with a rubber band from my purse, then turned the purse over and let the water pour out. After checking the position of the sun, I started walking cross-country in the direction of the Grand Strand.

I stumbled and fumbled through the swamp until I came across a dirt road running northwest to southeast. It wasn't a very pleasant hike. I'd lost my shoes, and though I'd spent most of my childhood barefoot, that had been many moons ago. Then there was the occasional snake one runs across in swamps. I didn't know I'd bummed up my leg until after all the excitement died down. After an hour of limping, sometimes hopping, then screaming in pain—when I wasn't looking where I put down my feet—I heard a pickup approaching from behind.

Unless I plunged back into the swamp there was no place to hide, so I took out my pistol, held it at my side in the folds of my dress and stepped off the road. Sweat ran down my face—it had to be a hundred degrees—my hair was something no one should have to see and one of my earrings was missing. I'd noticed that brushing back my hair.

The pickup was spotted with rust and had a headlight missing; its engine wheezed like an old man, or a young woman after a long hike through a swamp. The driver had greasy blond hair pulled back in a ponytail, a severe overbite, and wore a shirt covered with blood.

A rifle hung on the rack behind him. After coming to a stop, he called out to me. "Be needing a ride, ma'am?"

"As close as you're going to any highway." What highway I had no idea. The bozos taking me to see Nichols hadn't taken the direct route but wandered around on the back roads until I was totally lost.

Maybe that was the plan, Susan, you think?

"I can take you to the county seat. You can catch the Greyhound there." He glanced at his watch. "We oughta be able to catch the last one if'n we hurry. That bus goes to Myrtle."

Just what I wanted to hear. I climbed in, and as I did, saw a doe lying across the bed of the pickup.

The young man noticed my expression, got out of the truck, and threw a tarp over the dead animal, then slid back behind the wheel. Over the next couple of miles he ran through the gears, finally getting up to thirty miles an hour. After settling into third he looked me over. My dress was wet, my hair littered with trash, and I smelled, like, well, a swamp.

"Been doing some swimming, ma'am?"

Heat raced up the sides of my neck. "Yes, but that's still in season."

That shut him up—until he dropped me off in front of a general store, which included among its signs one for Greyhound Bus Lines.

"I'll wait right here, ma'am."

"No need to."

He did anyway, reinforcing the illusion that Prince Charming was out there . . . somewhere. Wait on, good prince.

I went inside, learned I was indeed in time for the last bus, and waved the young man off. As the pickup chugged away I was left with a new group of people

staring at me. If the sniper came looking for me, I'd left
an easy enough trail to follow. In the rest room I cleaned
my pistol before cleaning myself. Then I brushed the
trash out of my hair and underclothes and mopped
the slime off my dress with several wet paper towels.

The store had a sale on flip-flops. I bought a pair,
then paid for my fare with soggy money. I had a sand-
wich and a cup of coffee, and when the bus arrived,
climbed aboard to the curious stares of my fellow passengers. It was enough to give a person a complex and
caused me to move to the rear of the bus, where a pair
of teenagers held hands on the long back seat. They
sniffed the air, conferred in hasty whispers, and moved
forward. And me, I slid way down in my seat. Not the
grandest way to return home, but the sniper could be
anyone, including the next black guy to board this bus.

I got off before we reached Myrtle, called Pick, and asked
him to meet me at the Holiday Inn along the Waterway.
He said he'd be there. That's what I like about Pick: He
asked no questions, just picked me up in his skiff, and
ferried me to *Daddy's Girl*.

I must've looked a sight, huddled in the bow, jump-
ing at anything that moved. Before he left, I had him
make sure there was no one aboard. By now my clothes
were dry, my hair totally wasted, and my whole body
ached, especially my leg. I downed some aspirin with a
glassful of whiskey, then showered with the lights off,
after locking the door to the head and taking my pistol
into the stall. There's a hook in there just for that purpose and handier than soap on a rope.

I listened hard while toweling dry, then used a night
light to slip into jeans, a blouse, and a pair of running
shoes. While I was combing the tangles out of my hair,

the phone rang several times, then the machine answered: "This is Susan. Leave your name and number
and I'll get back to you."

It was Lt. Warden. "If you know what's good for
you, Chase, you'll get your butt down to my office and
right away."

The rest of the tape was a real circus. Doris Moffitt
had called again and wanted to know if I'd found Jenny.
She needed to see her, needed to see her real bad. Doris
was addicted—to something. Maybe I should tell her
what Jenny Rogers' addictions had led to. There was a
call from Mrs. Rogers, telling me she wanted her check
back. My boss said I was out of a job if I didn't report for
work the following morning (that's the sanitized version),
and the phony girlfriend had called again, asking me to
find her Eddie. Mickey DeShields left a message, saying
essentially the same thing as Warden, just nicer.

Hey, I was ready to head downtown, but I had all
these calls to return—not! I was listening to the last
message when Harry knocked.

"Susan, are you in there?"

The lights were off and I wasn't smoking. How'd he
know? Pick. I didn't want Harry to see me like this: one
hand holding the other, trying to calm each other down.

"Susan?"

I opened the door.

"You okay?"

"Uh-huh."

"Why no lights?"

"I—I was going out."

"Anything wrong?"

"Er—no."

Harry looked me over. "Anything I can do for you,
Princess?"

"I don't think so."

"Did you see Robert this afternoon?"

"Yes."

"What did he say?"

"Can I tell you later? I need to get into Myrtle."

"Are you going to see Lieutenant Warden?"

"Yes—yes, I am."

"Good."

I stepped on deck, closed the door, and locked it. When I turned around Harry was scrutinizing me with the help of a sentry light. In my hands was a dry purse and I was squeezing the devil out of that sucker.

"I was worried about you, Susan."

"And I'm worried about Jenny."

"What's happened?"

"She's confessed to killing O'Key. McGinnis is going to turn her over to the cops. I want to be there when SLED processes her."

"Susan, you're shaking."

"Dads, this thing has me rattled. I don't want to see Jenny go to jail, but I can't find O'Key."

He took my arm as we headed for shore. "What did her family say?"

"They think she's in Rio."

He looked at me sharply. "You didn't tell them what you'd learned?"

"Maybe I should've, but . . . ."

"And maybe you're being a little too clever for your own good? Want me to come along?"

"No—but I'd like to borrow your car. My jeep broke down and I don't want to have to hitch into Myrtle." God knows where my jeep was. Oh, yeah, parked in front of the Atlantic Towers—where I'd been kidnapped and taken for a ride into the country.

Shit! What had I gotten myself into?

Harry handed me his keys as we approached the Buick. Harry walked; I limped, but I don't think he noticed. The landing was dark. Very, very dark. Visions of headless men danced through my head.

"Susan, you're shivering. Are you sure you're okay?"

"Just cold."

He put his arm around me. "You should've worn a wrap. Want to go back and get one?"

I shook my head, then leaned into him as we approached his car—where I let him open the door for me. I had to get into town and see Warden, and I had to do it now, or the next time anyone went looking for me they'd find me hiding under my bed—or dead in it. Then I understood. The man who'd tried to rape me had done it to fire a shot across my bow!

"Susan?"

I slid into the car. And the bastard had followed me to Rio where he had tried to . . . what? Why was he after me? I shut the door behind me.

Harry leaned down to the window. "Are you sure you're all right?"

"Just a little distracted. I want this over with."

Harry smiled, patted me on the shoulder, then noticed something in the wood line. I reached for my purse before identifying the shape: the black Lab.

Letting out a sigh, I said, "Dads, if you don't mind how about showing the dog onto *Daddy's Girl*? There has to be something to eat in the fridge."

"I doubt that," he said with a chuckle. "I'll find something at my place."

The squad room was empty so Warden saw me coming. He pointed at a chair as I entered his office. "Sit."

On the way into town I'd regained my composure. Now, whenever I glanced in the rearview mirror, I didn't see some Swamp Thing lunging out of the back seat. "What's this, J.D.? No 'how you been, Susan' or 'gotten any lately'?"

"Cut the wisecracks. I want to know why you went to see Fast Bennie Lawson."

I was ready for just about anything but that. "What—what are you talking about?" was the best I could manage.

"I've got you on videotape. They had a camera in the lobby. Why were you there?"

"Why do you want to know?"

"It's a police matter, and stop answering a question with a question. Tell me what you were doing there and don't cite client confidentiality—Fast Bennie's dead."

"He is?"

"Yes—someone came down the side of that building on a window-washing machine left behind by workmen—we're checking them out now—and shot Lawson and the whore with him. His men didn't know anything about it until the following morning." Warden pointed a finger at me. "What I want to know is why *you* went to see him."

"He was seen talking with Kristy O'Key."

Warden's eyebrows arched. "You didn't find O'Key in Rio?"

I shook my head.

"You think she's back on the Grand Strand?"

Sagging into the chair, I said, "I don't know where she is, J.D. I have absolutely no idea."

"What's O'Key's tie-in with George Fiddler?"

"I don't know that either."

His eyes narrowed. "You leveling with me?"

"Yes . . . why shouldn't I?"

"Because you love being cagey. Your life has no meaning unless you're putting something over on this department."

"Don't be so self-centered, it's the mark of a shallow mind."

His eyes narrowed. "Why'd you switch from looking for Rogers to looking for O'Key?"

"I thought O'Key could help me with Jenny."

"Help you what? Find her?"

"Straighten out her life."

Warden sighed. "Chase, you don't have enough to do." He pointed at his in/out trays, full and overflowing. "That's the difference between you and me."

"Then why'm I here wasting your valuable time?"

"To be warned to stay away from Markey Nichols. Fast Bennie was part of Nichols' operation."

"Oh," I said, straightening up, "you think I'll get in the way of your precious investigation?"

"No—you might get hurt. I don't know how you do it, but you have a knack for turning up at the wrong place at the wrong time. The Chamber of Commerce isn't thrilled about your last escapade: chasing a naked girl through the lobby of the Host of Kings Hotel." He shook his head. "A half-naked girl chasing a naked one, that must've been a sight."

"I caught her at an inopportune moment."

"But you were after her, weren't you?"

"Not for her parents, like the girl thought. Her grandmother wanted her to come live with her."

"Well, you have one hell of a way of delivering messages and I'm not going to put up with it."

"You're lecturing me on frightening the tourists

when you can't close down Markey Nichols' gambling operation."

Warden shrugged. "We put him out of business and someone else takes his place. Besides, they're people in this part of the state who think blacks have a right to skim a little off white paychecks."

"A floating crap game—is that all you think Nichols' has going?"

"Of course, where do you think you are—Atlantic City?"

"No, I think . . . ." If Warden didn't grasp the extent of Markey Nichols' operation how would he sympathize with Jenny Rogers' plight?

Warden went on. "But the death of Lawson means some moron *thinks* this is Atlantic City."

"Which puts Fiddler's death on the back burner?"

"We don't need your help setting priorities for this department. Besides, I've got Coker and your friend Rogers for that."

"Then I guess you've chosen sides—since Coker's on the street."

He sat up. "How'd you know that?"

"Heard it on the street."

"Heard it on the street—bull! You pried it out of someone in this department and if I find out who I'll have their job. Was it DeShields?"

"No, it wasn't DeShields."

"It better not've been—I'll have his job, too."

"How'd Coker get out? You had her in here on a murder rap."

"The time of death was nowhere near when she fought with you on the stairs."

"Then it *was* her who knocked me down that flight of stairs."

"Right—and that's a perfect example of what I mean

about you being in the wrong place at the wrong time."

I leaned forward in my chair. "You're going to try to hang Fiddler's murder on Jenny, aren't you?"

"Try?" he asked with a smile.

I told myself to remain calm. Flipping out would get me nowhere. "What were you about to tell me about how Fast Bennie got killed?"

"If it'll get you to back off."

"Give it a try, J.D. Give it a try."

"A power struggle has broken out inside Nichols' organization. Word on the street is Nichols made the mistake of hiring some out-of-town talent to pick up his pull boards and the collector has more ambition than Nichols bargained for."

"Markey Nichols won't be sitting on his hands while all this is going down."

"And that's why I want you out of the line of fire. As far as I'm concerned Lawson's death was the first shot of a short but violent turf battle, and while I'd like to see the bastards kill themselves off, the director reminded me of the revenue this state derives from tourism. So I'm going to slap a lid on this thing before it gets out of hand." He pointed at me. "I'm warning you, Chase, stay away from Nichols. The last thing I need is some girl getting herself killed."

"If they kill me, they won't be killing *some* girl."

"It's that kind of talk that gets people hurt. By the way what'd you find in Rio?"

"Not what I was looking for." I stood up.

"Wild goose chase. No wonder her mother didn't want to foot the bill. Don't forget, I'm expecting you to turn over Rogers when you find her."

"I didn't think you thought that much of my ability."

He nodded. "I think private investigators can do

things legitimate law enforcement doesn't have time for, like locating runaways. I hope we never have time for that."

"Tell it to the parents, J.D."

But Warden was looking past me. Across the room came Mickey DeShields, dodging desks and chairs and coming to a stop by grabbing the door's jambs. I stepped back into Warden's office to keep from being run over.

"Got another casualty in our little war."

"Good God, why don't they just pass the damn lottery." There was pain in Warden's face. He could see himself explaining this to his boss—and the Chamber of Commerce. "Who is it this time?"

"Nichols' pull board collector was found in the Waterway with a bullet in the back of his head. Guess what else he was carrying?"

"A rifle with a sniper scope," I said without thinking.

DeShields looked at me. "How'd you know, Susan?"

"Er—heard it on the radio." There was no scanner in Harry's car. "Well, I've got to be going."

"Chase, I want you to stay away from Nichols."

"No problem. That's not where the action is."

Chapter 18

I drove down King's Highway to Georgetown. In Dads' Buick I made better time than I would've in my jeep. The O'Key compound was lit up like Christmas, but this time the guard was out cold on the floor of the gatehouse. I barreled ahead, running off the road in several places and leaving some of the plants the worse for wear, finally slowing down as I approached the house. Someone was trying to kick down one of those humongous doors and having little luck with the chore.

It was Emma Coker.

"Come out of there, you bitch!" she shouted at those huge doors. "I know you're in there!"

Coker saw me climb out of the Buick but couldn't make out who I was. I left the lights on, pointed at her. For some reason I felt I needed an advantage when dealing with this woman.

She shielded her eyes and her voice mellowed. "Kristy—that you?"

"Susan Chase."

Anger roared back into her voice. "Get away from

me, you little bitch! If it wasn't for you I wouldn't've spent all that time in jail."

I couldn't argue with that.

One of the doors opened and Lambert appeared. The elderly man's face showed considerable strain. "Miss Chase?"

Coker moved to stand between us. "I want to see Kristy and I want to see her now." Emma didn't look so good. Her hair needed combing, her blouse was half-way out of her jeans, and she was barefoot.

"As I told you over the phone, Madam, and just moments ago at this very door, Miss O'Key isn't here. She's out of the country."

"Don't give me that shit. I know she's in there. Send her out. I want to talk to her."

"Why don't you try her apartment on Pawleys Island?"

Coker's hands fidgeted; so did her feet. "I've been there. I've . . . ." She paused to catch her breath. "I've been everywhere. She has to be in *there*." Coker straightened up. "And I'm going to see her, so you might as well let me in." She grabbed the door and one of the old man's shoulders and tried to squeeze past.

Despite his age and build Lambert stood fast. "If you persist, Madam, I will be forced to call the police."

Coker grabbed his arm and tried to pull him out of the doorway. "You pompous old fool, call anyone you like, but I'm coming in. Kristy thinks she can hide from me . . . she can't. And you can't hide her from me!"

Lambert looked at me. "Miss Chase, can you help us here?"

I stepped up on the stoop, pulled Coker away, and pushed her to the other side of the stoop. "What are you doing here, Emma?"

She blinked. "Looking for Jenny."

"Why?"

"Because . . . because she belongs with me."

I shook my head. "Boy, you've got it bad, haven't you?"

Up went that nose again. "Who are you to judge? What do you know about people? About life?" She straightened her shoulders and faced the butler again. "Tell Kristy to send Jenny out. I order you to do so."

"You've got this all wrong, Emma. They don't have Jenny. I do."

She turned on me and I reached for my purse.

"I knew it! I just knew it! I had you checked out. You think you're the only detective around here? You hung around Pawleys and when Jenny wouldn't have anything to do with you, you went to her mother and told her you could bring her home. Her mother liked that, didn't she? She wanted Jenny home and you wanted Jenny all to yourself."

Lambert looked at me as if some of this made sense. I'm sure it did—to Emma Coker.

She took my arm. "Tell me where she is."

"Let go of me."

"You will tell me where she is," she said firmly.

"No, I won't. Now take your hand off me."

"I have to know."

"Sorry, Emma, but Jenny needs to find herself—before people start telling her who she is again." I took her hand off my arm. "Now get out of here and leave these people alone." I glanced at Lambert. "There's a sick man in this house."

Coker looked from me to the butler and back at me again. "You're in this together, aren't you?" Realization lit up her face. "Kristy's got Jenny down at the beach

house, doesn't she?" When I didn't reply she turned to
Lambert and saw the concern on the old man's face.
"That's where she is, isn't it? I knew it! Jenny's on the
key. Jenny's on the key," she muttered, stepping down
from the stoop and heading for her car.

Lambert followed her. "Madam, I don't think you
should go there."

"You people think you can put something over on
me?" She giggled, covering her mouth with her hand.
"There's no way—not you people . . . ."

I followed her to her car. "Go home, Emma. You're
not well and no matter what you do, you won't find
Jenny tonight."

"Yes," chimed in Lambert, "I agree with Miss Chase."

Coker looked at him—but swung on me. "You can't
tell me what . . . ."

I dodged, and using the inertia behind her swing,
caught her arm and twisted my body around, bringing
Coker up on my hip where she slid over me. Well, I
kind of helped her over or we both would've gone to the
ground, her on top of me.

Coker hit hard and shut down. And me? I shook
like a dog coming out of the water, then knelt beside
her and checked her pulse. Intense. Just like the
woman. I was beginning to dislike these artist types.

"Is she all right, Miss?" asked Lambert.

I stood up, tucking in my blouse. "Unconscious.
Call a cab. She's in no condition to drive."

He glanced at the car. A gunmetal BMW. "She could
come to before the cab arrives."

I went over to the car, reached inside, and released
the catch. After lifting the hood I removed the distribu-
tor cap and handed it to him. "Give this to the wrecker.
I believe you know the name of a good service."

To that he said nothing. Not even a smile.

"Let's put her in the car. You don't want her in the house, do you?"

"Absolutely not."

Lambert took her feet and I took her arms; we carried Coker over to her car and laid her across the front seat. She was as heavy as she looked.

Leaning against the car to catch my breath and to take the weight off my sore leg, I asked, "You wouldn't happen to have a drink on you, would you?"

Lambert smiled. "One double. Scotch. Neat. Coming up."

A few minutes later he returned with a glass in each hand. "It's been a most difficult night. I thought I might join you, Miss." He handed one of the glasses to me.

I took a swallow, then poured the rest across Coker's chest. "Now let her try to get behind the wheel of any car."

Lambert smiled, took a swallow of his own, and then poured the remainder across the unconscious woman.

He took my glass. "Thank you, Miss Chase, and thank you for taking care of this most disagreeable person." He glanced at the house. The mansion towered over us, its turrets casting Disney-like shadows with a half-moon behind it. "I couldn't have her waking up the master. He had a bad day and refused to take a pill."

"Tough old codger, is he?"

"Tougher than most."

"And it's crippled his relationship with his daughter, hasn't it?"

"I wouldn't presume to know."

I limped toward Harry's car. "Other members of the family on the key?"

He followed me. "I wouldn't go there if I were you."

After climbing into the Buick and closing the door, I asked, "Why not?"

"There's no way to reach the island this time of night."

"I'll manage. Somehow I always do."

He glanced at Coker lying across the seat of her car. "You do that quite well, don't you? I understand you're in the employ of Mr. O'Key."

I let him get out of that what he needed.

He pulled out some keys, took one off the ring, and handed it to me. "This opens the front door, but the screened door could be latched." He smiled. "On occasion I've had to use a knife to open that latch."

I dropped the key into my purse. "I'll keep that in mind." Shifting the Buick into gear, I added, "And, Lambert, have someone check on your man in the kiosk. He was out cold when I left him."

"And you, Miss Chase, you take care of yourself. I won't presume to tell you your business, but things aren't as they appear in this house."

"I was a little slow to pick up on that, but I'm doing much better."

Twenty minutes later I was at the marina. Hard to believe I'd been there earlier in the day. It felt more like last week. But no matter how late it was I had to do something to stop Jenny from turning herself in. Jenny would confess to anything. She wanted to be punished. For something. The punishing part I didn't mind. People have to live their own lives, but turning herself in for a murder she didn't commit—I don't think so.

I left the car in the parking lot, and under the light

from a waning moon, walked over to the pier. Along
the way I frightened a cat who thought it had the run
of the place, saw something break the surface in the
cove, and caused the gangway to squeak as I made my
way to the houseboat serving as the marina. There were
no lights so I fumbled around until I found what I
thought was the door and knocked.

No answer.

What I'd expect? It was close to midnight.

Rapping again, I heard someone say he didn't want
to be disturbed. Actually he was a bit more vulgar than
that and sounded a lot like me when I don't want to be
bothered. I rapped again and the door opened. Through
it stuck the business end of a shotgun.

"What you want?" asked my captain.

"It's me . . . Tip. Susan Chase."

"Who?"

I cleared my throat and kept my eyes on the shotgun. "Missy. You took me out . . . to the O'Key's . . .
earlier today."

The gun lowered, the door opened, and Tip peeked
out, then glanced behind him. The digital readout on a
clock radio told him I was out kind of late. With the
shotgun no longer in my face, I could speak in more
than sentence fragments.

"Tip, you remember the teenager injured in the car
wreck, the one who'll never get any older?"

"I remember."

"She kin of yours?"

He nodded. "A cousin. Somebody would have to
explain how many times removed."

"Well, I'm trying to save another girl's life before
the O'Keys screw it up." And I gave him a quick sketch
of what faced Jenny Rogers if she turned herself in.

"So I've got to go out there tonight."

"Want some company?"

"Nope. Just wanted to borrow the Chris Craft. It makes next to nothing in noise. Is it gassed up?"

"Always is. And it don't belong to no O'Key." Tip stepped out of the houseboat and brought along the shotgun. He wore striped boxer shorts but no shirt. His chest was hairless and he had on his nautical cap. Idly, I wondered what he'd picked up first: the shotgun or his hat. "I'll take you, Missy, if'n you got to go."

"Uh-uh. I only knocked on your door so you wouldn't shoot me while I was hot-wiring your boat."

"Hot-wiring my boat? I'd like to see you do that." He had started for the shelter. Now he glanced over his shoulder. "Well, maybe I wouldn't. But I'll take you out there."

"Won't work, Tip."

"And why not?"

"Would you hesitate to use that shotgun on any member of the O'Key family?"

He stopped. "I sure as hell wouldn't."

"Well, I would."

He considered this, then started for the shelter again. "It don't sound like much of an edge."

At the shelter he handed me the shotgun, then went inside where he unlocked the doors, cranked the engine, and maneuvered the Chris Craft out of its little house. When he brought the boat alongside the pier its engine hardly made a sound. I stepped amidships and he gave me a hand into the boat.

"Want to take along the shotgun?"

"I have a pistol. Besides, what's there to worry about? You know who's out there, don't you?"

"Yeah—I reckon you can handle it." He stepped up

on the pier. "Well, good luck, Missy. You gonna need the sheriff or anything?"

I whirled the wheel around, taking its measure. "You might bring him out if I'm not back by morning."

"You can count on it. And I'll be coming with him."

Nodding my thanks, I turned the boat seaward, added enough gas to break through the incoming tide, then motored past the smaller two islands, swinging out and away from the third. Fog had drifted in, making the house a blur against a darker horizon.

Out to sea I made a U-turn, then hit the gas. As I approached the island, I cut the power and let the tide take me in—where I brought the Chris Craft in beside the fiberglass beauty, doing my captain proud.

After tying up I found the walkway to the porch, and as Lambert told me, had to use a penknife to lift the latch on the screened door. I tiptoed across the porch, unlocked the door with the key, and eased it back, then pulled out my pistol. From down the hall came the sound of someone taking a gentle beating. I put my gun away and moved in that direction.

Chapter 19

There was a light on in the bedroom, a hushed, dimmed thing, and as I approached the door I heard Angeline encouraging her stepson to ride her. Peering around the corner, I saw Robbie trying his level best; that is, until I flipped on the light. He whipped around, sliding off his stepmother, his face full of fear, quickly replaced by anger.

"Chase! What the hell . . . ?"

Angeline propped up on her elbows, her glazed-over eyes focusing on me. "Interrupting our fun. That's why your father hired her."

She threw off the bedcovers, put her feet on the floor, and reached for her underwear. Robbie stayed in the bed and used the sheet to cover himself, but Angeline stood up and slid into her panties. I had to admit the woman had a nice body, if you liked them small. Beyond that I couldn't see the attraction and I'd seen several Kim Basinger movies.

"You can get dressed, Robbie. I won't look."

He cursed and reached for his pants—and almost fell out of bed trying to keep himself covered. I left before bursting into laughter. That really would've tightened the boy up.

In the living room I put my purse on the bar, built a drink, and sat where I'd sat earlier, propping my feet on the coffee table and sipping more of their fine scotch. It'd been a long day.

Angeline strode in, mixed a drink, and sat on the love seat across from me. She'd slipped into slacks and a blouse, but wore no bra or shoes. Maybe it'd been a long day for her, too, or simply an exhausting night. She smiled and I smiled as Robbie blustered in, cursing me and my sense of timing. He splashed some liquor into a glass and took a seat beside his stepmother, crossing one leg over the other; that leg bounced in a fit of nervous energy—or rage.

"All right, Chase, how much do you want?"

"I'm not interested in your money, Robbie."

"Bullshit! I know how you detectives operate."

I looked at Angeline. "I'm more interested in your stepmother."

"Me, Susan? I don't have any money. Robert controls it all. And if you're prepared to wait, well, what Robbie and I were doing wouldn't have any significance then."

"I don't think the O'Key family has enough money to bail you out of the trouble you're in, Angeline."

"I must say I have no idea what you're talking about, Susan."

"Murder, Angeline. I'm talking about murder."

Robbie's mouth fell open, but his stepmother just stared at me, her puzzled look replaced by a remoteness in those baby blues.

"Who's been murdered?" asked Robbie.

"Your sister."

He sat up quickly, almost spilling his drink. "Did she get involved in local politics again? I warned her about that."

"No—someone closer to you killed her."

"Who?"

I nodded at his stepmother.

When he finally understood, he said, "Chase, are you crazy?"

"Well, Robbie," Angeline said with a smile, "it appears we don't have to worry about your father believing anything this detective has to say."

"I'd be more worried about SLED believing what I have to say."

"What in the hell are you talking about?"

"Angeline killed your sister, Robbie."

His stepmother pouted. "Do we have to listen to this just because she caught us in bed together?"

Robbie stood up and threw a finger toward the door. "Out, Chase. Now!"

Putting my drink on the coffee table, I smiled at him. "Feeling like a man again, are you, now that Fast Bennie's no longer in the picture?"

"Who's . . . who's Fast Bennie?"

"Don't go simple on me, Robbie. The guy who's been blackmailing you."

"I don't know what you're talking about," he said indignantly. "First you talk murder, then blackmail—you don't make sense."

"Oh, but I do, and it's what you two don't know about each other that'll stop you from sharing a bed. I guess you could say I've accomplished what your father intended when he invited me here to see him."

"So the old bastard did hire you."

I shook my head.

"What do you mean? I saw the check."

"I can't think of any reason why Robert O'Key would agree to meet with some lifeguard and runaway finder, even if a former United States ambassador set up the appointment and he owed that ambassador big time."

"Wait a minute, let me get this straight." Robbie returned to his seat. "You're not going to tell my step-father what you saw here tonight?"

"I'd rather you tell me if either of you have seen the X-rays proving Robert O'Key's dying of emphysema or had a second opinion from a doctor who isn't under his thumb?"

Angeline and Robbie looked at each other.

"I mean, the uppermost deck of a beach home's not exactly the place I'd expect to have a conversation with a man who needs a machine to help him breathe."

Angeline shook her head. "I don't know what you're talking about, Susan, but you certainly have an active imagination."

Robbie stared at his empty glass. "I think she's nuts."

"You hope I'm nuts. Lambert wrote that check *after* I left. Your father told him to leave it where both of you would see it. And you both know what it means when Robert O'Key talks to a detective. He's checking on someone. You knew about the check, didn't you, Angeline?"

She didn't have to say a word. The answer was writ-ten on her face.

"If your father's not dying, Robbie, I'm willing to bet Lambert's been in on the charade from the get go."

He stood up, went to the bar, and mixed another drink, sliding my purse out of the way.

"Robbie, did you ever ask yourself how Fast Bennie knew you were screwing your stepmother?"

"There were tapes . . . made in the room you just caught us in."

"Is this true?" asked Angeline.

Her stepson nodded.

"What I meant was, who sicced Fast Bennie on you?"

"What? Oh, I don't know. Someone like Tip, I suppose."

"Tip may not look like much to you, but he can't afford to lose your family's business. That's why he hasn't told you that your stepmother's been sleeping around behind *your* back."

"What?" Robbie turned away from the bar.

"You're not Angeline's only sex toy."

"How disgusting. Susan, is this how you get your kicks: being a Peeping Tom?"

"Is this true, Angie?"

"I don't think that's important, my dear. We're simply back to how much Miss Chase wants. Evidently she wants some of that money to come from me, stemming from who I am and who she's not."

"What the hell do you want, Chase—if you aren't working for my father and you don't want my money?"

"I want your stepmother to turn herself in for your sister's murder—that way things will go easier on her."

"Susan, if you persist in this kind of talk you'll be sued for every penny you have, and that precious independence you're so proud of will vanish."

"Robbie, did you ever wonder why your sister became interested in painting with colors?"

"She wasn't," he said, returning to the love seat with his drink. "Everyone knows that."

Angeline stood up and I took my feet off the table. "You see, you've got this all wrong. Now if you don't mind I'll call a boat so you can leave. How did you get out here in the first place?"

"I borrowed a boat."

"Then whoever's boat you borrowed will never work for this family again."

"I doubt either of you will swing much weight around here after tonight."

"My dear, you make absolutely no sense at all."

"You've got that right," mumbled her stepson. He gulped down half his drink.

"Then let me put it this way—when I go to SLED tomorrow they'll come out here and arrest you for murdering your stepdaughter in a house she sublet in Francis Marion National Park."

"I've heard enough. Throw this disgusting creature out."

"Listen here, Chase, my stepsister's in Rio or some damn place. She may be dead, but it didn't happen around here. She's always taking off for parts unknown and always ticking off someone when she arrives. I should feel sad if she's really dead, but it's hard to feel anything about Kristy. She was my father's favorite and he played all kinds of games with her to make her come home. He couldn't take a hint—that Kristy wants nothing to do with us, and I'm the only family he has." Robbie glanced at his stepmother. "That Angie and I are the only people who genuinely care about him."

"And look how you treated him."

"Now listen here, Chase, I've had about enough —"

"When I went looking for Jenny Rogers I found her."

"So what? That's your job."

"She was in Rio posing as your sister."

"And why would she do that?"

"Because she thought she'd killed Kristy."

"Maybe she did," said Angeline, moving to the bar where she took down a glass. Her first drink sat untouched on the coffee table next to mine.

"Okay, Chase, for the sake of argument let's say my sister *is* dead. So where's the body?"

"In a sinkhole in Francis Marion National Forest, weighed down by an outboard motor."

"You have proof of this?"

Keeping an eye on the woman at the bar, I said, "Angeline wasn't strong enough to dispose of the body herself. For that she had to have some help and she called on the man Bennie Lawson saw her with."

"I don't follow . . . ."

"Jenny arrived in a cocaine stupor while Kristy's body was still there. Convinced she'd killed Kristy, she fled the country, posing as Kristy. If Angeline's friend— let's call him Eddie—had killed your sister he wouldn't've left the body lying around where anyone could find it. He would've disposed of it immediately."

"Robbie, do we have to listen to this?"

Yes, you do, my dear, because I'm on a roll.

"You know, Robbie, I have a friend who thinks my education is lacking. Because of this he lends me books. One of those books discusses how new planets are discovered. If existing planets don't act as they should, following their usual orbits, then scientists look for what might be affecting that orbit, perhaps Planet X. And you're right, none of this makes sense unless someone tried to rape me, someone followed me to Rio, and someone tried to kill me when I left Markey Nichols' gambling joint this afternoon."

I turned my attention to his stepmother. "The police will want to know where you were when George Fiddler was killed. Perhaps you were with him, demanding to know where Rogers was. And I'm sure a woman with your money can afford any number of wigs. The little girl who lives at the hotel with her father recognized your face but not your hair color."

Robbie sat there, mouth open, drink cradled between his legs. Things were moving too fast for the boy and I wasn't about to make it any easier.

"After the break-in was reported it was safe to have the apartment cleaned. Something you supervised, too, Angeline. Rich people don't do that either. And if Lambert had known what you were up to he wouldn't have allowed it."

"But Lambert's with Angie all the time," said her stepson. "My father assigned him to help her . . ." he glanced at the floor, ". . . smooth out the rough edges."

"Fair enough, but any woman cheating on her husband knows the easiest way to bury those adulterous episodes is in long afternoons of shopping. And if we had Lambert here he'd have to admit there have been hours, even whole afternoons, when Angeline's slipped away from him, especially at Waccamaw Pottery. All she'd have to do is walk across the mall and be gone."

I looked at Angeline leaning against the bar, her fingers white from gripping the edge. "Unfortunately, once Lambert had proof of your indiscretion, who could he tell? Certainly not Robert. That would upset *their* relationship. That's why Lambert made sure you two saw the check made out to me for the thousand dollars."

Angeline said, "According to you, I'm one smart gal, not the dumb blonde everyone takes me for."

"Smart enough to get away with killing your first husband. That's why you thought killing Kristy would be a piece of cake. Everyone was so taken in by your act, but this husband fought back. Fought back the only way he knew and without further embarrassment to the family. Robert's isolated you with his emphysema, Angeline. Can't you see that or are you too busy counting all those millions you'll inherit when he dies?"

"Angie," asked Robbie, "you aren't sleeping with Reggie and Trent, are you?"

"What would it matter if I was?"

"But I thought once he was dead, we would . . . ."

His stepmother only smiled.

"What's she need you for? Once your father's dead she can sleep with anyone she wants."

Robbie looked sick. Angeline looked put out.

"When trying to rape me didn't work, Eddie sent a girl to hire me to find her missing boyfriend. Now I wonder who told Eddie about me?"

"What girl? And what does she have to do with this?"

"She sings for Markey Nichols. She saw me at his place this afternoon and alerted Eddie. As I returned to town, Eddie ambushed the car and tried to kill me."

"Sounds like it would've been better for all concerned if he had," mumbled Angeline.

"What are you saying? My sister has connections with the mob?"

"Not even as much as you do with your gambling. Bennie Lawson met with Kristy to tell her who her stepmother was sleeping with: 'A colored guy' is probably what Bennie said for shock effect. You can imagine how that went over. Bennie knew how tight Eddie had become with Markey and he was looking for a way to pry him off when he saw Eddie with your stepmother. But Eddie isn't all that slick. He simply killed Fast Bennie and the unlucky woman with him. After your sister had that meeting with Bennie, she gave Angeline an ultimatum: Don't be here when I come back from painting a picture, in color, of the one place my parents adored when they were first married. Because Kristy had walked away from money, she thought her stepmom could do the same."

Angeline snorted. "Kristy doing something for this family—that'll be the day."

I ignored her. "Though your sister was determined to live her own life she still had enough compassion for her father to paint the one scene he fondly remembered. And if Robert wanted to believe his daughter was mending her ways, painting with colors, a step toward reconciliation, fine. But Kristy wouldn't tolerate Angeline sleeping with a black man." I sat back in my seat. "Or perhaps Kristy simply wanted the satisfaction of showing her father he had no control over his daughter, his life, or his new wife. Whatever, Kristy was way too naive. Angeline couldn't walk away from all that money and Kristy didn't know she was dealing with a cold-blooded killer."

"You've got a lot of nerve, Susan. Aren't you afraid I might order this Eddie person to kill you?"

"Eddie can't help you anymore, Angeline. The police fished his body out of the Waterway a few hours ago. Evidently Eddie misjudged how Markey Nichols would react to his killing Bennie Lawson."

I think the woman's face whitened. It was hard to tell under such a splendid tan. Robbie shook his head. He didn't know what to think—until his stepmother snatched up my purse and began to dig around inside.

I got to my feet. "It's time you and I went to see SLED."

Angeline pulled the Smith & Wesson out and pointed it at me. "Stop right there, Chase, or I'll shoot."

My leg was stiff from sitting too long. "It's not loaded, Angeline."

She pulled the trigger several times, then shouted,

"You bitch!" She threw the gun at me and ran out of the room.

I ducked and my leg gave way, the one I'd injured in the swamp. From down the hall came a crash, and as I turned the corner, I found the grandfather clock blocking my way. I crawled over the clock as it bonged away, then hustled down the hall, into the bedroom, and into the muzzle of a .22 target pistol.

"When you're older, Susan, which isn't likely, you'll learn to keep more than one gun around the house." She gestured at Robbie, who had followed us into the bedroom. "And I still have a man to help me dispose of anyone who gets in my way."

Chapter 20

"Tie her hands," ordered Angeline.

Instead, Robbie gulped like he was going down for the third time. In the hallway the grandfather clock pleaded for help, making sick-sounding bongs.

"You two don't have the nerve—"

"I don't know about Robbie, but I've done all this before." Angeline showed me the pistol again. "And *this*, this will give Robbie all the nerve he needs." She unhooked her belt, jerked it out of its loops, and threw it at him. "Tie her up I said."

Robbie stared at the belt, which had hit him across the chest and fallen to the floor. He looked at me, then back at Angeline; his mouth moved but no sound came out. But his legs could move and he ran out of the bedroom and down the hall.

"Robbie!" shouted Angeline. "Robbie, come back here!" She motioned me out of the room with the pistol.

But the boy hadn't gone far. We found him at the bar, drinking straight from the bottle. His stepmother snatched the bottle away and threw it across the room, where it smashed against the black marble fireplace.

Robbie coughed and wiped a hand across his mouth, "But, I need—"

"The belt! Get in there and get the belt."

"I—I can't, Angie."

She swung the pistol around on him. "Do it, fool! You don't and we're finished."

"You're the one who's finished, Angeline. Don't confuse the boy."

"Think about it, Robbie. Chase found us in bed together and now she's going to tell your father."

"But she said she wouldn't—"

"Don't be a fool!"

"It's her word against ours."

"And what if it's true—that your father's not dying? He could cut us off and we'll have nothing."

"I'll—I'll still have my trust fund."

"You'll have nothing when Robert's through with you. We'll have nothing."

"But we don't have to kill her."

"Angeline has to kill me. You don't have to help her."

The pistol returned to me. "Not another word or I'll shoot you where you stand, Chase, and worry about getting rid of your body later."

Not only did I shut up, but I felt myself blink.

"Well, Robbie, are you in or out?"

"I—I'm scared, Angie." He trembled. "I've never done anything like this before."

"Of course not. You've always slipped out the back door when you heard the husband coming home. Well, this time you can't sneak out because the husband is your father."

"I don't know . . . ."

"Don't know what—if you want us to be together or

if you're man enough to do anything more than take money from your father?"

Robbie said nothing. He didn't even look at her.

"You don't want me?" asked Angeline, her voice softening. And I'll be damned if Angeline didn't open her arms to give him a better look at the merchandise.

"You don't want me all to yourself? Helping me dispose of Chase—what better way to ensure I'll be yours forever?" She reached over and cupped his face with her free hand. "Don't you remember what we were doing before she interrupted us?"

"I remember." He looked at her. Jeez, it must be true: When the prick stands up, the brains fall out.

"Well, I'm yours, all yours. You're all I've ever wanted since I met your father. You know that, don't you, darling?"

Robbie nodded. His breathing had become labored. Now I understood why Kim Basinger was such a box office draw.

"Robbie," I said, "you don't actually believe . . . ."

The gun swung around to me. Angeline's face was no longer as sweet as an angel's but looked meaner than the devil.

"I—I still don't know if I can do this."

She stuck the pistol under his nose. "But you'll do what I say so I won't have to shoot *you*, right?"

Robbie nodded and avoided my eyes as he left the room and disappeared down the hallway.

When he was gone, I said, "You don't have to do this, Angie."

"Not one word, Chase."

"With that little girl act of yours—"

She jammed the pistol in my face.

Robbie returned and snatched up a bottle, dropping the belt on the wet bar. "I need a drink."

Angeline waved the pistol around. "Just do it!"

He drank too much and drank too quickly. Bourbon ran down his chin, dotting his shirt like so many spots of blood. He coughed, then took another drink.

"Robbie!"

He put down the bottle, almost tipping it over, then caught it and righted it. He picked up the belt and took my hands without looking me in the eye.

"Tie them in front so she can move where I want her, and tie them tight."

Robbie whipped the strap around my wrists while I tried to find my voice, maybe even locate my nerve. Angeline certainly gave the impression she had done all this before, and a pouty face giving such orders sure looked funny, but nobody was laughing—least of all me.

Hands shaking, Robbie pulled the belt tight. It was one of those woven leather things and I just might slip out of it if I didn't get the damn thing wet.

"Okay, Chase. We're going for a ride."

Oh shit! Out here that could only mean by boat.

"I have to have another drink," whined Robbie.

"No!"

He snatched up a bottle and tried to kill it. When Angeline saw what he was doing she knocked the bottle out of his hands and it fell to the floor, dribbling its contents across the polished wood.

She motioned us toward the hall. "Get the door for her. Follow him, Chase."

I followed Robbie through the archway, out into the hall, and onto the porch. He went ahead of me, opening the door like a kid on his first date—or murder. There he stopped.

"I don't know if I can do this. I don't know if—if I can be a party to murder." A puddle formed at his feet.

Angeline pushed me ahead of him. "Then get back inside! I'll take it from here. Eddie showed me what to do. Can you believe it? A colored guy was the only real man I've ever loved. I'm going to enjoy killing you, Chase. You took away the only man I ever loved."

"Wrong. You've never loved anyone but yourself."

Robbie retreated into the house, probably heading for the bar.

"You call anyone, and I'll come back and kill you. And I'll be back long before the cops arrive."

"I won't call anyone. I'll stay right here. Near the bar."

See what I mean?

Angeline returned her attention to me. Actually, she'd never taken her eyes off me. "Down to the pier, Chase. Try anything and I'll shoot you. I've got too much to lose to stop now." She nodded toward the house. "Something that fool would never understand."

"Oh, I think Robbie understands you're the one with the most to lose." And I turned on my heel and walked into the fog. It had thickened considerably but was still no place to hide, and don't think I didn't consider it.

On the pier Angeline motioned toward the fiber-glass beauty. "Get in."

I did and stood amidships.

She regarded the Chris Craft, then shook her head. "Tip—you shit." To me she said, "Move to the rear and sit down."

"It's called the stern, Angeline."

"Yeah—right. We'll see how tough you are when I'm dumping you over the side. Now put those skis on the pier—from the sitting position—and don't get any funny ideas. I can shoot you before you can get to your feet, much less swing a ski."

I followed her orders as Angeline loosened the lines.

Finished, she stepped into the boat.

"Think about what you're doing, Angeline. Turn yourself over to me. I have friends at SLED. I'll speak up for you."

She gave a sick little laugh. "Nobody ever spoke for me, but to say I'll take the blonde, and take me they did. Well, I'm doing the taking these days and I'll take my chances. I don't think anyone'll come looking for you. You're a loner like Kristy. As for Robbie, well, I've always been able to handle any man."

I cleared my throat. "This has gone far enough. Stop it. Stop it right now."

She stooped down and stuck the gun in my face. "What's wrong with you? Haven't you ever seen what a bullet can do to someone?"

Matter of fact I had—earlier in the day; before that I'd been a cherry. Maybe that's why my knees wouldn't stop knocking. "Angie, please don't do this."

She laughed. "Now don't disappoint me by whining. I thought you were a real tough girl."

I thought I was, too, but tears had formed in my eyes. I openly trembled.

Angeline laughed again and stepped into the boat, one careful foot at a time. Facing me, she reached behind her and turned the engine over. It caught, and without taking her eyes off me, she slid the boat into gear and backed it away from the pier. Once she'd brought the boat around and changed gears, she steered with her free hand, glancing over her shoulder from time to time to see where we were headed. Actually, you couldn't see shit in the fog.

Raising her voice over the engine, she said, "You know, Chase, one thing I learned living here is if you go out far enough there's a point where things dropped overboard won't wash ashore."

"You don't have to do this, Angeline."

"You're starting to repeat yourself. You know how us rich folks hate to be bored. A fate worse than death." The moonlit fog turned her smile into a ghoulish grin. "But I'll give you one thing, you're wise beyond your years or one hell of a fisherman. That husband of mine, the first one, got us into a fix. I warned him, but would he listen?   No, sirree, he would not. Dumb blonde-married-for-her-looks, what would she know?   The bastard said he'd been busted before and clawed his way back. Sorry, but I wasn't interested in doing any clawing. I'd done plenty before."

I wondered if I could fall overboard and disappear in the water. Could I do that before she got off a shot? Get underwater before she fired a second time? Maybe the fog would hide me. The lights from the beach house were as dim as those from Georgetown.

"What if Robert doesn't die?"

"Oh, he'll die, don't you worry about that. You won't be around to see it, but Robert's going to die. You may have bought him some extra time, but nobody's going to ruin this for me."

"Robbie's the weak link . . . ."

"Robbie's always been a weak link, but he knows where his bread's buttered."

"What if he thinks turning you in is the best way to win the heart of his father?"

She shrugged. "Robbie thinks I'm tied in with the mob—you did that for me. He knows no amount of money can save him from being killed if I have a hit lined up—taking effect after he turns me in. Then where's the government's witness?"

"Jenny Rogers will tell her story—"

"Oh, that's good, Chase, really good. Jenny Rogers is a flake. You know that as well as I do."

"SLED won't be able to find Kristy. They'll have to check out Jenny's story."

"You mean about Rogers thinking she killed my step-daughter. I guess she did and dumped her body in a sinkhole in the national forest." Angeline laughed. "You see, without you around there's not much of a case."

"And how will you explain my disappearance?"

"People like you disappear all the time. You've been tempting fate ever since your father died—Eddie told me all about it. I don't think anyone'll give a damn what happened to you. By next year they won't even remember your name."

"I told Lambert I was coming out here, Angeline. He gave me the key to the house."

"I'm not worried about Lambert. Any notoriety reflecting on the O'Key family reflects on him. Lambert's very sensitive about that. Robert's marriage to a much younger woman was a real embarrassment, if you can believe that."

"Lambert might turn you in himself."

"Not without the go-ahead from Robert. As you said, they have a special relationship. They're so close, at first I thought they were queer."

"Robert—now there's someone who's going to have questions."

"Not about his daughter. Jenny Rogers killed Kristy while on drugs. He won't want to stir this up for the papers. Being ridiculed isn't something Robert relishes. He went through that with his first wife. You should see how he reacts whenever some reporter dredges up his father's clear-cutting." She smiled. "And I'm sure Robert doesn't want it to become common knowledge that his wife turned to a black man when he couldn't satisfy her. So my husband doesn't like me sleeping around. Okay, I'll be more discreet, but when he's dead, I'll sleep with whomever I want. You know what's great about being a woman these days is we girls can sleep around until we find a man who satisfies us."

We motored along for a few minutes. "You hooked up with Eddie in New Orleans, didn't you?"

She nodded, her mind on other things, but the .22 always remained on me. "Yeah. When I moved to New Orleans I still thought I was dirt poor, even with all that insurance money. But people treat you differently when you've got money. I liked that feeling. Finally, I liked that feeling more than I liked Eddie."

"Such a touching story."

"You don't want to hear the rest?"

Actually, I was wondering if I had the nerve to leap over the side—if I was faster than a speeding bullet. "I can figure the rest. Before you blew all your money you came to Charleston and started doing charity work—where more than one woman's caught a rich husband. Men never suspect women are on the make doing charity work; men never suspect women are always on the make, for themselves or others. Your mistake was telling Eddie you'd killed your first husband."

"I didn't tell him. You think I'm an idiot?"

I studied the fog. I could barely see the water. Angeline was a blur in the darkness. "Oh, you didn't confess exactly, but you hinted around enough so a guy like Eddie got the message. You knew you'd have to do something special to impress a hard case like Eddie. Sex wasn't enough."

She laughed and held out her arms again. "You're right, but this bod does a pretty good job. Robbie, his father, Trent, Reggie, all the others are proof of that."

I flexed my legs. They were still sore, but they'd have to do. "You moved here to get away from Eddie, but he followed you. You thought he might queer the deal, but Eddie was fascinated with you. He'd never met a black widow before. How you got away with killing your first husband, then marrying O'Key for his money gave Eddie the idea he could make a move on Markey Nichols. When deceit didn't work for Eddie like it had for you, he started killing people."

"For Eddie, it would always take killing people, a lot of people."

"But it only took your first husband, then Kristy, to protect your investment."

"Kristy didn't give me an out. Said she'd tell her father I was sleeping with a black man if I didn't ask for a divorce and damn little alimony. You were right about Lawson telling her about Eddie and me. I don't know when he saw us. It was only once or twice and that was in Charleston."

"Wouldn't you notice a salt and pepper couple in this part of the country?"

"It wasn't a problem in New Orleans."

"Killing your first husband and collecting all that money went to your head. You thought you could get away with anything."

"I had nothing when I was a kid, Chase. Nothing. You don't know what it's like."

"I know. Believe me, I know."

"Your father fucked you? And fucked you up good?"

"No—but it wouldn't have turned me into a killer."

"You don't know, Chase. You're the same as me, scamming people, especially those who have more than you, and citing your virtue as coin of the realm."

Angeline glanced behind her and when she turned around, I was flying over the side. A bullet whistled by my head, then I was in the water and fighting the belt to get free. Surfacing, I saw the boat coming out of the fog and Angeline leaning over the side, pistol in one hand, wheel in the other. I took a breath and went under again. When the boat passed overhead I popped up, grabbed the side, and jerked down. Well if you're strong enough to drag grown men out of the surf, you should be able to tilt more than a pinball machine. I tried to hold on to the side, but my hands were numb from being tied too tightly and I had to let go. Robbie would've been so proud. He had finally done something right.

Angeline tumbled into the water, and when she surfaced, the boat was twenty feet away and as good as gone. She swam for it but quickly gave up and came after me. At least she didn't have a pistol anymore. But in my eagerness to trap her, I'd trapped myself. With my hands bound I could only make my escape by dog-paddling and the next thing I knew she was crawling up my back, trying to get her hands around my neck.

I broke away, but a lot of good it did me. All I could do was paddle and kick, and not very well. We went under again—Angeline let go—but she was waiting for me when I surfaced, catching me from behind.

"You think . . . I'm leaving you out here?"

She pushed me under and held me there. I twisted to one side and fought my way to the surface. Angeline laughed, grabbed me, and shoved me under again. I couldn't keep this up forever—so when we surfaced this time I stuck my fingers in her eyes.

She screamed and let go, and I dove under, twisting away, kicking, feeling the depth in my ears. It brought back memories of when I'd been diving for the

Margarita and Daddy had had to bail me out. I didn't
think Daddy would like it if I drowned. He'd think I
hadn't learned a thing.

Angeline heard me surface and raced over but lost
me when I went under again. Next time she found me,
she grabbed my leg and followed the line of my body to
my throat. She wrestled me to the surface, facing me,
her hands on my neck. Much more of this and I wouldn't
have the energy to swim ashore—if I ever got away.

She shoved me under, and as I went down, I grabbed
her between the legs, pinching her through the thin
fabric of her slacks. She yelped and her hands loosened, then tightened around my throat again. I pinched
harder and Angeline let go—with a roar!

I threw myself back and away, hands over my head
and surfaced, trying to get a breath, but Angeline came
after me, throwing herself against my chest and forc-
ing me under. I kicked and fought, but I'd been at this
too long. I was growing weary and those damn hands
wouldn't go away. Well, if I had to go I was taking this
bitch with me. Maybe no one would miss me. Maybe it
was time to rejoin my family. I hadn't seen any of them
for an awfully long time.

I hooked my hands around the back of her neck,
holding her head in place, then pulled back my head
and came forward, smacking her in the face with my
forehead. In soccer it would've been a terrific header.
The blow stunned her and she was in the middle of an
"Oh!" when I forced her under, my arms around her
neck, legs around her waist, weighing her down. I hoped
she hadn't taken in much air, maybe even taken in
some water. Now it was between her tennis lessons
and my early morning swims. Angeline was still pum-
meling me as we drifted toward the bottom.

Chapter 21

Harry was drinking his usual bottle of water while I was working my way through a bottle of gin. It was the afternoon I had come home from the hospital, and contrary to what Angeline had said, plenty of people had been worried about me. (I oughta keep that in mind for future reference.) But my mood was glum and finally they drifted off, not only Pick, my boss, and Mickey DeShields but even J.D. Warden. Gee, I didn't know he cared.

Harry stayed behind to cheer me up. "Why not look on the bright side, Susan? You located Jenny, got her into therapy, and she's painting again, maybe not with the same old fire, but her work's selling and you cleared her name. Wasn't that enough? More than what her mother hired you for. More than what she paid you for."

"I killed someone, Dads."

"How many more times do you have to say that?"

"I don't know."

"Is saying it supposed to help?"

"I don't know that either."

"Angeline was trying to kill you—would've liked nothing better."

"I know that."

"And she'd killed before."

"I know that, too."

"Then what's bothering you?"

All I could do was stare into my glass. I was sitting on the sofa, shoulders slumped, hands cradling my drink. Harry sat in the rocker, the gin bottle between us on the coffee table, the dog at his feet. I wanted another drink but didn't have the energy to move, and Harry sure as hell wasn't going to pour it for me. Mounted behind me was *Day's End*, a trade with Mrs. Rogers. She never paid my fee and I never returned her daughter's painting.

"Dads, nothing anyone says makes me feel better about killing that woman."

"And it won't until you want it to."

"Plenty of time for that. They haven't even found the body."

"That man found you. That's all we care about."

"His name is Tip."

Harry smiled. "Now there's someone you can be angry with. Tip came out to the O'Keys' when he promised he wouldn't. Otherwise you might've drowned. Said he was worried about some kid borrowing his boat."

I made a face at him.

"Maybe what's bothering you, Princess, is that you finally overstepped your bounds. If I remember correctly you said you were on your way to see Lieutenant Warden or I never would've allowed you to borrow my car. You also said your jeep was disabled. You didn't tell me it was parked where some gangster and his girlfriend had been murdered."

"You don't have to worry about me, Dads."

"Good. I don't want to have to come around and have these daily little pick-me-up talks."

Outside someone laughed as a boat left the landing. Moments later the swells rocked *Daddy's Girl* and I found myself crying. The dog came over and tried to comfort me, putting his head in my lap. I wiped the tears away, but they still flowed.

"I don't get any respect, Dads, so to prove I could do the job, I killed someone. I set it up that way. Now maybe people will take me seriously."

"Susan, what you did—"

"Please, Dads, let me finish. I could've told Warden my suspicions and Angeline would be alive today, but did I? No. I had to give her a chance to go for my gun. That would clinch everything—because it would've meant Eddie had told her about the Smith & Wesson I carried."

"Susan, don't do this to yourself."

"What I'm saying is: Without the authority Warden carries the only way I could finish this job was doing what I did and now Angeline's dead and I have to live with the fact a cop might've handled it differently. Hell, maybe a man would've handled it differently. Maybe Angeline wouldn't've tried anything with a guy. Maybe she would've tried to seduce him. At least a man wouldn't've been carrying a purse."

"Susan—"

"No—let me finish."

The dog had had enough. He returned to lie at Harry's feet.

"I didn't ask for anyone's help, because of the way I was treated by Jenny's mother and the police chief on Pawleys Island, even J. D. Warden—like they thought I couldn't do the job."

"He was just trying to protect you. Warden didn't want to see you get hurt."

"I don't need a father and you can tell him that for me."

"All of us worry about you—"

"I can take care of myself, Dads."

"You've said that before, but what are you going to do when some young man wants to take care of you? You know, Susan, men enjoy doing things for the women they love. Men like to think women need them."

"I don't need a man."

"Nor do I know one who could put up with you. Young men are much too insecure these days."

I just sat there, chin on my chest.

"People don't know what to make of you, Susan. You're always going for the jugular and never letting up. I wasn't there when you confronted Angeline O'Key, but I want to think you gave her a chance to turn herself in."

"I gave her a chance to turn herself in, Harry."

"Then maybe there's hope for you after all."

"I hope so. I'm all the Boomers have until their kids come along."

"Then maybe you should find a job other than lifeguarding? Show respect for what the older generation values so they'll respect you."

My chin came off my chest. "Dads, are you trying to tell me what to do with my life?"

"Don't you want someone to?"

"Of course not. I can take care of—"

There was a knock at the door.

When Harry went to open it, a brown-haired guy with good shoulders, a strong chin, and a pleasant smile stood there. He wore tan slacks and a gold pullover.

"Susan?" He put his hand over his eyes so he could see through the screen.

In a flash I was off the sofa and at the door. "Yes?"

"I heard you almost drowned. I wanted to see if you were okay so I dropped by. I hope you don't mind."

Harry said it was time to walk the dog, and as he and the Lab went through the door, the young man made way for them. That was nice, showing respect for his elders.

"Would you like to come in?" I asked.

He did and stood there ill at ease. "I wasn't sure I should come over, since I don't really know you. I asked your boss where you lived. I hope that's okay." He glanced at the floor. "I didn't know when you'd be back at work. How are you feeling?"

I gave him my very best smile. "In the hospital I kept thinking if I ever got out of there I was going dancing—that very night so I'd know I was alive."

He chuckled. "You know what, Susan, you're funny."

"Think so?"

"Sure."

He looked me over, and as he did, I wondered how I looked. Thank God my friends had cleaned up the place. I'd have to thank them for that.

"Are you sure you're okay? I don't want to tax you your first night out of the hospital."

"Hey, if I pass out, we'll know I've overdone it."

He chuckled again.

"Really," I said, taking his arm—he had quite a fore-arm—"I'm okay."

"Well, I could come by about eight. We can get something to eat, you know, one-stop-it at the House of Blues if you're up to it. You don't have to get up early, do you? You're not working tomorrow, are you?"

"I'll be ready by eight. By the way, I don't even know your name."

At the door he smiled. "I never told you, did I? It's Chad Rivers."

"Your father's the one who builds boats."

"Er—yes."

"I remember your boat. It had great lines."

"Thank you. That was my own design."

"Really?" I followed him through a door held open for me and out onto the deck. "You'll have to tell me all about it."

"You're interested in boats?"

"Actually, I'm more interested in their designers."

He laughed and said he'd pick me up around eight.

As he left, I held onto the railing to stay on my feet. No way was I going to miss tonight, even if we had to double date with the staff of Grand Strand Regional. At his car—a black Corvette—he waved before climbing in. I waved back.

Could Missy see me on such short notice? Maybe if I told her I'd almost drowned. No—that wouldn't be right. I still valued my virtue—my coin of the realm, as Angeline had called it.

"Susan?" asked someone beside me.

I was watching the Corvette disappear up the road. "Yes," I said, finally breathing again.

"I have some new books for you."

I took Dads' arm and walked him back to his schooner, the Lab trailing along behind us. "Really, Harry, I don't think I'm going to have much time for reading."

He leaned over and gave me a peck on the cheek. "Now I know you'll be all right."

"I don't know about that, but I'm going to be something, maybe even a real private eye."

ABOUT THE AUTHOR

A member of the Mystery Writers of America and Sisters in Crime, STEVE BROWN is also the author of *Radio Secrets*, a novel of suspense about a radio psychotherapist with a secret past; *Black Fire*, the story of a modern-day Scarlett and Rhett facing a church-burning in South Georgia; *Woman Against Herself*, a suspense novel in which a single mom takes on a drug kingpin; and six novels in the Susan Chase Mysteries series.

Steve lives with his family in South Carolina. You can contact him through www.chicksprings.com.

COMING FEBRUARY 2004

COLOR ME GONE
A SUSAN CHASE MYSTERY
by Steve Brown
ISBN: 0-7434-7997-1

All four women were strippers between the ages of twenty and thirty-five. And they were blondes.

So it stands to reason if I had a job at the Open Blouse—if I could actually stand to work there—and got into a fight with the owner, I would also disappear. Without a trace.

Because I'm a blonde....

"It's a rare man who can write from a woman's point of view and make it work, but Steve Brown succeeds beautifully!"

—**Gwen Hunter**,
author of *Betrayal*

"It's another wild ride with Susan Chase. You'll like her new adventure."

—**Barbara D'Amato**,
President, Mystery Writers of America